Under the Frog

For all those who fought.

(Not just in '56
Not just in Hungary.)

Under the Frog

A Black Comedy

Tibor Fischer

The New Press
New York

Published in the United States by The New Press, New York
Distributed by W. W. Norton & Company, Inc.,
500 Fifth Avenue, New York, NY 10110

Originally published in the United Kingdom by Polygon,
Edinburgh.

Library of Congress Cataloging-in-Publication Data

Fischer, Tibor, 1959–
    Under the frog : a black comedy / Tibor Fischer.
       p.   cm.
    ISBN 1–56584–148–4
    1. Basketball players—Hungary—Fiction. 2. Young
men—Hungary—Fiction. I. Title.
PR6056.I772U5   1994
823′.914—dc20   93–46679
                                            CIP

Established in 1990 as a major alternative to the large,
commercial publishing houses, The New Press is the first
full-scale nonprofit American book publisher outside of the
university presses. The Press is operated editorially in the
public interest, rather than for private gain; it is committed
to publishing in innovative ways works of educational,
cultural, and community value that, despite their
intellectual merits, might not normally be "commercially"
viable. The New Press's editorial offices are located at the
City University of New York.

Printed in the United States of America.

94 95 96 97   9 8 7 6 5 4 3 2 1

Contents

November 1955

It was true that at the age of twenty-five he had never left the country, that he had never got more than three days' march from his birthplace, no more than a day and a half of horse and carting or one long afternoon's locomoting. On the other hand, Gyuri mused, how many people could say they had travelled the length and breadth of Hungary naked?

They always travelled naked. He couldn't remember how or why this started, but it had become the irrefrangible rule for the Locomotive team as they traversed the nation for their matches. They always travelled in their luxury wagon (custom-built by Hungarian railways for the Waffen SS to facilitate them in their Europe-wide art-looting, and well known to the authorities on rolling-stock as a peerless carriage for riding the rails) and they always travelled naked.

Róka, Gyurkovics, Demeter, Bánhegyi and Pataki were playing cards on the mahogany dining-table, an ex-antique (according to Bánhegyi, who had served in his father's removal business) it had been mutilated out of value by years of liquid rings, inadvertent and advertent lacerations, the burrowing of burning tobacco. Left as an object unsuited for pocketing in time of rout, the table had been proudly kept by the Locomotive team despite its great (if progressively diminishing) value as a symbol of corporate excellence.

Who was grassing? Who was the informer?

Róka was shifting about, as if uncomfortable: because he was being tapped of his money like a rubber tree and because of the commotion in his blood stream.

Basketball, for Róka, was essentially an aid in disseminating his chromosomes across the country. Basketball, and in fact any activity that got Róka out the front door, served as a bridge between him and members of the opposite sex. Abstention from sexual relations for anything longer than twenty-four hours would result in Róka getting extremely agitated, and doing things like running around in small figures of eight, ululating. Even in a habitat like the Locomotive carriage where women were over-represented in the conversation, Róka's devotion to gamic convolutions was remarkable.

But Róka was too decent to be a brick in their wall.

That is, Róka was good-hearted, and Gyuri, like everyone else, liked him. So it was hard to imagine him as a delator, grassing up the team. Indeed, it was hard to imagine anyone in the team snitching. Except Péter. But as the only card-carrier Péter was surely too obvious. Pataki, he had known from the age when you start knowing. Gyuri couldn't see any of the team informing. Demeter – too much of a gentleman. Bánhegyi – too jolly. Gyurkovics – too unorganised. And all the others were ... singularly uninformer-like. However, Gyuri contemplated, turning the proposition on its head, perhaps it was Róka's decency that had snared him. If you don't do this, we do that to your motherfathersisterbrother.

As always, when Róka wasn't humping, he consoled himself by talking about it: 'So I explained to her it was okay by me.' That was Róka. He wasn't elitist. He was generous, egalitarian. He scorned petty bourgeois concepts such as *beauty*, *desirability*, and *youth*. He was relating his tryst with a recent conquest, a lady whose attractiveness, he emphasised, was in no way impaired by her artificial arm. The dénouement of Róka's anecdote was that the lady had become dismembered and Róka had found himself with an extensive annex to his tool. This, apparently, had occasioned great distress to the lady, despite Róka's chivalrous assurances that it could happen to anyone with an artificial arm.

Nevertheless, the chief punchline, Gyuri sensed, hadn't been reached when the narration was guillotined by Róka's fury at losing a heavily-wagered hand to Pataki. Gyuri wasn't playing cards, because he found it boring, and additionally, Pataki always won. They only played for small amounts of money but as he only possessed very small amounts of money, he didn't see why he should hand it over to Pataki. It was a mysterious process, but an inevitable and obvious one, like droplets of rain guided down a window-pane, how all the currency gravitated towards Pataki. Pataki would lose a hand every now and then but it was at best courtesy and looked more like blatant entrapment.

Tired of trying to crack the problem of the informer, Gyuri settled down to think about being a streetsweeper while he gazed out of the window at the countryside that went past quite lazily despite the train's billing as an express. The streetsweeper was a sort of cerebral chewing gum that Gyuri popped in on long journeys. A streetsweeper. Where? A streetsweeper in London. Or New York. Or Cleveland; he wasn't that fussy. Some modest streetsweeping anywhere. Anywhere in the West. Anywhere outside. Any job. No matter how menial, a windowcleaner, a dustman, a labourer: you could just do it, just carry out your job and you wouldn't need an examination in Marxism–Leninism, you wouldn't have to look at pictures of Rákosi or whoever had superbriganded their way to the top lately. You wouldn't have to hear about gambolling production figures, going up by leaps and bounds, higher even than the Plan had predicted because the power of Socialist production had been underestimated. Being a streetsweeper would be quite agreeable, Gyuri reflected. You'd be out in the open, doing healthy work, seeing things. It was the very humility of this fantasy, its frugality that gave the greatest pleasure, since Gyuri hoped this could facilitate its coming to pass. It wasn't as if he were pestering Providence for a millionaireship or to be handed the presidency of the United States. How could anyone refuse a request to be a streetsweeper? Just pull me out. Just pull me out. Apart from the prevailing political inclemency and the ubiquitous shittiness of life, the simple absurdity of never having voyaged more than two hundred kilometres from the spot where he had bailed out of the womb rankled.

The train went into a slower kind of slow, signalling that they were arriving in Szeged. This was, he knew from his research, 171 kilometres from Budapest.

Just next to the railway station in Szeged was a high, red-brick building which now advertised itself as a hotel. It had been, as everyone knew, one of the most renowned brothels in Hungary before such dens of capitalist iniquity were closed down. Town, gown, yokels in their Sunday best (only worn at church, in a coffin, or at the knocking shop), commercial salesmen and royalty (admittedly only the Balkan variety) had all made their way through its portals.

There was no doubt that it was pure hotel now. The girls would have been dispersed to some more dignified toil. Gyuri recalled the Party Secretary at the Ganz works making quite a ceremony out of it when the factory had taken on four night butterflies. Welcoming the new arrivals, Lakatos had launched into a heated denunciation of how the loathsome capitalist system had dragged these unfortunates into the lustful sweatshops of hypocritical bourgeois depravity. How capitalism had perpetuated the *droit de seigneur*, how capitalism had taken young male proletarians to be slaughtered in wars for markets and how their sisters were thrust into strumpetry. It had been, especially for Lakatos, a sterling performance. He had obviously read it somewhere; he was probably parroting a section in the Party secretary's manual, 'upon receiving former whores on the shopfloor'. The girls had listened to Lakatos's fulminations demurely, wearing factory overalls. The diatribe had ended with Lakatos wiping the rhetorically-induced sweat from his brow and disappearing into his office while the girls had been led off to learn the ropes.

Within a fortnight the girls had been once again plying their trade inside the huge coils of copper wire the factory spun. That really was the heart of Communism, Gyuri decided: it made it harder for everyone to do what they do.

Róka threw his cards down in disgust as Pataki made off with another hand: 'In the words of the Grand Provost of Kalocsa after he had had both his legs sheared off by a train, "Aren't you going to take my dick too?".'

'We can talk about that jazz record of yours,' replied Pataki, patiently shuffling the cards.

Róka, as the son of a prominent Lutheran bishop, was the carriage authority on all matters ecclesiastical, plus Horace's odes. Every time Róka's father had seen one of his three children, he had greeted them with a line from Horace; the offspring had been enjoined to respond with the subsequent line, on pain of an imminent clip around the ear. The bishop was not completely severe. A slice of chocolate cake was on offer for anyone who could catch him out on Horace's texts; Róka claimed he had never eaten chocolate cake until he was sixteen.

Like Gyuri, Róka was class-x. But Róka seemed unperturbed by this, and certainly didn't allow his political handicap to interfere with his mission in life. Methodically, he scanned the platforms at Szeged station for any woman who had the sort of look on her face which suggested that she might be thinking about a vertical liaison against a secluded wall with a basketball player en route to Makó. Aside from his interminable hormones, Róka had also acquired a haul of excellent (i.e. Western) jazz records that was now almost entirely in Pataki's clutches, and he was looking out in the hope of a deliverance that might prevent another disc from taking up residence in Pataki's collection. Róka's countenance grimly, faultlessly, registered the absence of a woman under sixty at Szeged's railway station.

'We haven't blessed Szeged, have we?' remarked Bánhegyi. It was childish, but cheap, and sometimes amusing. Katona leaned out of a window further along, so he could capture the scene while, as the train pulled out of the station, Róka, Gyurkovics, Demeter and Pataki promoted their posteriors up against the carriage window next to the platform. A gallery of photographs starring bewildered or outraged rail passengers from all over Hungary adorned the carriage walls.

Szeged was a little disappointing. One elderly ticket-inspector got the full blast of the four-bum salute but she remained unmoved. Myopia perhaps, or an overdose of war; it looked very much as if some misfortune had spooned the zest out of her. Or possibly they were inured to basketball teams in Szeged.

Gyuri looked out on the river as they crossed over, still ruminating on the attractions of being a streetsweeper. 'The border's too far to walk from here,' said Pataki, continuing to preside over the impoverishment of his team-mates. 'Make your break from Makó.'

Gyuri's aspirations, though he had never opened them up, dripped out over time and had been fully divined by the others. Keeping secrets from those you travelled around with naked wasn't easy. 'It's really not that wonderful out there, Gyuri.' Gyurkovics kept on repeating this. Gyurkovics was a liar – not in the same league as Pataki but competent. But while Pataki turned on the falsehood principally for entertainment and only used it as a shield at the last resort, with Gyurkovics you knew as soon as his enamels parted, his lying was to exile the truth.

Gyurkovics had got out. In '47, before the borders had been sealed up tighter than a louse's arse, Gyurkovics went off to Vienna. It had been about the same time that Gyuri had gone to see Pataki about skipping the country. Wearing newspaper for underwear, Gyuri was spending most of his time worrying about when his next foodstuff would be making its appearance. He had been going upstairs in the hope of catching lunchtime in the Pataki household when he bumped into Pataki coming down the stairway. Pataki was wearing his US Army sunglasses (clandestinely obtained and one of only a dozen pairs in the whole of Hungary). Pataki was better off in that his loins weren't girded with newsprint and he had a mother and an employed father to assist him in the obtaining of meals. But Gyuri doubted that was the crucial factor. 'Let's go. Let's get out of this country,' Gyuri had urged. Pataki paused, mentally fingering the proposal. 'No,' he said, 'let's go rowing.' That had been that. Gyuri had no doubt that if it had been yes, they would have strolled down to the station without any ado, but it had been no and a saunter to the boathouse.

Gyurkovics however had snapped the homeland umbilical cord, but incredibly had returned six months later, when there were even fewer reasons to return. He had an uncle in Vienna, who from Budapest looked immeasurably rich, having coined it in the shoe business. Many an evening had been spent in the throes of unrestrained envy, but Gyurkovics had reappeared looking gloomy and sporting an unimpressive suit. The rumour had been that only insanity or murder could have brought him back; his brother had passed out the truth. Gyurkovics had demolished the shoe empire. In his suicide note, Gyurkovics's uncle had written: 'You have incredible gifts – anyone who can destroy an enterprise built up over forty years with love, diligence, early rising and an unequalled regard for the customer, in the space of a few weeks, has extraordinary talents. I trust that one day these powers will be harnessed for the benefit of mankind.'

Still biding his time with a bit of basketball before redeeming humanity, Gyurkovics played down the West. Probably there were further embarrassments littered around Vienna that he didn't want any acquaintances to chance on. Besides, this stretch of border around Makó wasn't worth the effort of crossing it. Who wanted to go to Yugoslavia or Rumania? Both red star affairs. Yugoslavia – a bunch of knife-wielding Serbs and Rumania...

Gyuri had been miffed at not going on the Rumanian tour. Okay, Rumania wasn't really a country, but it wasn't Hungary and it was infuriating that bourgeois lineage should have deprived him of the trip when crypto-fascists and rotten decadents like Róka and Pataki had gone. They had wanted the team to win, so they couldn't leave Pataki behind, but they didn't want anyone too class-x passing the ball to him. By some incomprehensible ministerial process the level of class-x in Róka had been deemed more acceptable than his.

Rumania hadn't had a good press though. Years before, Józsi from the ground floor had returned from a summer holiday visiting relatives in Transylvania and recounted in horrified tones: 'They actually fuck ducks. I'm not joking, I saw it'. 'Don't be ridiculous,' Pataki had riposted, 'it must have been a goose.' Józsi had seemed genuinely aghast and when you thought about how all the great Hungarian generals, all the true hard men of Hungarian history had come from Transylvania, it seemed plausible that rising in the morning to discover your neighbour with his breeches around his ankles making some fowl howl could toughen you up.

Gyuri had also quizzed István, who had been the last soldier out of Kolozsvár, 'the last but the fastest', about Rumania. István just laughed and carried on laughing. Elek, who had taken the Orient Express to do business in Bucharest before the war, when he heard that Gyuri was angling to get on the Rumanian tour, commented: 'My son is an imbecile. This is the cruellest blow.'

Still, Gyuri was subjected to an air of distinct smugness as the others made their preparations to depart for Rumania. Róka managed to acquire a Rumanian phrase, which he went round chanting all day, which, he believed, translated roughly as 'put your hole on my pole'. Pataki packed extra toilet paper and took a small, aged guide book on Rumanian gastronomic delights.

They went, they saw, they lost, but at least they came back. Gyuri had met the returning train at the Keleti railway station.

Róka was the first off. Always reedy, he had noticeably lost weight, a skeleton painted a white skin colour, totally out of place for August. 'Let me put it this way,' Róka summed up, 'if you gave me the choice of spending two weeks in the waiting room here at the Keleti, with nothing to eat, or a night in Bucharest's best hotel, I wouldn't have to think very hard about it.'

They had lost the two matches they played. Largely because Pataki had been out of action. Pataki, who had never had a day's illness in his life (the closest he had got to being ill was when he had invented ailments to dodge various duties), who had only ever come into contact with doctors for the obligatory check-ups on all players, had spent the duration of his stay in Bucharest, on his knees, spewing incessantly, vilely betrayed by his sphincter muscles, bowing to the lords of disgorgement, hugging different immobiles in his bathroom suite, pleading for divine intercession. The others had had ruthless alimentary disruptions but had just succeeded in getting out on court; the Locomotive players had all felt as if their legs were encased in lead casks – they bitterly regretted getting possession of the ball since that forced them to run or try to do something. They would have happily forfeited the match at half-time, if it hadn't been for a fervent appeal to national honour and auroral threats of unprecedented strength by Hepp. Despite losing irremediably from the first second (or perhaps because of it) Locomotive were soundly booed by the crowd and one of the darts thrown by the spectators had skewered Szabolcs's ear.

When Demeter, as acting captain (on account of Pataki's indisposition), had offered to trade tops with the opposing captain as was the custom with international fixtures, the Rumanian had insisted on haggling, with the result that Demeter ended up with three unwanted Rumanian tops and the Rumanians left congratulating themselves on having gulled the Hungarians.

'I never thought we were going to get back alive,' Róka had said, kissing the platform. On the home leg of the fixture, they had had their revenge, beating the Rumanian Railway Workers' Union but only by two points, a puny margin, acutely disappointing when one took into account that Róka's brother, who was in charge of the kitchens at the hotel where the Rumanian team was staying, had applied injudicious amounts of rat poison to their goulash.

* * *

The train rolled into Makó, the last stop for both the train and the Locomotive team. They were due to play the Makó Meat-Processors that afternoon. There was a minor abattoir in Makó which helped to supply flesh to the salami factory in Szeged. Their opposition was entirely drawn from the small-bone cleaning unit of this abattoir.

No one was there to greet them at the station, but Makó wasn't really big enough to make finding anything too much of a problem. They arrived at a school sports hall for the match to find the meat-processors out on court, clumping about in what had the appearance of a desperate attempt to learn how to play basketball half an hour before play was due to commence.

As they were changing, Hepp gave the team a pocket edition of his pre-match exhortation. It definitely wasn't needed, since they knew without setting eyes on the meat-processors that they couldn't be any good. Unknown, provincial teams couldn't be any good, since any hot player would be immediately siphoned up, lured into the grasp of one of the big teams that could offer huge betterments. This was a friendly match to appraise the meat-processors, a newly formed team, who had probably lined up the first-division Locomotive via political channels. A Makó Party secretary had phoned another Party secretary to whom he had slipped a crate of salamis, who would in turn phone another Party secretary, a soon-to-be proud owner of a crate of salamis, and so on, till at the end of the chain Locomotive chugged into town.

Thus there was no need for Hepp to flex his admonitions, but the thing about Hepp, which could be quite irritating at times, was that he was a professional: he took his job seriously despite the fact that ten million other people in Hungary didn't. He was good in every way as a coach, manager and mentor of the team, but he did have one grave fault. He always got up at 4.30 in the morning, and after fifty years on the earth, still couldn't grasp that other people didn't. His direst threat was circuit training at 5 a.m.

One morning, not long after he had joined Locomotive, and not long after he had burned his bed, Gyuri woke up on the floor with the awful knowledge that Hepp was expecting him at 5.30 for some track work in what was a bottomless black October freeze. Wondering why so much of existence consisted of getting up in the cold dark to do something you didn't like, he resolved he wasn't having it. Normally Gyuri was exemplary about training, indeed, that was why he had burned his bed, in an attempt to incinerate his laziness. It hadn't been a great bed, but it had been serviceable, it had worked, and lying there in the mornings Gyuri had found its temptations preferable to running about in the winter. He lay there in its fortifying warmth and comfort, thinking about the training he should have been doing, repeatedly previewing it instead of doing it. Gyuri knew he had to train, and train much harder than anyone else because he was a self-made athlete, unlike someone like Pataki who was a natural. To get the rewards that accrued from basketball, Gyuri had to work.

That was why he had lugged the bed down to the courtyard and burned it with a sprinkling of petrol, to make sure that his will wouldn't buckle in the future. The neighbours hadn't batted an eye, because, by that point, if they hadn't had their throats slit as they slept by Gyuri or Pataki, categorised as the crazies of the block, that was good enough for them.

Gyuri placed his hopes on a groundsheet and the floor encouraging him to get up briskly and to log a few hours' exercise before the other preoccupations of the day. But even the floor could grow on you. And that morning, he had thought 'you can't rush reality' and dived back into sleep, having written off Hepp's proposed cross-arctic running. The doorbell rang at around six (as it would turn out). Elek, who was up, even though he had no convincing reason to be, opened the door to Hepp. Hepp handed Elek his card, which he always carried – 'Dr Ferenc Hepp, Doctor of Sport' – and asked to be shown to Gyuri's room. Lying, Gyuri lied reflexively that he was ill, whereupon Elek expressed surprise as Gyuri hadn't mentioned feeling poorly the previous evening. This somehow removed the sparse vestiges of veracity from Gyuri's statement.

'Well,' Hepp had said good-naturedly, 'if you can manage to triumph over this unwellness, if you can bring your body to heel, because a hard mind makes a hard body, and get to the track in twenty minutes and do ten more laps than the others, to show this illness you're not going to take it lying down, I think I can do you a commensurate favour: I can sign your military deferment papers.' That had been quintessential Hepp. Other coaches would have sent someone else round to threaten him but Hepp was unwavering in doing things himself.

'It goes without saying you're going to win this match,' said Hepp, 'so I'm not going to say it. These meat-processors have undoubtedly got webbed toes and if they're in basketball gear, it's because they brought their mothers to help them change. I don't want to be accused of being unreasonable, I don't want to be the target of petulant rumblings but gentlemen, I have to insist on a twenty-point victory.

'They say you shouldn't judge a book by its cover but as far as I'm concerned that's exactly what it's there for – this bunch couldn't find themselves in the dark. So I have to insist, even allowing for your not inconsiderable indolence, I have to insist on a twenty-point, no, a thirty-point margin of victory. Otherwise it's sit-ups in the City Park on the rainiest five o' clock in the morning that I can find.'

Hepp then erected his blackboard, which he always carried around, and chalked up a few plays, selected from his notebook as thick as a hammer-thrower's thigh (Gyuri once glimpsed a play with a number as high as 602). This was often the hardest part of any match, paying attention to Hepp's schemes, since, certainly when dealing with a collection of small-bone pickers, the required tactic was simply to get hold of the ball, pass it to Pataki and watch him obligingly run down the court and propel it into the basket. This was a tactic stunningly effective against all but the top three or four teams in the first division who had the brains, talent, speed or foresight to impede this model operation.

But there in Makó, it was hard to attend to Hepp's phenomenally involved machinations. You had to put one or two into action, regardless of whether you needed to or whether there would be any benefit from using it, such as collaring a couple of points. Hepp was the coach, and basketball was better than a real job where you were expected to work for the money they didn't give you. A certain amount of explaining away was possible – 'Doc, the marking on Pataki was too fierce, we couldn't use the Casino egg play...' – but if there wasn't some evidence of orders being obeyed, Hepp's favourite remedy for disregard of his specially-bound leather notebook was half an hour of stadium steps and it didn't make any difference how fit you were, your legs would become solid outposts of pain.

And of course there were times when Hepp's scheming won matches, such as the Great Technical University Massacre, when the better team hadn't been allowed to win because of Hepp's plays. When the end whistle had blown, the Technical University team had stood on court, unmoving, unable to believe they had been beaten, viciously beaten, by a team five places further down in the division. But it wasn't so much to do with the winning, as with control. Gyuri had learned from his own coaching in the gimnáziums that the greatest part of the pleasure was seeing the invisible strings pulled, relishing the remote control, like being a theatre director or a general. You wanted to recognise your handiwork.

Róka, as was the custom, went out alone onto the court with the gramophone player. They all knew that this showmanship was wasted in Makó, but this was the point of being professional amateurs – you went on with the show even if there was no one to watch, or if the spectators were too thick to appreciate it. The gramophone player was István's. István and the gramophone player were about all that was left of the Hungarian Second Army. István had got the portable gramophone player as a present from Elek when he set off to the front in '41. Gyuri had no idea how much it had cost, but fortunes were involved; there had been German generals who didn't have the sort of musical recreation enjoyed by the Hungarian artillery lieutenant. The Hungarian Second Army, like all Hungarian armies, had the unfortunate habit of getting wiped out. István returned, flayed and dented by shrapnel, even though 200,000 other Hungarians didn't. Even more miraculously, the gramophone player had been returned home months later by one of István's comrades-in-arms. István had no objections to Gyuri permanently borrowing it.

Róka put on one of the jazz records, to the sound of which Locomotive trooped out and started their warm-up, bouncing around and sinking baskets. The records they performed to were all of American origin, which could have been tricky, but before they had thrown away a load of records presented to them by one of the visiting Soviet railway teams, they had steamed off the labels and refixed them on the jazz records. So the Western decadents were then camouflaged by rubrics such as 'Lenin is Amongst Us', 'Our Steam Engine', and the biggest hit 'In the Front-Line Forest' performed by the Song and Dance Ensemble of the Soviet Army (the original credits for the jazz had been long forgotten). Any snooping eyes would only meet estimable red cyrillic whatever the reports of their ears.

The small-bone cleaners were visibly taken aback by this. Somehow, Gyuri felt, they weren't going to break into the big time of big-bone cleaning. One of them loped up and announced that they could only provide one referee. 'My other uncle couldn't come.'

A towering player, some six foot six, the Meats' not-so-secret secret weapon, lined up with Pataki for the jump-off, pouring down a look of smug contempt on the five inches shorter Pataki. It was funny – the Meats thought they were going to win.

They were very surprised when Pataki disappeared with the ball but instead of whizzing downcourt to deposit it in the boardbank as was his wont, he passed it back to Gyuri. For a bit of fun, Gyuri tried to drop the bomb, taking a shot from under his basket at the opposition basket. Normally, this was only attempted as a desperate measure with only seconds to go before the end of a match. The odds practically blocked the ball going in but as Gyuri knew the match was Locomotive's anyway, even if they'd only been playing two men, he had a go. The ball flew across the court and shot through the net without touching the ring or the backboard. Any experienced player would have diagnosed it as magnificent, once in a career cheek, but the Meats were flummoxed and rocketed from bucolic swagger to abject panic. Instead of piling on Pataki (not that it would have greatly hindered him) they crowded around Gyuri. After Pataki had eased his way through to ten straight dunkings as if he were practising on an empty court, the twenty points hinted to the Meats that they should keep an eye on Pataki but this was of little help. The Secret Weapon lumbered about trying to pillage passes to Pataki but he was too big an opportunity for gravity to pass up and Pataki always got higher or lower faster to pluck the ball.

Bias, the like of which none of the Locomotive players had seen, flabbergasting bias from the referee which gave the Meats impunity to foul, trip and punch, along with several completely unwarranted penalty throws, resulted in a final score of 68–32 to Locomotive. It seemed obvious that the total export capacity of Hungary's salami industry would be needed to thrust the Meats into the first division.

The pleasure of the good result that Hepp was looking forward to had been greatly marred by the referee's behaviour, going for his whistle whenever someone from Locomotive neared the ball. Hepp went over to the referee to discuss the one hundred and eight infractions of correct refereeing he had noted down during the course of the match. Gyuri could tell by the look on the referee's face that he didn't realise that he really was going to have to go through the one hundred and eight points one by one in exacting and atomic detail.

Hepp's persistence was one of the pillars of Locomotive's high ranking in the league but despite all his cunning, expertise and drive, there was no way he could push Locomotive into beating the Army's team, which had the championship trophy riveted down in its clubhouse, as there was no need to move it. The Army's strengths were self-evident: an infinity of boons for its sporters, innumerable facilities, the ability to draft anyone they wanted and above all, the bonus that playing for the Army meant that you didn't have to be in the Army (the real one where you didn't eat, lived out in sub-zero temperatures and dug ditches). In fact one of the most agreeable ways of avoiding the Army – a pastime that, after bonking, was the major preoccupation for healthy young Hungarian males – was to join the Army.

The life of the Army's basketball players, as indeed of all its sporting practitioners, was cushy. On the first day they might go as far as to show you what a rifle looked like but that was as far as military science went for the sporters. Anyone who played in the first division had a nominal job handed out by their club, the duties being mainly collecting your wages (there were also the little brown envelopes at the clubhouse containing 'calorie money'). For example, Gyuri had visited his place of employment on numerous occasions and had learned the Morse code in the course of his railway career. In the Army, shamateurism reached full speed; the only duty that impinged on the Army's athletes was putting on a uniform once in a while. Plus, if you were of an international standard, a high rank and a fat salary were thrust on you. Puskás, the football genius, not only had a car, but a chauffeur.

In their changing room, Locomotive were joined by their vanquished opponents. The atmosphere was not one of sporting benevolence and fraternity; the hope of obtaining some home-brewed pálinka, as often happened on trips to the provinces, was dashed. The demeanour and conduct of the small-bone boys was indisputably bunko; you would have thought they could contain their surly clod-hopping to their own changing room but they couldn't stay away from the excitement from Budapest: ergo, there was nothing else to do that weekend in Makó except bait the Locomotive team.

The Meats had chosen Demeter as the principal subject of their attentions. Demeter was tall and aristocratic, as befitted someone who came from a long line of tall aristocrats. Whether because seven hundred years of appearances behoved him to do so, or whether it emanated from his nature, Demeter emitted a constant poise: you could imagine him being bombed and pulled out from a pile of rubble without a hair out of place. If you were wearing a dinner jacket and Demeter was stark naked, you'd still feel underdressed.

Demeter was also excessively equitable, which was why he hadn't responded to the Meats' unimaginative abuse. If it had been Pataki or Katona, or indeed any other member of the team on the receiving end, fugitive teeth would already have been scuttling across the floor. Why was it always the friendly matches that ended up unfriendly? thought Gyuri looking around the changing room for some handy blunt instrument such as a length of iron piping.

The universal punch-up Gyuri expected didn't in fact come to pass. The Meats' spokesman was working his way through a loop of observations such as 'You think you're pretty good, don't you?' and 'You think your shit doesn't stink, eh?' As he was engaged in this, Demeter adjusted his tie, and then, with such purpose the movement seemed slow, administered a slap resoundingly on the spokesman's face. Not a punch but an open-handed rebuke, without any follow up. Demeter then carried on packing up his kit-bag. The Meats flocked out in silence – rather as a martial artist was reputed to be able to summon fatal strength to one finger, so Demeter had conduited a crushing amount of contempt into that slap that had incontrovertibly spelt out their fourth-divisionness in all aspects of life. The irony was that it was Demeter who insisted on politely bidding farewell to their hosts.

They had to hunt around for Hepp before they could leave, but they located him eventually, somewhat out of breath – he had run a mile down the road pursuing the referee who had taken to his bicycle at point forty-eight. Hepp was in excellent condition for his age, indeed he was in good shape for someone twenty years younger, and he could have carried on much further had it not been for the awareness that his strictures were not being accepted constructively.

Returning to Szeged to spend the night, the bulk of Locomotive opted for an inspection of the town's main square to see if there was a restaurant willing to serve them. They remembered that they had run out of a restaurant in the centre of town without paying the bill, doing a Zrínyi, as it was known in the Locomotive ranks, in memory of the great Hungarian general Miklós Zrínyi, who had rushed out of his castle, admittedly to do battle with a Turkish force that outnumbered him ten times (to be completely wiped out). They remembered they had zrínyied out of a restaurant, but having been so legless and brainless they couldn't remember which one (they had been so inebriated only half the team could walk, and had only made good their escape by locking the staff in the kitchen). But what was the point of being away from home if you didn't behave disgracefully? They chose the restaurant on the left hand side of the square, where having reassured the management they weren't anything to do with water-polo they were shown to a table. 'When I hear the word water-polo,' said the head waiter, 'I know it means ... refurbishment, hospital, the police, a loss of teeth ... years of painful, slow recovery.'

Hepp was busy back at the hotel, writing letters about the one hundred and eight points to everyone even remotely connected with the governing of basketball and some to people who weren't. 'I definitely think you should write to the Ministry,' Pataki had said, knowing that Hepp's epistolary exertions would save the team from a few hours of post-match analysis which on previous occasions had driven people to climbing out of windows to evade Hepp.

Gyuri had gone off to the main post office to see about a phone call to Budapest. Three days before, he had been stopped in the street by a striking Swedish girl who asked for directions to the Museum of Fine Arts. The miracle of such an encounter, of a girl who was from the outside and who was good-looking, just walking up to him without any advance notice from fate, had stupefied him and he almost let her go without assaying further acquaintance. She was visiting Budapest for some youth festival organised by one of the countless peace committees but that was immaterial. She was a two-legged ticket out of Hungary and worth a four hour wait for a phone-call. Stay calm, reasoned Gyuri, stay calm for a few more days and then if she hasn't fallen insanely in love with me, there's always the expedient of falling at her feet, pleading for marriage, offering half of his salary for life, offering anything, to kill people she didn't like, to beg desperately and shamelessly.

Bugger the informer, he concluded entering the post office, I'm breaking out. Joining the queue for phone calls, a familiar figure in front of him was mnemonically focused into recognition. It was Sólyom-Nagy, the champion shoplifter of the Minta school. Sólyom-Nagy's prowess at pilfering, mostly chocolate bars, had been such that the entire third year, as a result of the gargantuan amounts of cut-price Sólyom-Nagy-supplied chocolate they had consumed, had been unable to view a bar without feeling ill. Although they had lost touch, Gyuri had got on well with Sólyom-Nagy and had been very grateful to him for specially stealing a multi-faceted penknife, subsequently lost when Keresztes, who had said he just wanted to borrow it for a minute, had left it in a gypsy at the fairground.

Sólyom-Nagy, it transpired, was studying Hungarian literature at the university in Szeged. 'This is Jadwiga, by the way,' he said indicating a slim girl next to him who was letting her boredom with waiting show. The surname was something Polish that Gyuri didn't bother trying to retain but he was disappointed that Jadwiga didn't seem more delighted to meet him. One didn't get anywhere by overlooking introductions to women. However, according to the instant classification of the back-room boys in Gyuri's cranium, Jadwiga only scored a keep-on-file anyway and he had more pressing Swedish women to phone.

It took a portly three hours to get through to Budapest and she wasn't at the student hostel. It was going to be hard work becoming a streetsweeper in Stockholm.

December 1944

The German soldier was trailing behind the others, clutching in his left hand a good portion of the intestines spilling out from an otherwise quite smart uniform. To Gyuri, he didn't seem greatly distressed – it was rather as if the unTeutonic untidiness of runaway guts was far more troubling than any physical pain.

Of course, fussing or expecting any sort of sympathy or attention would have been a waste of time – like everything else sympathy and attention were running out. The Germans, pedestrian or motorised, still pretending that the war wasn't over, were heading to the river and crossing over to the castle where it was rumoured they were going to hole up and fight it out with the rapidly approaching Russians. Gyuri had watched the Germans arrive in force, months earlier, when they had helped themselves to Hungary's government. The Germans had poured in with their heroic motorcycles and other items of snappy transport, swaggering around in beautiful leather coats.

The Germans weren't looking so confident now, the prospect of getting mashed by the Russians not agreeing with them. It would have been fun to watch if it hadn't been for the fact that the mashing was going to take place in Budapest. From the direction of the City Park Gyuri could hear the distant rumbling of artillery, the mighty footfalls of the Red Army.

Military training, even for fourteen year-olds like Gyuri, had been stepped up since the Hungarian High Command, having lost one army, was trying to get another to play with. Gyuri's instructors had placed exclusive emphasis on running around a lot in gas masks and then crawling back and forth over some prime cow pats. 'The Russians will be in big trouble if they try to defend themselves with cow shit,' one of Gyuri's fellow soldiers had remarked.

They were also shown the much-hailed 'Panzerfaust', the shoulder-launched antitank missile that was the latest secret weapon from the German scientists, and the piece of kit that everyone wanted to get their hands on. Their instructor had taken the Panzerfaust out of its box and held it out to them like some sort of talisman. 'There it is, lads, the Panzerfaust,' he had said, packing it back into its box so it could be taken off to be exhibited elsewhere and launching into a lengthy description of sundry hush-hush techniques for getting a truly first-rate shine on your boots.

Some of the duties were more pleasant. There had been a boom in requisitioning, presumably on the premise of doing your looting while you could. The notoriously stupid Hankóczy, who having made it to fifteen, was in charge, had led them on a stripping tour of properties in the Jewish quarter.

Supposedly searching for items that would help the war effort, Gyuri and Dózsa had an exceptionally good pillage in a pharmacy, recruiting lots of soap. Dózsa's presence had been rather odd, since his father was Jewish and had been issued with a yellow star and one evening had been taken away. Gyuri had spotted him being escorted away, carrying one small suitcase. But a day or so later, Dózsa's father had returned, and although he hadn't been tap-dancing on the roof, he had been left alone.

Coming out of the pharmacy, Gyuri and Dózsa had heard a shrill protest from the other side of the street. From a fully-opened second floor window, a diminutive, but vocally powerful old lady unleashed a savage tirade against their appropriation of toiletries: 'Filth, termites, bloodsuckers. Have you no shame? Stealing like this in broad daylight?' The woman had the appearance of being irritating on a full-time basis but Gyuri had been startled by the vehemence of her denunciations, which were surprising: against the background of wholesale export of Jewish families, the emptying of a pharmacy didn't really rate a mention. Also Gyuri didn't see why he should get the blame for the Nazi goings-on. Was the woman out of touch, or was it her pharmacy?

But she was very loud and very persistent. People stopped to watch the show. The most annoying thing, Gyuri suspected, was that she was right. Hankóczy had materialised and taken stock of the situation: 'Right, Fischer, shoot the old bag.' Gyuri had been issued with a vintage revolver, as a sort of official warrant, which he enjoyed wearing. 'Go on,' Hankóczy commanded in a senior, military sort of way. Gyuri pulled out the revolver from its holster. 'Shoot! Shoot! Shoot!' insisted the old lady, weary of the world, but Gyuri, after reflecting that at that distance he'd probably miss, had decided to be merciful.

'Your mother, dear madam, was a whore,' he had shouted belligerently. This massive and out-of-all-proportion rudeness had pleased Hankóczy even more than a round through the old girl would have. It had certainly blown her back into her flat, ripping apart her lace-curtain world. Hankóczy slapped Gyuri on the back approvingly but a creeping feeling of shame soon overtook Gyuri. You're brought up to be polite to little old ladies, Gyuri thought, but all you want to do is to shoot them.

Tired of watching retreating Germans, Gyuri set off for home. He was curious about what war would be like close-up. Their first instalment had been yesterday, when he and Pataki were looking out from the tiny balcony that the Patakis had, a sort of a concrete slab that jutted out of the building. Pataki's mother called them in for a few samples of the parliamentarian pastries she had been baking. A minute later, there was a faint thump and they went back to the balcony to see what it was, or rather they wanted to go out on the balcony, but they couldn't because it was gone, seized by a long-distance Russian shell that hadn't felt like exploding.

Gyuri had heard a similar story from Gergely. Gergely's family were down in the shelter during an air raid and when it was over went back upstairs to their top-floor flat, opened the door, and found the whole flat gone. All that was left were the front door, its hinges and a view of dusty debris four floors down. 'At least we didn't have to bother tidying up,' Gergely had commented.

Gyuri had also quizzed István about the war. István had spent three years on different fronts, always bringing back in an elder brotherly way some mementos for Gyuri: bullets, bayonets, helmets and one Russian revolver that sadly didn't have any ammunition. 'What's it like at the front?' Gyuri asked. István hesitated, uncharacteristically, and then replied: 'You try to shoot first ... otherwise it's like anything else. Some people love it, some people hate it.' Elek, who had been highly decorated the last time round, never discussed the war, but then he never discussed anything with Gyuri. Dealing with his children came as naturally to him as juggling pineapples. Gyuri had inquired once about the decorations, to which Elek had volunteered the information: 'As a soldier in a war, you end up highly-decorated or dead, though some manage to overlap.' The imminence of the Russians had coaxed one further military, paternal revelation from Elek, however: 'Listen, if it comes to the point where someone is stupid enough to tell you to fight, just vanish and hide somewhere till it's over.'

As Gyuri walked down Damjanich utca, he saw a limousine with army insignia parked outside number ten. Wondering if this signified anything for the family, Gyuri spotted Kálmán, one of István's closest friends, now something influential at the High Command, wearing a fancy dress uniform. Kálmán was taken aback to see Gyuri and you could see him reviewing

a number of approaches before going for the shortcut:
'István's back. He's badly wounded.'

Inside the flat, Gyuri got a glimpse of István lying on the
dining-room table, looking like an eleven stone steak. Elek was
next to him with one of his old army chums, Krúdy, a doctor
who was taking instruments out of a black bag. Gyuri knew,
although he knew that he shouldn't know, that Krúdy had
made a fortune out of pussy, angel-making (conducting
abortions) and reconstituting hymens to produce born-again
virgins for the best families in Budapest. Just before Elek shut
the door in his face, István, who had somehow noticed Gyuri
standing there, shouted: 'Sorry, I didn't bring you back
anything this time.'

When Kálmán returned with another officer, Gyuri was still
floating around outside the dining-room. 'We couldn't find
any anaesthetic,' he said undoing his uniform, 'this is going to
take a long time. He's got more metal in him than a cash
register.' During the intermissions in the surgery Gyuri
learned from Kálmán that he had found out that morning
that István's unit had been strafed by Russian planes near
Gödölő, just outside Budapest. Kálmán had phoned Elek and
they had gone out to search for István. It was a good thing,
Gyuri realised, that his mother was away in the countryside
getting supplies, otherwise Elek would be taking full
responsibility for the Second World War.

Much later, Krúdy came out: 'Now we can start worrying
about the Russians.'

* * *

In some ways István had been very lucky. They put him on the
last train to get out of Budapest, moments before the Russians
completely encircled the city. He didn't have to spend six
weeks in a cellar while the Russians and Germans argued over
Budapest.

There were some consolations to living in a cellar. First-floor Noémi who had been unrequiting Gyuri's love for some time was forced into proximity with him. But the diet of tedium, unwashedness and intermittent horsemeat was hard to take. It was also hard to think well of anyone with whom you had spent six weeks in a cellar The only person to come out of the cellar episode with any credit was Mrs Molnár, venomous in peacetime but now that war had expunged the basis of her displeasure with society – namely the lead everyone else had in such fields as youth, pleasure and more expensive patisserie – sparked cheer and encouragement. Pataki had a huge supply of books and seemed content with the opportunity for a good read. Elek had sat stoically smoking cigarettes for as long as there were cigarettes. After that, he just sat stoically.

It was not long after Noémi had complained about not having washed in recent history, that the bleak observation of old Fitos, the head pessimist in a cellar strong in pessimistic competition, 'Cheer up, when you think things have become unbearable, they are going to get worse', came true. The Russians made their way into the cellar.

Depending on how drunk they were, they either removed the women to some separate room or they did it on the spot. They were fair. They didn't just rape the young and attractive women but distributed the violations equally. It was a day when Gyuri was glad that he didn't own a vagina.

The Russians took anything of value, anything portable; Gyuri even noticed one eyeing the huge boiler greedily.

Elek negotiated with them in German, as far as circumstances and linguistic abilities allowed. This rather boiled down to Elek translating the Ivans' request for booty. The legendary fondness of the Red Army for wristwatches proved to be well-founded: everyone, including Elek, lost their timepiece.

The Russians left bouncily, doubtless feeling the cellar at number ten had been well worth the visit. Gyuri hadn't been upset or concerned about his mother's jewels or Elek's watch;

after all, Elek could buy replacements after the war. However, he was glad he had hidden his own wristwatch, a large Swiss model with so many dials he couldn't remember what they were all for, around his right ankle, beneath the protection of a thick sock. 'They didn't get my watch,' he reported to Elek, showing its concealed position. Elek stared at him in disbelief, slapped him around the head, took the watch and rushed out to give it to the Russians.

* * *

In the streets it looked as if it had been raining dead Russians. As Gyuri and Pataki wandered around they didn't notice any dead Germans; perhaps the German horror of disorder had prompted them to tidy up as they retreated. All the corpses were frozen solid and many of them had left life in the most ridiculous postures. It reminded Gyuri of the pictures of the bodies from Pompeii, frozen in time by the lava from erupting Vesuvius, that István had brought back from his school trip there. Gyuri was looking forward to visiting Pompeii, mainly because of the more artistic murals, as István said the guide had labelled them, one of which reputedly featured a guy with a dick the size of an oar.

A lorry pulled up and before the idea of running away had even occurred to him or Pataki, a Soviet soldier jumped out, a fat Ukrainian peasant. (If he wasn't one he should have considered that profession because he had the looks for it.) Waving his submachine gun, the davai guitar, in the winning way the Ivans had, he succinctly expressed his wish that they should load up some of his fallen comrades onto the lorry. Having made clear the task, the soldier set off for some investigative looting. For weeks after the fighting ended, they were quite accustomed to Russians strolling into the flat and liberating some item that caught their eye, anything from one of Elek's suits to his Mother's eau de cologne, usually consumed on the premises. There had even been one individual who had stayed for a long time trying to work out how you were supposed to drink from the toilet bowl.

Józsi joined Gyuri and Pataki and gave them a hand loading up the defunct soldiers. The floor of the lorry was frozen and you could slide the corpses along as if you were curling. There were some really ludicrous poses – one corpse had a hand cupped to his ear as if straining to hear something. 'What's that, Sergei?' Pataki supplied the line. 'The wrist watches are definitely in the next block.' Another corpse they managed to get upright, and leaning him slightly against a wall managed to return a semblance of animation to him. Pataki sacrificed a last cigarette to give a more life-like appearance to the figure. 'Sure, I've got a light,' said Pataki holding a match to the cigarette inserted between cadaverous lips. From a distance it really did look a Russian soldier having a smoke. It was as they were trying to get one corpse to give a piggyback ride to another that they discerned, by the augmenting sound of swearing, the return of the soldier, who was rather angry to see that he didn't have a lorryful of corpses and that Gyuri, Pataki and Józsi were slowly, sombrely, respectfully, gingerly and tenderly placing the mortal bits of a fallen hero on the back of the lorry. '*Malenky robot, malenky robot,*' (a phrase everyone now knew meant 'a little work') he repeated furiously, '*bistro! bistro!*', waving his gun to indicate the rapid tempo of work he desired; evidently, he had an important looting to attend. The remaining bodies in the vicinity went in faster than sacks of potatoes.

Having filled up the lorry, they were about to bid farewell when the soldier indicated, again through the eloquent means of the sub-machine gun, that they should clamber in the back as well. They thought about objecting, but very briefly. They got on board and watched as the lorry drove out to the City Park. It was an uncomfortable trip. 'These stiffs are stiff,' remarked Pataki.

They were taken into some administrative building where they were shown to the basement and locked in. An ugliness was noticeable in the atmosphere and because Pataki had some bean soup waiting for lunch, they decided to decamp. There was a small window that with great difficulty they could just about climb out of (another portion or two of horseflesh the previous week and they wouldn't have made it). They emerged at the back of the building, without any Russians in view. After they had run all the way home, they didn't set foot outside for a couple of days. Mr Pártos from the first floor, who had ventured into town since he had had a tip-off about some milk, had disappeared that day. A week later he managed to get a message home from the cattlewagon he was in at Záhony, near the Hungarian–Soviet border, through the kind medium of a railway worker. He had been invited to do a '*malenky robot*' by a Russian soldier, and obviously there was some mistake which he was confident he could sort out.

* * *

A lot of Gyuri's fellow pupils had been killed, so the first roll call of school recommencing was rather grim. Annoyingly, none of the teachers had snuffed it. In particular, Gyuri had been hoping that Vágvölgyi would have copped a direct hit from some Russian artillery or an American bomber, but there he was, bald as a snooker ball, unsmiling, blocking Gyuri's path down the corridor, patently expecting the project on Kossuth which was already a week late when the Russians had arrived to give Gyuri a breathing space. If anyone else had said: 'I trust you used the extra time to broaden your background reading?' he would have been joking. Vágvölgyi wasn't. As Gyuri floundered in his explanation of how reading one more book on Kossuth's American exile had prevented him from entirely completing his opus, Vágvölgyi shook his head with a wounded look. 'Fischer, Fischer, this is deplorable. You can't let a little war interfere with serious scholarship. You know our history. As a Hungarian you should be prepared for the odd cataclysm.'

October 1946

Pataki was having a lucubratory crap when they came to arrest him.

He was comfortably perched, working his way through a first edition of Tompa's poetry, a splendid gold-embossed publication printed in 1849 that had come from a bombed-out Jewish flat. Tompa was the sort of poet Pataki liked, plodding and second-rate, and this was precisely why Pataki was investigating his rhyme schemes. Tompa's mediocrity was rather reassuring. Tompa had been *there*, Petőfi's sidekick, in the middle of the 1848 revolution, the highlight of the century, bobbing up and down in the cauldron of era-making, handed all the great moments of existence, and he had fluffed it. All Tompa had managed to do was to knock out greeting-card verse, a chain of tum-tee-tum.

Tompa was what you wanted in the way of a literary predecessor, solid, reliable, uninspired, doing some useful groundwork, warming up a few promising stanzas, passing on the baton to his successors so they could make the dash to glory. A spear-carrier. A stagehand. Not like that bastard Petőfi who had fenced off most of the language, who had confiscated most of the things worth poetising about, creating Hungarian literature in the lunchbreaks between his revolutionary activities; the man who (according to some authorities) had declared the 1848 revolution open, monogrammed all the best poetic forms, tossed out entire school and university syllabuses as a sideline, and fought with the Hungarian revolutionary army which thrashed the Habsburgs, the army which looked as if it had ironed out the jinx, when whoops, it got wiped out.

Then Petőfi had the nerve to die, looking sharp in a white shirt, alone, on foot against Cossack cavalry at twenty-six. A man whose verse was embossed on every Hungarian at the factory.

That was what you didn't need – some rotten genius queering the pitch, eating up all the literary glory on the table. Pataki had two recurring dreams. One was rather nightmarish: he would be drummed by a heart-rending fear that he couldn't remember either the names or the addresses or the telephone numbers of two or three staggeringly attractive women he had met: their details were always just out of recall, the fingertips of his memory couldn't reach the shelf they were kept on, so he had no way of tracking down the beauties. They were out there, waiting for him, but he couldn't get his memory to cough up. He would wake in a sweat.

The other dream featured a bookcase. It was the type of dream where you knew from the kick-off it was a dream. The pre-eminent book was a thick volume of poetry. The whole form of this book spoke of great literature, it was stuffed with world-class stuff, the sort of thing that would be in everyone's collection, even those people who don't read. So Pataki would read the book, thinking, this is brilliant poetry, it could muscle its way into any anthology of verse, it leaves Petőfi at the starting-line and it doesn't *exist*. All I have to do, thinks Pataki, is memorise it, write it down when I wake up, and hey presto, instant immortality.

Nevertheless, although he trotted through the dream again and again, he could never capture a chunk. Once, exceptionally, he returned with a line 'The dog is in the dogcase', which despite long consideration, wasn't any good on its own, and Pataki was unable to do the sequels. There was a variant on this dream where he came across a heap of gold coins, and despite furiously concentrating on bringing them back, he would wake up with a fist full of nothing.

Pataki did try writing without the shortcuts but although he would get enthused during the writing, as the ink dried, so did his satisfaction. The ideas, the visions that turned his ignition were exciting but it was like taking a pebble out of a river where it gleamed and watching it become matt and boring. Pataki tried to splash with ink the invisible men that only he could see, so that others could detect their outlines, but he always missed and was merely left with a mess.

He hadn't succeeded in penning anything he wanted to show other people. It was so frustrating to see something like a beautiful girl and then to end up with something like a matchstick figure scrawled on a wall.

Thus, drawing comfort from Tompa's mechanical poetry, Pataki was surprised to hear a jarring knock on the toilet door (not really designed to take the force of a heavy fist) and an unfamiliar male voice calling his name. He was surprised, but not as surprised as he would be when he discovered it was the AVO outside waiting for him.

As secret police went, the AVO weren't terribly secret about what they did – half the business of being secret policemen is people knowing about you, word-of-mouth-publicity. Pataki's mother was, fortunately, even more astonished than he was; she was flabbergasted into silence and so there was no scene as they left the flat. Even more fortunately Pataki's father was still at work. If he was going to talk his way out of this problem he didn't want any interference. The problem was, what was the problem? The two AVO made a point of not telling him why he was wanted for questioning; they were milking the superiority of their knowledge, that Pataki could tell. Until he discovered the cause of the trouble, it was going to be difficult to decide which fraud to unpack; he readied two or three all-purpose disclaimers so as to have a good story at hand.

They passed Mrs Vajda on the staircase lamenting with Mrs Csörgő the demolition of the church that had stood at the end of Damjanich utca for over a hundred years. 'This can't go on much longer,' she was saying.

The AVO car was long and black, and Pataki tried to enjoy the short ride. There was something flattering about being arrested, the entourage did testify to one's importance, but being in custody was becoming a habit; he really had to cut down. There had been the corpse-collecting incident – the window had got them out of that. Then he and Józsi had accompanied Gyuri to his mother's cottage in Erdőváros. The first day in the countryside they had walked out of a forest slap into a Russian camp. Pataki immediately feigned intense pain, on the lines of acute appendicitis, and got the others to plead for a doctor and medicine. This appeal had the desired effect, the soldiers had told them to go to hell and shooed them away.

They had been reliving that escape the following day, chuckling over Russian gullibility as they fired a revolver at some bottles they had carried out to a local beauty spot for target practice. This was when there had been notices everywhere, in newspapers, on walls, in railway carriages warning that anyone caught with a firearm would be considered a bandit, a fascist, someone to be shot forthwith. It was probably the shooting and their chuckling that obscured the sound of Russian patrol until it was right behind them.

One of the four soldiers, a true short-arse, who looked about twelve, was extremely jolly. The Red Army manual for troops stationed in Hungary obviously contained the phrase 'We are going to shoot you' (just to prevent any misunderstanding) since the midget kept on repeating it with an appalling accent, adding various onomatopoeic execution effects, like 'bbubbbbuabbaa'. This he did, interspersing delighted laughter, all the way to their headquarters in the village of Jew. The people who lived in Jew didn't look at all Jewish, nor were they, otherwise they'd have been long dead.

Not for the first time Pataki reflected on the imbecility of Hungarian village names and how idiotic it would look to be shot in Jew.

They were left in a small room, with a window so minute none of them could have managed to get more than an arm out, and besides which their titchy escort was on guard outside, still rehearsing for the firing-squad. It was going to be a tough one to mendacity out, Pataki had reflected, bearing in mind that none of them had a greater command of Russian than 'fuck your mother'. Józsi was beginning to smell badly and Gyuri's eyes were on stalks of terror. 'Don't worry,' Pataki said in an endeavour to bolster morale, 'they're not going to shoot us.' 'It's not that,' replied Gyuri, 'everyone saw us being brought here. My mother's going to kill me.' Pataki then recalled that Gyuri's last word to his mother before going out the door had been 'no' in response to the irate question 'You haven't still got that revolver, have you?'

Pataki was exploring two lines of thought: first, that they had found the revolver and were on their way to hand it in, precisely because they realised how illegal and dangerous such an object was and how it could easily fall into the wrong hands. Or there was the hunting down of a Nazi soldier reputed by the locals to be scavenging in the forest, harbouring wicked anti-Soviet ideals, with the jackpot line 'we wanted to bring him in ourselves as thanks to the Red Army for having so selflessly liberated our country of evil scum like this'; it was a better yarn but sadly less believable.

Then the commanding officer came in. Pataki divined from the crestfallen look on the midget's face that perhaps they weren't going to be fattened up with lead. None of the fabrications were given a chance to come into play but an abrasive, sandpaper severity lecture skinned them alive (through an interpreter) and to Gyuri's disappointment they were released and had to go home. That captivity had been just over an hour; how long would the AVO hold him?

At a stately pace, the driver took the AVO car down the

boulevardous Andrássy út and turned right at number 60, their headquarters. Pataki cut off his reminiscences with the thought that the entrance to number 60 looked familiar and recalled that he had seen it in a newsreel, showing captive Arrow Cross leaders and other assorted Nazi assistants being led in, handcuffed, having a good idea of how their trials were going to go: hangings all round. The car pulled into the side entrance, the tradesmen's entrance as it were and Pataki suddenly ran out of nonchalance; fear made itself comfortable in his mind.

He was ushered up a long, ornate staircase, with incapacitatingly thick carpet. The opulence of the interior was all the more striking since Pataki couldn't remember seeing a freshly-decorated wall or indeed one without bulletholes or some sort of martial damage for years.

He was shoved into a large room, with a ceiling almost out of sight from which was suspended a chandelier the size of a crystal yacht. 'Go and stand in the corner,' said one of his escorts. Pataki then noticed someone else in another corner with his nose pressed into the right-angle of the walls. Even though he only got the rear view, from his red hair, bolt upright like a thistle, he recognised Fuchs. This revelation and the schoolmasterly injunction to stand in the corner brought on a fit of laughter which had a high hysteria content. This, in turn, produced a fist in Pataki's ear, which was still smarting when it got dark outside but Pataki was quite happy to stand like a dunce because he now knew what it was all about and he could get the juices of expiation, protestation and misrepresentation ready to flow; moreover, for once, he hadn't done anything.

It had all started with the rowing trip down the Danube with Gyuri. They stopped for a bite of lunch on Csepel Island and as they relaxed on the verdant riverbank Gyuri spotted a small container of the type that usually housed grenades. To their joy, it was full of grenades. They did some fishing – grenades producing unbeatable results – no wasting time with maggots, bits of line, hooks, weights, waiting. But after you've harvested a good haul of zapped fish, the fun diminishes.

They were good grenades, German grenades, so Pataki, having acquired Gyuri's holding through a boat-counting wager, decided to sell or trade them at school, as he had done a roaring trade at the close of the war, arms-dealing for a little pocket-money.

During one of Hidassy's physics lessons Pataki started his retail exploits. Hidassy was, no matter how many times he had taught a topic, passionate and excited in his exposition, so much so that as soon as he launched into density or atomic eccentricities he didn't even notice what the front row was doing, and as far as the back row was concerned, with Pataki and the grenades, it could have been on the other side of the planet. One week they had even managed a small scale football match using a rolled-up paper ball without Hidassy intervening.

Hidassy made a pleasant change from the other masters who loved to supervise every aspect of a pupil's existence, for example someone like Horváth, whom it was rumoured had been stripped of his Army commission because of the embarrassing number of conscripts who had died in his charge. Horváth was always caning people or grooming them for expulsion on grounds of insufficiently perpendicular spines. Snoozing on the workbench however didn't bother Hidassy, who just carried on waving sections of rubber tubing or sticking things into a bunsen burner. On the occasion Pataki had ignited one of the laboratory benches, purely experimenting to see if it would burn, Hidassy's only reaction had been to open a window to let the smoke out.

One day, an hour after school had finished and the class had filed out, it was claimed Hidassy had been seen still conducting a lesson on electromagnetism: he loved physics. And he was liked by his pupils, not only because he left them in peace, but because, when it came to exam time and mouths were left gasping like landed fish, he would give a good mark for 'understanding the principle'. In fact what usually happened during the oral exam was that he asked the question and then, even before you had time to supply an answer (should you have happened to have had one), however feeble or conquering, he would beamingly answer it, requiring at most a little nodding in agreement from the examinee.

'Teller was telling me that if you split the atom, you'd blow up the whole world: the least he could have done was write to apologise,' Hidassy was rambling as Pataki sold his grenades. Keresztes, as well as Fuchs, came round to examine the goods, which Pataki wished they wouldn't do. Keresztes was an unwelcome customer as he was perilously unpredictable. During the siege, Soviet machine gunners had found Keresztes at their elbows, asking for a go. Once Pataki and Gyuri had been at a fairground when Keresztes had latched on to them. A gypsy, without carelessness or malice, entirely through the natural Brownian motion of public place, had brushed into Keresztes. Courteously asking for Gyuri's celebrated penknife, Keresztes had run through the different attachments and, having selected the longest blade, sunk it into the gypsy. 'Thanks,' he had said politely.

That was the only occasion, though, that Pataki had seen Keresztes exhibit good manners. Fuchs wasn't great as a prospective customer either as he had an unblemished reputation as penniless. In any gathering of thirty youths, there is always one who gets sat on. Someone, anyone, would call 'time for a Fuchs' and immediately a quorum of eight would sit on Fuchs; more might be interested, but Fuchs wasn't very large, and even with ten there would be a couple only sitting on a brace of fingers, a hand, a nose – something peripheral like that. It was a rather simple, but an inexhaustible amusement. Fuchs was also good for locking in cupboards, and because it was public knowledge that his mother would phone the police if he was two minutes late home, on one side-splitting occasion he had been handcuffed to a rail in the number forty-seven tram, where he had stayed despite his impassioned pleas until the driver took the tram back to the terminal.

Even more amusing than doing things to Fuchs was doing things to his briefcase. He had acquired a very sober, expensive leather briefcase through a family belief that such an accoutrement would boost his scholastic achievement. Because the briefcase was pompous, very expensive and above all belonged to Fuchs it came in for a lot of attention. Fuchs had a curious spiritual oneness with this briefcase that transcended merely trying to protect it. Since it was kicked on sight Fuchs had to walk around with the briefcase clutched to his chest, but as he couldn't maintain such tight security all day, the briefcase would disappear. Invariably, the moment it fell into hostile hands, no matter how distracted he was, Fuchs was telepathically alerted and he would have to be sat on while his briefcase was filled with liquids, trampolined on, nailed to a wall, or on one memorable occasion during one of Sólyom-Nagy's chocolate gluts in early '44, topped up with chocolate melted over a bunsen burner to the accompaniment of Hidassy's discourse on the spectrum.

They were sitting on the window ledge at the rear of the classroom where Keresztes pawed the grenades much to Pataki's discomfiture. The lab was on the second floor and there was a drop of twenty feet to the pavement. A vogue was sweeping the school for jumping off the top of the music block, which was a twelve foot drop onto grass, started by Gombóc, whose elder brother had been a paratrooper, resulting in an epidemic of sprained and broken ankles. Keresztes lobbed a grenade up and down thoughtfully: 'I tell you what. I bet you this grenade that you can jump out this window and walk away.' Keresztes never explained what he was going to put up but in any case Pataki wasn't having it, since whether or not Keresztes broke his neck, such an escapade could only add to Pataki's detention time, which was already heavily curtailing his rowing on the Danube.

Pataki had already said no three times when Keresztes, who

needed to be told things six times as a minimum, threw Fuchs out of the window. Fuchs looked surprised at the physics lesson having run away from him but had got up swiftly and dusted himself off. 'See,' said Keresztes, 'my grenade.' Whereupon he pulled out the pin. Row upon row of boys ducked under their benches as awareness of the unpinned grenade spread.

After a good three or four minutes, Pataki crawled out from underneath the neighbouring bench to see Keresztes holding the grenade up to the light. 'All right, how did you know it was a dud?'

'I didn't,' replied Keresztes. Just then Fuchs walked back into the classroom. Hidassy, who hadn't missed a word of his eulogy on the electron during the grenade scare, rounded on Fuchs. 'How dare you leave the classroom without my permission? Double detention.' That lesson was the last time they saw Keresztes. Two rumours made the rounds. One that the headmaster had Keresztes on a retainer to stay away from school; the other that Keresztes's vanishing was due to having bet someone at Kőbánya railway station that he could head-butt the 4.15 from the Keleti, which didn't stop at Kőbánya, into submission. Pataki definitely preferred the latter version and found the detail verisimilar.

Fuchs had been doubly depressed by the double detention: he had never had a detention and Hidassy, to the best of everyone's knowledge, had never given a detention.

As they left their punishment, Fuchs bent double with woe, his briefcase pressed to his chest, Pataki, since there was no one else around to witness it, felt compassion and tried to cheer Fuchs up. 'It's no use,' moaned Fuchs, 'I'll never do the great stuff like you, selling grenades. No one sits on you.' Pataki strived to play down the kudos of arms-dealing but as they waited for the tram, his sense of humour pushed in front of his compassion when Fuchs suggested: 'Look, couldn't I help you sell some?' Pataki looked contemplative for a theatrical moment, then agreed. 'Okay,' he said.

Pataki outlined the hidden underground German arsenal he had discovered which was brimming over with top SS gear, ammunition, weapons, grenades etc., which would make the two of them a fortune.

'What you need to bring is rope ... a lot of rope, fifty feet. A miner's helmet or if you can't get one, a very powerful torch. And lots of sorrel.'

'Sorrel?'

'Yes. You know, the green stuff. Sorrel is the best thing to pack explosives in; it relaxes them,' elucidated Pataki with an infallibly serious face. The rest of the way home, after he had farewelled Fuchs, Pataki kept lapsing into laughter at the thought of Fuchs working his way through the shopping list. And on the appointed Thursday, when Fuchs showed up at school hidden under enormous coils of rope, a miner's helmet at a rakish angle on his head, carrying two huge baskets full of fresh green sorrel, Pataki was truly afraid that he was going to injure himself or pass out. He had also primed the rest of the class about the proposed weapons-quest, so there was universal merriment, but it was the touch of the miner's helmet, which must have potently taxed Fuchs's ingenuity, that finished Pataki off. He couldn't control himself and earned three detentions for inexplicable spasms of mirth. By the next afternoon he had managed to compose himself as he read his Tompa.

* * *

The schoolish atmosphere at number 60 Andrássy út was further heightened by an instruction, after he had been standing in the corner for hours, to cover two sides of paper with his curriculum vitae. Pataki was calm now, if not utterly confident of talking his way home that night. The grenades he had actually sold would be long gone, deniable. A blanket refusal to acknowledge them was the tactic there, and as for the subterranean German arms cache, since there wasn't one, he could reveal it as a schoolboy prank, apologise profusely and go home. It was a pity he hadn't had a chance to liaise with Fuchs to harmonise their narratives, but he polished various emotional stages, fear, incredulity, repentance, with a few stand-by lies in reserve. Mentally, he adjusted the tones of denial and set the level of horrified innocence he wanted to draw on at key junctures.

They were interrogated separately. Pataki was allowed to sit, and this he did as respectfully and helpfully as humanely possible. His interrogator was wearing the new blue-insignia uniform of the AVO and he started off the session with: 'Of course, we know all about you, Pataki.' Pataki paid no heed to the contemptuous tone and smiled steadily, working on the theory that smiling might reduce the chances of getting hit. The interrogator looked at his life story with conspicuous disgust. He put it down with what Pataki as a consummate dissimulator instantly spotted as an artificial hiatus; he had the feeling that his interrogator wanted to go home. It was nine o' clock after all. 'Fuchs has confessed everything about the weapons. He told us you wanted to be his assistant in organising an armed struggle... 'No,' said Pataki as uncontradictorily as possible, 'there aren't any weapons, it's...' 'What's this then?' asked the interrogator, slapping a German sub-machine gun on the table. He counted the beats and said: 'An oversized and extremely impractical toothpick? Part of a lawnmower perhaps?'

Pataki found himself, for the first time in his life, out of stock of any suitable fabrications. Were they going to frame him? Whatever was going on he realised he wasn't going to get any of the good lines. 'But as I said,' continued the interrogator, 'Fuchs has turned on his mouth. He explained that you didn't know anything, that he was just bringing you in to help distribute. We've nipped this one in the bud, which is as well for you.' Here it is, thought Pataki seeing it coming, he wants to go home. 'We know all about you. That's our job. But you're young. We're going to overlook this mistake though it's a weighty offence. We're going to give you another chance.' Whatever you say, thought Pataki. 'You're in the scouts, aren't you?' It wasn't a question.

They didn't give him a lift back home. Andrássy út, bleak and black as it was, looked tremendously beautiful to Pataki. He inhaled a generous amount of night air. A poem about freedom was coming on, given his new qualifications in valuing it. The prop with the gun had been a little crude, he judged, but he had been really afraid they were going to stitch him up. But if they deemed waving a gun necessary to get his co-operation, that was their business.

Ladányi was then in charge of the scout troop. The other Jesuits took part, but it was Ladányi's principal duty, fitting enough, as he had worked his way up through the ranks. He looked the part of the Jesuit, tall with sober eyes that could gatecrash your thoughts. Pataki had to remind himself that although Ladányi was dressed in black, he was still on probation; there was some ridiculously long apprenticeship for the Society of Jesus, advanced altar-kissing and so on.

'I know you may find this hard to believe …' Pataki began.

'Let me guess: the AVO want you to spy on the troop,' Ladányi volunteered.

'Er … yes, frankly. How did you know?'

'Someone would have to do it. Your fondness for getting into trouble makes you the obvious choice. May I suggest copying out the troop's newsletter? It'll save you a lot of time. Just give a little more space to any particularly noteworthy knots, any really intriguing bonfires. Those people are very keen on paperwork. Anything else?'

Pataki met Fuchs on the way to school a week later, the first time he had seen him since their joint incarceration. Fuchs seemed terribly frightened and upset to see him. 'I'm sorry, I thought you were joking about those guns: that's why I took them to the caverns; but I think I managed to convince them it was me who found them. I'm sorry.'

Pataki and Fuchs never talked about it again. They never

really talked again. And Pataki certainly never talked about it with anyone else. But he noticed that people didn't sit on Fuchs any more.

September 1948

The ant-training had been typical. Gyuri knew he should be studying much harder. Unlike all previous exams, whose certificates of importance he had never found convincing, this was frighteningly, windpipe-constrictingly important, and he really should have been studying much harder. He had wanted to study much harder. The intention had been beautifully formed, it had been everything an intention should be, but it remained an understudy, never getting on stage.

He had rowed out on his own to a quiet stretch of Margit Island with a whole boatful of textbooks, leaving no clue as to his whereabouts. It was just him and the mathematics. One on one. Lying in the heat of the elderly summer, Gyuri opened the books to lay himself bare to calculus, to bask in the equations, but while his tan deepened, somehow his erudition didn't. He felt cheated. Like jumping off a cliff, he had hurled himself at the distant algebra, but instead of plummeting down to impact with those formulae, he just hovered above, aloft, some covert anti-gravity repelling him from the maths.

Relishing the unrationed sunshine, he succumbed to a bout of ant-shepherding. Prior to this, his only dealings with ants had been stepping on them, either by accident or squashing them when they invaded his possessions or edibles. He had partitioned himself at the intersection of a number of formic caravan routes and spent the better part of three hours devising olympianly a series of obstacles and tests for the ants with the aid of twigs, leaves and extracts from his lunch sandwiches. He toyed with the idea of becoming a great entomologist, a world-leading zoologist. As far as he knew, biology was an area unpolluted by Marx though some of his disciples, like Lysenko, had tried to make up for Marx's silence on the phyla.

The fascination of the ants had run unabated as long as there was no other distraction from the maths. Mathematics had this to recommend it, if nothing else: it made everything else, ants, English, push-ups, ironing, washing-up, beguiling and wonderful. Whole new galaxies of interests had popped open now that the maths exam was drawing close; anything unconnected with maths was irresistible.

He rowed back to the boat-house to discover that Pataki had been sculling up and down the Danube looking for him in a fruitless attempt to gloat over his revision.

Gyuri lugged the maths books home. He was used to carrying the heavy weight about as a sort of tandem intellectual and physical toning, helping his stamina and also, he hoped, the proximity of the knowledge would help it to spill out on him. There were many dogs in Budapest that weren't as well-walked as his maths textbooks. Entering the flat, Gyuri noted that Pataki wasn't around, because Elek was on his own. Pataki had taken to frequenting the Fischer flat, because he found Elek most congenial, as unlike Pataki's father, Elek had no objection to Pataki smoking; indeed, he would hoard up cigarettes, ear-marking sole survivors of a delivery to be reserved for an appearance by Pataki.

More and more often Gyuri would return from training or a run to find Elek and Pataki in a nicotine partnership, making the most of scanty tobacco; Elek usually testifying to the callipygian glories of a set of buttocks he had encountered as long as four decades ago. Gyuri didn't smoke. The odds against him playing first-division basketball were already so great that he couldn't afford any handicap however small, so he didn't begrudge the extrafamilial sharing of the cigarettes.

What was irritating was Elek's equanimity.

Elek would now be regularly on duty in the large armchair which was almost the last remnant of their prewar furniture, indeed virtually the last of their prewar property. Stationing himself in this armchair, abetted by a cigarette if available, Elek looked unbelievably good for a man completely ruined. His hair and moustache were so disciplined it was as if they had been sculpted into place; however the grey pullover which was now the core of his wardrobe did have two impossible-to-miss holes. Other men having seen all their assets evaporate overnight, especially having an entire fortune fly by night, would have protested bitterly at the unseen forces reducing their wealth to the small change in their trouser pockets. Destitute at the age of sixty, even allowing for the common denominator of a world war and vast industries of suffering and misery, you would have expected some cursing and shrieking. A gnawing of fists. A denouncing of higher powers.

But Elek didn't issue any unseemly lamentations. He simply sat in the armchair, at ease, as if enjoying a day off. He tried to resurrect his fortunes after the war, and more crucially, after the hyper-inflation, which Hungarians proudly pointed out had been the fastest and greatest in economic history. Once the inflation was over, Elek went to the bank where he had deposited millions, emptied his unfrozen account and bought a loaf of bread, hardly getting any change back. The gutters of Budapest had been clogged with discarded banknotes, the fallen leaves of an old order.

What tortured Gyuri even more than Elek's tranquillity, what racked him night and day, was the sheer inanity of the loss. It could have been so different, a tiny stash in Switzerland, a loose gold ingot buried in a field, some well-cached jewellery and things would have been different enough for them to eat and even eat well. But everything had gone in what would amount to no more than, at best, an eyebrow raising footnote in abstruse economic journals.

Funnily enough for a bookie who had made a very good living out of people losing their money on horses, Elek's first ventures to recoup some money saw him going to the track for a string of flutters. Gyuri could distinctly remember Elek before the war coming home with the takings from the races (in a small brown suitcase, the money all jumbled up for Elek's staff to sort out) and exclaiming: 'Human folly – it's the business to be in. You can't go wrong.' His turf accountancy riches had been less the result of his astuteness than the fact of bookmaking being a virtual monopoly and one of his old army chums being responsible for handing out the licences. Nevertheless, incited perhaps by his inside knowledge, Elek remained adamant that the gee-gees would provide, if not a regular income, a start-up capital for some future, nameless, hardship-solving enterprise.

Elek's excursions to the track were, in the main, shirt-losing exercises but now and then he must have won since there were evenings when there was something to eat. More direct action took place too. One day Gyuri came home to find that his books, all his books, were gone; all that was remained was a patch of lighter wallpaper 'I had to sell them,' Elek replied to Gyuri's inquiry: 'we have to eat you know.' Which was fine, but Elek could have asked first, and the galling thing was not that the books were gone but that whatever the going market value of his library was Elek would have been bamboozled and only got a tenth of it. Elek's business sense, if he ever had any, seemed to have been mislaid somewhere during the war. The grocery shop that he had run for a month was the best example; it nearly destroyed the family because they had to rise before dawn to buy stock and not only did they not make any money, they lost it. They lost a staggering amount, more than if they had just jettisoned the greens in the street. Grocers weren't keen on other people becoming grocers.

Ambitious projects like grocering were behind Elek now, the armchair was enough. Since Mother died, Elek had demonstrated less of a need to be seen doing something. There were mysterious absences from time to time, which spawned packages of food, but Elek treated life largely as a spectator sport.

This lack of remorse and of pleading to rewrite the script could be accounted in some quarters as admirable, but Gyuri found himself unable to applaud: 'How does it feel to have one of the most sat-on arses in the universe?' he inquired after a very forlorn day. Elek shrugged: 'My father lost everything,' he said, as if this were a lucid explanation, appending by way of conclusion, 'You'll dig me up when I'm gone.'

Gyuri hadn't seen much of his grandfather. Memories of his grandfather's visits in his furthest childhood had two components: nice cakes he wasn't allowed to touch and a bullet-headed, dangerous-looking old man who kept asking who Gyuri was. His grandfather had, according to Elek, stood surety for a friend's gambling debts. The friend had been unable to pay and instead of doing the done and honourable thing, passing a bullet through his brains, went off to Berlin to open a Hungarian restaurant, leaving grandfather to fork out. But if nothing else Elek and grandfather had handled fortunes. Somehow Gyuri feared that he wouldn't be given a fortune to lose.

Nevertheless, Elek's snap pauperdom had certain benefits for Gyuri. Having a father who had stepped down from life meant there was no friction over the exam business. Elek had never been excessively concerned about Gyuri's schoolwork; sometimes Gyuri wondered if Elek knew which school he was attending. In a rare and ephemeral flare of studiousness, Gyuri once asked Elek to test him on some Latin verbs. 'Do you know them or not?' Elek had queried, and when Gyuri had responded that he thought that he did, Elek had retorted: 'Then why do I need to test you?'

Still, Gyuri reflected, as he shaved in the first of his preparations for his evening out, at least he only had to sit one subject again to get his matriculation certificate. Next door, while he decapitated his bristles, he could hear Mr Galántai repeatedly complaining about the nationalisation of the factories which really must have been exercising him since it had happened some months ago. 'This is too much – it can't go on much longer.'

Gyuri had no doubt that things would go on for some time yet. Enough to get him in the Army. This was the sole encouragement to study – and it was a truly major carrot. No pass, no university. No university, yes Army. Yes to years of not eating, standing out in the rain, digging ditches, not seeing anyone you knew, anyone you liked, prison with salutes and worse beds. People preferred to commit suicide before being conscripted as it was more agreeable to die at home in comfort, rather than truncating your arteries in some dingy barracks.

It was a good thing that mathematics was the only remaining weight threatening to drag him down into all that; after all there had been many fails nuzzling up against him in the exams. Hungarian literature had been a real case of digging himself out of the grave. Luckily, Botond had been conducting the oral examination, albeit with a couple of other teachers who didn't like him as much, or probably at all. The set text was Arany's *Toldi*. Either he had never had a copy or he couldn't find it but the evening before, when Gyuri had resolved to read a bit, his sudden desire to read Arany was foiled so he turned up dutifully at the exam to collect a fail.

Botond was sitting with his feet up on the table. The other teachers' faces were strongly broadcasting that this detracted from the decorum of the occasion but Botond was the head of the Hungarian Department and what was more was unchallengeable in Hungarian literature. He had read everything twice, and when it came to poetry could recite nearly every published verse. If you were lucky, if something sparked him off, he would enter a Hidassy-like trance and declaim flawlessly for twenty minutes, giving the class a much-needed break. As befitted someone deeply implicated with art, Botond had long unruly hair, so remorselessly unruly that pupils and staff suspected he engineered his coiffure to look like a starfish every morning.

'Well, Fischer,' Botond had said jovially staring up at the ceiling, tapping a cuspid with the earpiece of his spectacles, probably running through some juicy texts at the back of the cerebral shop while he was going through the tedious business of testing the pupils. 'It's always a pleasure to see you, but I regret that you'll have to give us some of *Toldi* before we can let you go.'

'To be honest, I can't,' Gyuri owned up. 'I'm sorry; but I don't know any.'

'Ha, ha. Always modest. Always modest. Any section, just fire away.'

'No honestly. I don't want to waste your time,' Gyuri had insisted.

'Exam nerves, eh? All right, just recite any one of your favourite poems.'

It was a reasonable request, but it caught Gyuri by surprise. He rifled his literary knowledge but the drawer was empty. 'No, sir, I'm afraid I can't recite anything.'

'Ha, ha, Fischer, your sense of humour will get you into trouble one day. I'll put you down for a pass. Send in the next candidate, please.' Botond was extremely avuncular to everyone (except those who evinced a sincere enmity to poetry). He was one of the few masters who was liked, a fondness fuelled by the biographical information, passed on year after year, that Botond had got drunk with all the major figures working the Hungarian language since the turn of the century. He had starved with Ady in Paris ('Bandi and I were arguing who should peel the potato for supper') and with eight other unwashed and less posteritied Hungarians shared one bed on a shift basis in an unheated garret, got drunk with all the major literary figures again, punched Picasso in an argument over prosody and was, despite his senior teaching post, available at short notice for drinks with any major (or minor for that matter) literary figures left after two world wars and a plethora of emigration. Literary criticism was more compelling when you knew that your teacher had dragged the author out of a bar by his legs.

No, Botond was not the type to hand out a fail lightly, especially since he still owed Elek a five figure sum.

Once out of the exam, in the corridor, with post-incident clarity, it did occur to Gyuri that there was one poem he could have rounded up, by Botond's old pal, Ady, on the pleasure of seeing the Gare de l'Est in Paris; one of Ady's most appealing themes being that the noblest prospect a Hungarian could see was the way out of Hungary. Good but sozzled poet. István had been in Érmindszent, Ady's birthplace, during the war and had been surprised to find not so much as a plaque to Ady's memory, whereas, by comparison, Hungary was littered with commemorative notices such as 'Petőfi walked past here' and 'Petőfi almost walked past here'. When István pointed out this omission to a local the rejoinder was 'Why should we put up a monument to a second-generation alcoholic?'

The maths exam was first thing the next morning but it was too craven to stay in, despite the frittering away of time caused by the afternoon's ant-circus. Elek was in the armchair, in some difficulty without a cigarette. As Gyuri was heading out, Elek caught him in the back with 'You're going to love the Army'.

* * *

The first time he sat the mathematics exam, he had prudently taken the precaution of smuggling in the textbook. The main reason he failed at the first attempt was because he hadn't known enough to know he hadn't known enough. Gyuri dipped into the textbook in the hope of succour, but had found its pages totally unintelligible. He angrily registered that if he had worked a bit harder he would have been able to cheat properly.

The second time around, his preparations at least gave him

enough expertise to understand the questions, even if the answers weren't jumping into view. It was possible for him to do something about these questions, even if it was like fighting a forest-fire with a thimbleful of water. An all-pervasive desperation not to do military service saturated his being. He had seen a group of conscripts the previous week, ideally cast for the role of a chainless chain-gang, miserable, bones veiled in skin, carrying a loaf of bread that had long ago lost its credibility in the civilian world, that required a pickaxe rather than a knife.

Gyuri liked to think he was tough but knew he didn't have the resilience for hardship so well-planned, so non-stop; although things were rough, there was always the prospect of something good happening to you if you were outside the Army, no matter how remote that prospect might be. In the Army you weren't going to be bothered by any comfort, cheer, or anything that could be classified under the heading pleasant; there would be no appointments with pleasure.

The others in the exam hall, from a distance anyway, seemed to be beavering away confidently. Did he look in control to those two rows back? Gyuri wondered. The first question offered a few footholds, so he hastened to put something down on paper, before the wisdom he had fished out slipped away, and in the hope that if some apocalypse should curtail the exam after ten minutes, he might have enough answer to pass.

He had unrolled as much of the answer to question one as he could, when a glance to his left established that his gaze had a direct flight path to the left breast of the young lady there; either she had forgotten to do up her blouse or the buttons didn't feel like working but light was taking off from untextiled skin and crashlanding into Gyuri's retinas. His loins underwent a stepping-on, all the mathematical erudition he had convoked was summarily banished. To deliberately have arranged such an alignment, to visually sidestep the clothing barrier in other circumstances could have taken hours, but now, at such a delicate moment, his composure and her mammary impacted. Simultaneously, he looked away, but it was too late – the chemical heralds hit the road, stirring up a global ache.

Crippled by this unwarranted intrusion into his concentration, he returned to the maths and found he was locked out. The second question scarcely acknowledged his greeting.

Surveying the 180 degree view on his right, Gyuri ruminated on a group from one of the People's Colleges. These were the special institutes where individuals predominantly from the bottom of the bucolic barrel were crammed with learning to provide the Party with man and womanpower. Peasant lads, in the main, who had ties fastened around their necks, copies of the *History of the Communist Party of the Soviet Union (Bolsheviks)* stuck in their hands, along with a ticket to the centre of the universe, Budapest, where accommodation in some appropriated bourgeois building would be waiting. They were loud in their endorsements of Marxism, as anyone in their new shoes would be.

Gyuri needed, as a minimum, three attempted answers to pass and while he had one attempt and a feint, the remaining questions looked hermetically sealed, inscrutable. A girl on his right, one of the People's College contingent, kept staring over at his paper which Gyuri found droll. How could she think there was anything worth examining on his laughably blank paper?

He was coming to the conclusion that glaring at the questions in the hope they might crack was a waste of time and he might as well enjoy a display of swagger by walking out and perhaps fooling a few despairing souls into believing he had done brilliantly, instead of squirming around like a maggot on a hook.

The People's girl was still looking at his paper and what was worse, looking as if she was looking. Being disqualified for cheating wasn't going to make much difference to Gyuri but it might to her.

'I can't help,' Gyuri mouthed to her. 'Don't look or we'll both...' he drew a finger across his throat. The girl reddened and threw her regard down onto her own sheets of paper. Now that he had conceded the mathematical match, Gyuri adjourned to treat himself to a spot of ocular plundering from the chest of the girl on his left, but was disgruntled to find that a fold of blouse was now refusing his glance admission, barring any further visual trespass.

Having decided that he wasn't going to sit like a cabbage any longer, he was putting the top back on his pen as a prelude to departure, when the supervising rays from the invigilator were momentarily diverted and a square of paper made its way from the row on the right to his desk. Opening up the paper, Gyuri found it contained a neatly written solution which although he couldn't entirely follow it, had such aplomb that he couldn't doubt its correctness. He copied out the answer and sauntered out of the exam-hall knowing he had vaulted the pass, although, with hindsight, he conceded the ant-training and other diversions had drained the blood from his luck.

In the aftermath, several congregations of maths discussions formed. Numerous people were slumped around, with crumbled faces, as if auditioning to illustrate the caption 'despair'. For the first time in his life, Gyuri felt like going to church to say thank you.

He certainly thanked his immediate saviour. He was in good form with her since she was so unattractive that there could be no question of making an overture and he could relax. Pataki appeared, closing in and frowning to see Gyuri wasting verbal effort on a young lady lagging so far behind the pack of beauty. Pataki, of course, hadn't failed any of his exams. He had strolled down to the exams, dipping into a textbook or two as he walked, packing bites of knowledge into his cheeks like a hoarding hamster and then spitting them out at the examiners. By the time he walked out of the exam, he already knew less than when he walked in. In basketballing terms it was like a one-armed blindman throwing the ball, the ball hitting the ring, circling around, wobbling, teetering but then finally slumping into the net. Lucky, very lucky, travelling to the border between luck and miracle, but two points nevertheless.

Gyuri could see Pataki taking his time, lining up a whole afternoon's witticisms about his poor choice of female interlocutors, but it wasn't going to bother him. 'Thanks again for the help,' said Gyuri as his valediction, 'you must be phenomenally good at maths.'

'Oh no,' said the girl modestly and endearingly, 'they gave us all the answers last week. We had plenty of time to learn them.'

* * *

They took the watch to the brothel. His mother's watch which had incredibly not ended up on a Soviet Army arm, which was probably the only pre-liberation timepiece left in Hungary and which had once been worth an awful lot, was on that particular evening enough for two beachings, one for himself and one for Pataki.

Gyuri had been fervently determined to celebrate and to have the much-respected good time but once the negotiations over the gold watch's weight in harlots were over, Gyuri felt oddly detached, as if he'd left his dick at home. He would never have believed he could appraise so academically femaleness being exposed.

Whores were so often associated with ugliness, sadness and debasement but the girl who had introduced herself as Timea was young, vivacious and if not intelligent had an alertness that could pass for it. 'You're very beautiful,' Gyuri remarked, repeating the observations of his eyes. 'Oh, my breasts are much too small,' she replied as she continued to undress for work. It wasn't true. She had the sort of beauty that removed the possibility of difficulties; she could have had anything she wanted from hordes of men genuflecting in submission. Her employment in the brothel was strange, since you would have thought she could have easily bagged a couple of millionaires to have a less demanding lifestyle.

Considering the inordinate amounts of time he spent in contemplation of four-legging, Gyuri found it hard to account for the sudden amputation of his desire. Watching Timea was delightful, worth the money in itself but a curiously abstract experience like admiring some art in a museum. Gyuri suggested that Pataki go first.

It was terrible. His callousness had simply packed up on him: out of order. He was annoyed with himself for wanting to do it, and at the same time, he knew that once he was out of range of the brothel, he would be annoyed with himself for not doing it. When Pataki re-emerged, all he could suggest was that they should leave. 'Are you out of your mind?' Pataki expostulated. 'You can't throw away a perfectly good fuck!' He returned to claim the unused coitus.

Gyuri learned there are people who can take their deceased mother's watch to a brothel and there are people who can't. And if you're one of those who can't, you can't. It was an expensive lesson and one that was not likely to have any future applications because he wasn't going to have any more deceased mothers or deceased mothers' watches.

He wished Pataki would hurry up. He wanted to go home since he had the feeling he was going to cry.

January 1949

They spent the last hour telling camel jokes.

'The new Foreign Legion officer arrives at the fort in the middle of the Sahara desert,' explained Ladányi. 'And he's being given the introductory tour by the sergeant and he listens attentively but eventually he says: "This is all very interesting, Sergeant but there's a rather delicate matter I'd like to inquire about. We're going to be out here for years. I mean what does one do when the *juices* start to build up?" "Well, sir," says the sergeant pointing to a camel tethered in the yard, "when an officer is missing the ladies' company, that's what we have Daisy, the regimental camel for." The new officer is rather shocked to hear this but says nothing. Months elapse and finally after a year in the Sahara, he snaps, runs screaming across the yard and flings himself on the camel. As he's pumping away, the sergeant comes up and coughs discreetly. "It's none of my business, sir, but the other officers prefer to ride Daisy to the brothel in the next village."'

For a Jesuit, Ladányi had an astonishingly good fund of camel jokes. Gyuri and Neumann could hardly get any in. Ladányi was rather hogging the camel section but it was a very long journey, and Gyuri certainly didn't have enough camel jokes at his disposal to cover a fraction of the trip to Hálás.

Ladányi had been a little vague at first about what he had to attend to in Hálás, the hamlet where he had been born and raised. 'I might need a bodyguard,' he had said to Gyuri. Gyuri would have been glad to do a favour for Ladányi anyway but it was flattering to be thought of as large and dangerous (though Gyuri had brought Neumann along in the event of any bona fide bodyguarding being required. As a water-polo player and a very large person, Neumann was going to have the last punch on any subject. Gyuri had seen Neumann, when two drunk and quite large firemen had merrily announced that they were going to thrash the living daylights out of him, pick them up and throw them across Rákóczi út where they had hit a wall with unpleasant bone-breaking sounds. It had to be some sort of record, but sadly throwing firemen wasn't a recognised sport.)

'The new Foreign Legion recruit arrives at the fort in the middle of the Sahara desert,' Ladányi resumed. 'And he's being shown the ropes by an old sweat, and he finally summons up the courage to ask the question that's on his mind. "Look," he asks, "we have to spend years out here, what do you do about the *urges*?" "What we do," the old sweat elucidates, "is we go out, find a bunch of bedouin, ambush them and find relief with their camels." So time passes, the troops go out into the desert, they hide behind a sand dune and bushwhack some bedouins. The old sweat immediately runs down towards the camels and the new recruit asks: "What's the rush? There are plenty of camels for everyone." "Yes, but you want to get a good-looking one."'

At the railway station at Békéscsaba, a wiry, behatted peasant who kissed Ladányi's hand, was waiting for them. A cart, luxurious by local standards, but bottom-grating for an hour's journey – the time the deferential peasant assured them it would take to reach Hálás, conveyed them.

Going back to his origins didn't seem to excite Ladányi greatly, but as Gyuri surveyed the territory, where the shoe was still seen as a daring new fashion idea, where only the sound of crops growing disturbed the peace, he could comprehend the lack of enthusiasm. There was nothing to be said about the landscape apart from that it started where the sky finished.

Ladányi was coming home because of Comrade Faragó. Faragó had been, apparently, an egregious feature of life in Hálás for a long time. Ladányi had vivid memories of him although he left Hálás at fourteen to study in Budapest. 'Faragó was both the village idiot and the village thief. In a small place like Hálás you have to double up,' Ladányi recounted. But the small village had great tolerance for home-grown trouble.

The war and the Arrow Cross changed that. October 1944 was the last time the villagers of Hálás had expected to see Faragó. He had evolved from subsistence misdemeanours such as sunflower-stealing, apricot-rustling and abducting pigs, to running the district Nazi franchise. Ladányi didn't expand on what Faragó had been up to. 'You don't want to know.'

Hálás's citizens had not expected to see Faragó again after October 1944 as that was when he had been shot in the chest six times and taken by cart to the mortuary in Békéscsaba where the police deposited inexplicable and unclaimed cadavers. It was still a time when stray bodies attracted bureaucracy; a little later no one would have bothered.

It was when they put Faragó on the slab at Békéscsaba that he began to complain, quite loudly for a corpse, that he wanted a drink.

The villagers were very surprised to see him again. 'You gave me a revolver with only six shots, is it my fault?' a reproachful voice was heard in the csárda. This hadn't been the first attempt on Faragó's life. A month earlier, as Faragó was enjoying the hospitality of a ditch which was a lot closer to where he had got leg-bucklingly drunk than home, sleeping soundly in the cold, someone had chucked in a grenade to keep him company. The grenade had failed to get rid of Faragó, though it did get rid of his left leg but even this didn't slow him down in his duties for his German mentors, hence the subsequent target practice.

It was the village priest who then suggested an auto-da-fé.

Again, when it was known that Faragó had his nose pressed to his pillow by an enormous volume of alcohol, anonymous hands set fire to his house in the middle of the night. Faragó must have been in the grip of a true carus because he didn't lose a snore as the fire charred his front door and then burned to the ground the two neighbouring houses. 'The priest suggested that?' observed Gyuri. 'Who knows?' Ladányi said. 'If we had the original text of the commandments, there might well be a footnote concerning exemption in regard to Faragó.'

When Hálás learned that Faragó had signed up to become the local Communist Party Secretary following the changing political wind, it was decided to stop messing about. Faragó was dragged out of his house in the dead of night, dead drunk, a dead weight. His hands were tied behind his back, a rope was thrown over a branch, a noose attached to Faragó's neck. He was hoisted up, the branch snapped and Faragó's yells drew a passing Russian patrol that came to investigate.

The outcome of this nocturnal suspension was that Faragó ended up with a blister necklace and a revolver as he sensed there were people who didn't entirely approve of him.

'I shoot,' Faragó had announced in the csárda, 'and I'm not even going to bother asking any questions afterwards.' This statement came after the death of the villager credited previously with the six-fold ventilation of Faragó.

The cause of Ladányi's return was a small vineyard of two hectares well away from Hálás that produced a wine so acrid that Faragó was almost the only person who would drink it. This vineyard had been left to the Church (probably maliciously) although it barely earned enough income to have the altar dusted.

Faragó as first secretary and mayor of the Hálás-Mezőmegyer-Murony community had decreed that the vineyard should be removed from the charge of the pushers of the people's opiate and handed over to the hegemony of the proletariat. The village turned to Ladányi because he was someone who had been to Budapest, who had seen the innards of books, because he had breathed his first lungfuls in Hálás, because he was a fully paid-up member of the Society of Jesus and because he had broken the fifty-egg barrier.

Although he had left the village fifteen years ago and had only been back for one weekend in the interval, Ladányi was still big news and a source of immense pride. How many other places could boast that the village Jew had become a Jesuit? And then there were the reports that meandered back, as Ladányi made his way through his law studies at university, of the omelette jousts and of Ladányi's participation in the goulash wars that had broken out at the end of the thirties in Budapest's restaurants. Ladányi was six foot two and this copious frame in conjunction with a student's appetite created an enormous parking space for edibles. He started to pay for his studies and his mother's upkeep by taking part in eat-outs with a side-bet going to the greatest devourer. His first contests were on the student circuit where the wagers merely covered the cost of the food consumed (usually dittoed three-course meals) but his unflinching digestion soon took him to the big time of the New York Café where leading journalists would be hard at work stretching the human capacity for eating omelettes. When Ladányi polished off a forty-five egg omelette with a couple of kilos of onions and ham thrown in for flavour, devastating the drama critic of the *Pester Lloyd*, who had thrown in his napkin at thirty-eight, Hálás knew all about it. When Ladányi with his custom-built cutlery was invited to Gundel's to test the new hyperstrength goulash, which was eventually billed as 'even Ladányi only had three bowls' and had been certified by the Technical University as containing 30,000 calories, Hálás had all the details (if a month later). When circus strongman Sándor the Savage thought he could take Ladányi with drum cakes, everyone had a good chuckle about that and the Stradivarius violin Ladányi had won.

But Ladányi had hung up his knife and fork, having broken the fifty-egg barrier for the second time, after the editor of the *Pesti Hirlap* dropped dead on the opposite side of the table, his cardiac arrest not unconnected with the forty-six eggs' worth of omelette he had just consumed. This abrupt prandial demise and Ladányi's realisation that he wanted to join the Order brought his gastronomic career to an end, without diminishing his fame in Hálás. So when Faragó heard that Ladányi was coming to plead for the vineyard, he simply issued the challenge 'Let's eat it out.'

The population of Hálás was hardly past four hundred, according to Ladányi, and despite the cold and pluvial weather, most of them were gathered outside in the rain waiting for the Jesuit-laden cart to arrive.

It was, Gyuri comprehended, the highest accolade you could get. 'Now I know what the nineteenth century was like,' he thought. The best thing about visiting a place like Hálás was that it made you very grateful for living in Budapest. Gyuri hadn't been out of Budapest seven hours and already the charms of electricity, pavement and a greater choice of genetic material were becoming overpowering. For a day, when he got back to Budapest, he would be very happy. Feeling he had grown to the dimensions of a tycoon or a film star, Gyuri stepped off the cart and watched his best shoes (not much to brag about, but the most powerful in his sartorial arsenal) disappear in mud.

They were shown into the csárda, a wooden affair, with a stove in the centre dispensing a little heat into the interior, which was really going to be warmed by the crowd outside funnelling its way in. Ladányi held a whispered confabulation with the village priest in a confessional, sombre manner. As Ladányi's retinue, Gyuri and Neumann took the brunt of the local hospitality. This, of course, had been in Gyuri's mind when he agreed to come to Hálás: the countryside meant unrestrained food. They might go short of excitement, but not of eats. Gyuri had firm intentions of swallowing along with Ladányi as long as he could and if people insisted on pressing presents of foodstuffs on them when they departed, Gyuri could put up with that.

The scale and ferocity of peasant cuisine could be overpowering if you were out of training. Gyuri knew how the breakfasts alone could put feeble urban dwellers in hospital. At Erdóváros, the summer he was thirteen, when Gyuri had been entrusted to one of the local families, they poured him a generous pálinka for breakfast along with a brick of fat garnished with a dash of paprika. Thinking well of their liberality, he drank the pálinka before walking out the door into the ground. It had taken his legs hours to remember how to walk but his stomach only a few minutes to evict the solid elements of his meal. That sort of morning fuelling was tolerable only if you had grown up on it and if you had a day in a field ahead of you. Even as an athletic thirteen year-old, harvesting for an hour had given him so much pain in so many places that all he could do was lie in the field and pray for an ambulance, while the heavily pregnant woman who had been working alongside him kindly offered to go and get him a drink.

The hospitality was unleashed straight away. Gyuri hadn't seen so much food, so much good food since the point when the war had got noticeably war-like, and it was quite possible that he had never seen that much food in an enclosed space ever before. The depressing thing was that he wouldn't be able to make up for five years' going hungry in one evening, however hard he tried. Even the expansive Neumann was looking awed by the food, since people had unmistakeable designs of inflicting several servings on them. If Gyuri tried to slow down his consumption, the villagers who had appointed themselves his personal troop of waiters would hover around and if he ate up, the consumed items would be swiftly replaced. Within half an hour of mastication commencing, Gyuri was already seriously worried about parting company with consciousness: surrounding his enormous plate, which had grown a stalagmite of sausage, cured pork, pig cheese and boxing-glove-sized chunks of bread, were two glasses of wine, one red, one white, two glasses of pálinka, apricot and pear, and two glasses of beer in case he got thirsty. Behind him he could hear enraged villagers fighting to get to his side so they could pour out more of their pressings and distillations.

Ladányi was also offered some refreshment and a selection of food but noticeably halfheartedly. No one wanted to wear out his alimentary muscles. He was principally occupied in giving his hand to be kissed by the queue of people that had formed to pay its respects. Ladányi was far from pleased about this, Gyuri could tell, but the villagers' veneration was reasonable enough, bearing in mind that there were university professors who were terrified of Ladányi, who would duck into doorways to avoid a searching question from Ladányi, a question that would home in on their ignorance. The story Gyuri had heard was that when Ladányi collected his law degree the faculty offered to throw in a doctorate to save everyone's time.

The concurred time for the blow-out had been five o' clock, but Faragó and his sidekicks didn't show up till half past. Ladányi's request to Gyuri for him to come to Hálás to manage any violence hadn't been made out of concern for his own safety. 'The villagers would protect me, and that's exactly what I don't want. If things turn nasty, I'd like someone from outside, who won't have to stay there.' However Gyuri's apprehension about roughhousing was completely subsumed in his amazement at Faragó's appearance.

'No one's going to believe us,' Neumann whispered to Gyuri who concurred with a nod. No amount of assertions that what they were saying was strictly in the bounds of veracity would help, Gyuri knew, when he saw Faragó walk in; no one back in 'Pest would believe them. Faragó rolled in with two lanky lackeys, a pistol tucked into his waistband. His hue was so ghastly that Gyuri could imagine corpses being dissected by medical students looking fresher. Faragó was drunk. He stank. His suit, a pinstripe, looked as if it had been buried, circa 1932, and only dug up the day before; in any case it clashed with the string vest he had on underneath. His tie was the most successful part of his outfit; it made an eye-catching belt.

The hatred that rose when Faragó entered was so solid, so sinewed, Gyuri was surprised that Faragó was able to walk in. He realised he was going to be treated to something special that evening.

It was hate at first sight for Gyuri which made him reflect that Faragó must have taken the villagers on an almost endless argosy to undreamed-of lands of human anger. This was the absolute zero of human turpitude. He deserved to be exhibited, but it was probably for the best that he was shackled to Hálás. 'I thought we had it tough,' observed Neumann taking in Faragó, 'but the rest of the country should write a thank you letter to Hálás for keeping him here.' Gyuri had been teasing Ladányi on the train down about how the Church should surely adapt and adopt a forgiving attitude to Faragó and gladly renounce worldly possessions. Smiling quietly, too capable to be caught red-handed with any unJesuit emotions, Ladányi had replied: 'Whether or not we should have such properties is a good question, as is what should be done with them, but they shouldn't be handed over to bandits. And while our Lord did enjoin us to turn the other cheek, it should be borne in mind that he never met Faragó.'

'So the black beetle has come to be crushed by the people's power?' roared Faragó, missing the chair he had been aiming to sit on and vanishing from sight. Installed in the chair with the assistance of his seconds, he continued his welcome address. 'As First Secretary of the Hungarian Communist... the... er... the Hungarian Working People's Party of the Hálás-Mezómegyer-Murony community and as mayor and as Chairman of the 'Dizzy with Success' collective farm, in the words of Comrade Stalin, reporting on the work of the Central Committee to the Eighteenth Congress of the CPSU(B).' Here Faragó petered out ideologically, paused and having run out of things to say, reached for his pistol to illustrate a point and shot himself in the leg. To general disappointment, it was the wooden leg.

'And,' Faragó resumed, 'and in a scientific manner, with a bolshevik tempo, I'm going to eat you into the ground.' He snapped his fingers and the proprietor of the csárda approached the table and erected an enormous balance with scales. 'They used that in the Békés county fried-chicken championships,' someone interjected in Gyuri's ear, as the proprietor measured out two vast bowls of steaming bean soup for the kick-off. Ladányi had said nothing more than 'good evening' so far, while Faragó continued to glasshead, letting everyone see his thoughts. 'You're trying to impress us, aren't you? You think you can carry on sucking the blood of the people, you leech in a dog collar?' Here Faragó halted as his eye chanced upon the village gypsy standing in the front row with a good view of the proceedings. Emitting a thoracic-cleaning rasp, Faragó then expectorated a slab of phlegm so huge and forceful that the unsuspecting gypsy was knocked sideways. 'No gypsies,' Faragó elaborated. Which Gyuri found odd since Faragó looked more gypsy than the village gypsy, with an extended stomach of such paunchity you might think he had a huge watermelon stuffed under his vest; his nose had gone in for extra growth as well, hanging like an overripe raspberry. Gut and conk were unimpeachable witnesses to Faragó's feasting in lean times; he saw himself as an omnivore, as a megalovore, for whom eating was a measure of virility. Faragó had no doubt he would leave his opponent stalled on the first course.

Ladányi said grace and Faragó retaliated by clenching his fist and growling the communists' salutation: 'Freedom!'. It was obvious who the crowd was backing on this occasion, Gyuri thought, as the two contestants started to shovel in the bean soup but it wasn't always easy to sort out who to back in the Rome vs. Moscow conflict. The Church in Hungary was heading for a kicking indisputably. Mindszenty, the Cardinal, was stuck in a nick somewhere in Budapest, while they adjusted the charges to get a good fit (Gábor Pétér, the head of the AVO, had been a tailor): spying for the Americans, plotting to bring back the Habsburg monarchy, breeding Colorado beetles, sneering at socialist realist novels. And they must have had the survivors from the scriptwriting teams from Hungary's prewar film industry on contract to concoct the evidence, because no policeman could invent as fantastically as that.

It was hard to sympathise with the Cardinal, Gyuri reflected, because Mindszenty was a buffoon, however wronged. The Catholic Church in Hungary wasn't topheavy with brilliance. It would be so nice to have a real choice, fumed Gyuri. It was like Hungary being between Germany and the Soviet Union. What sort of choice was that? Which language would you like your firing squad to speak? In these circumstances, of course, a brilliant Cardinal might not be any more useful. Being clever and far-sighted wasn't always of use. Does it help being the clever pig on the way to the abattoir?

Stupidity could be quite advantageous now and then. Mind you, stupidity (with which he was well-equipped) hadn't done Mindszenty any favours either. If you're falling off a cliff, the quality of the brains that are going to get dashed doesn't hugely count.

When Gyuri discussed the position of the Church, Ladányi was grave but not worried but it was very hard to imagine Ladányi worried about anything. Being burned at the stake would all be part of a day's work for him, even if other clerics would jib at the prospect. It was hard to imagine Father Jenik, for instance, gearing up for martyrdom, much as Gyuri liked him. Jenik firmly held to the philosophy of getting the best out of things: why had God created first-class hotels if he didn't intend us to use them? Just after the Russians had tied down Budapest, Jenik had taken the entire scout troop out into the countryside. The hundred kilometre trip had taken two days by a train that had gone so slowly that, when one of the younger boys had fallen out of the open-doored wagons, one of the older boys had plenty of time to climb down from the train roof, rescue him and throw him back on. Jenik had led the troop to a village where he had some tenuous kinship, and had begun to spin a yarn, relying heavily on hyperbole, expounding at length the horrors and degradations of war and how sadly the tender youths in front of them had been marked. Jenik wasn't lying, but he wasn't doing anything to restrain misunderstanding. Father Jenik, who had been laughing all the way down on the train, and whom Gyuri suspected as the original begetter of Ladányi's camel jokes, had become sombre and pained. His discourse on the ordeals of war had been rolling along for quite a while before Gyuri realised that Jenik was talking about the troop. Jenik had his hand on Papp's shoulder as he conjured up the tortures of hunger and deprivation. Papp did look as if he had been constructed out of knitting-needles glued together, shudderingly thin and haggard, despite the fact his father was a butcher and he and his family got more meat than all the carnivores in Budapest zoo. Tears had peeped out of peasant eyes, and until Hálás, Gyuri had never eaten so much at one go. That night he had had the firm belief he would never need to eat again as long as he lived, and he wandered around in the dark, keeping his legs moving in a desperate attempt to festinate digestion and to eschew puking, to grind down the anvil in his stomach.

However, in other ways Father Jenik was the traditional avuncular priest, always rolling up your sleeve to check your spiritual pulse, working his way through the club regulations: attendance at mass, confessions, observance of holy days. Ladányi would never mention religion, unless you brought it up or it cropped up naturally in the course of conversation. There was no badgering, no impresario-like push to get bums on seats, no ticking off a list with Ladányi. He seemed unconcerned whether you turned up or not and this was what was so pernicious. Gyuri had dropped church much in the same way as he had stopped believing in Santa Claus; there came a point where it was impossible to take it seriously. And that was what was so worrying about Ladányi. He was so clever, he had a bird's eye view of everyone's actions – even Pataki wouldn't try modifying reality with Ladányi, because Ladányi would have read your diary before you'd written it. Gyuri couldn't help feeling when he was doing something totally trivial like cleaning the bathtub or buying some groceries that it was all part of some master-plan, that cleaning the bathtub and buying groceries were all part of Ladányi's machinations (it was just that he was unaware of it) and that one day he would wake up wearing black with a white collar.

Perhaps because of his order, perhaps because of his Ladányiness, Ladányi operated quietly. The summer before, in an excess of compliance, Gyuri had offered Katalin Takács to pick up her new dress from the dressmaker. It was bruited by her changing room companions that she had no pubic hair. So he journeyed out to the dressmaker, helping to dress the girl he wanted to undress to verify the canard about her cat.

The favour was a double goodwill since the dressmaker lived in the Angyalföld, off the Váci út. It was said that when the American Liberators had carpet-bombed Angyalföld at the end of '44 by mistake as they searched for the factories on Csepel Island, no one had minded because no one could tell the difference. It was also maintained that both the Waffen SS and the Red Army had stayed out of the Angyalföld because they hadn't wanted any trouble.

Although Gyuri knew Budapest well, he had never ventured into the Angyalföld and was flabbergasted to discover that the stories were true. Having quit the tram, he passed people lying in gutters, like piles of autumnal leaves in smarter quarters, booze having severed their relations with the known universe. As he walked along, he was regarded with an unconcealed hatred by groups of natives milling around; reflexive dislike and aggression he had experienced before but never with such cannibalistic fervour. Gyuri had considered, before setting out that morning, pocketing a knife on account of Angyalföld's notoriety but as he turned the corner into Jász utca, he couldn't help noticing two men fighting with what could only be described as cutlasses, long heavy swords of the type favoured by Hollywood pirates. A semi-circle of barefoot spectators were monitoring, not greatly impressed by the quality of the hacking. Carrying a knife wouldn't have helped, the result would have been that he would have had his knife stolen as a supplement to getting stabbed, and a good knife like everything else was hard to get in those days.

Gyuri had lots of time to ruminate on how his untimely, unremarked demise on the streets of the Angyalföld would be due to his yearning to let his gaze ski down Katalin's smooth slopes, killed by curiosity about a bald cat. He had also ruminated on his way up to the fifth floor, how people he visited always lived on the fifth floor of liftless buildings. The dressmaker, a sprightly lady of eighty plus, clearly of the work-twelve-hours-a-day-till-you-drop variety, and who was cosily unaware of what went on in the rest of Angyalföld, congratulated Gyuri on the cut of his trousers. The trousers were the last pair of Elek's Savile Row trousers, indeed the only fully-qualified trousers that Elek had left, lent to Gyuri since Elek had come to the conclusion that he wasn't getting out of bed that day, or that should he rise, he wouldn't be progressing beyond the armchair. The dressmaker bustled away to prepare the dress for its journey while Gyuri reflected how sad it was that she couldn't bequeath her industry to him.

It was as he rushed back to the tram that he chanced on Ladányi talking with some of the Angyalföld's denizens patiently listening to him. They patently considered Ladányi as someone who had stepped down from the moon. Ladányi seemed slightly peeved at being caught in the act of doing good, but he accompanied Gyuri to the tram and reluctantly disclosed that he haunted Angyalföld before the first mass of the day. It was the sheer lunacy of his faith, Gyuri thought, that enabled Ladányi to leave with all his physical workings intact. Greatly relieved at having emerged from Angyalföld with his functions uninhibited, Gyuri was waiting outside the

Nyugati station to change trams to deliver the dress, when a group of five youths his age came up and one, without any preamble, with a pair of scissors, swiftly cut the tie Gyuri was wearing, the last of Elek's silk ties, the last of Elek's ties and the only tie then residing in the Fischer household. The trimmer then handed over the snipped sections to Gyuri with the invocation: 'Cerulean'.

At that point Gyuri recalled there was a vogue in Budapest, particularly amongst those who went round in fists of five, for prowling the boulevards with a pair of scissors to amputate ties and then to say 'cerulean'. The tie hadn't been a great tie, the design hadn't really been to Gyuri's taste and there had been of late a painfully visible soup stain on it, but the desire to punch the scissor-operator in the mouth had been quite breathtaking in its intensity, especially since he was clearly expecting Gyuri to have a laugh over the dividing of his tie. Gyuri thought how much he would enjoy punching him in the mouth, then he thought how much he wouldn't enjoy getting it back as a fivefold minimum. He resorted to what he hoped was a look of contempt. The five got on the next tram remarking how some people had no sense of humour.

* * *

When, at Faragó's suggestion, they switched to chocolate ice cream, Gyuri knew it was all over.

Ladányi and Faragó had warmed up with a couple of litres of bean soup before moving on to the main course – fried chicken – its consumption meticulously measured on the scales. 'We in Hálás have always been famous for our fried chicken,' Faragó rambled on, 'and now under socialism, the fried chicken is even more fried.' He reached for a plate of slender green tubes. 'The paprika is optional,' he announced loading a couple into his mouth.

Three kilos into the chicken, Faragó began to sweat, though whether this was due to gastronomic exertion or the calorific effects of the paprika it was hard to judge. He was also beginning to look uneasy, perhaps because it was dawning on him that the reports of the Jesuit's unearthly wolfing had some foundation. Faragó was oozing effort while Ladányi was methodically and calmly stripping drumsticks with such ease that he hadn't taken the trouble of dialling his willpower yet.

'I'm just going to shake the snake,' Gyuri informed Neumann. He was becoming increasingly anxious about losing contact with several outposts of his body. Draining two of the four glasses of pálinka awaiting his attention, he made his way out of the csárda into the sheltering darkness and voided the burning liquid from his mouth in an aerosol flurry to dodge some of the enormity of Hálás's hospitality. A standard peasant, an elderly gent with the inevitable black hat that peasants had stapled to their heads and a massive handlebar moustache, came to join him in watering the planet. 'Good evening, sir,' said the peasant, causing Gyuri to note that only countryfolk could be so courteous while airing their dick. Conversation turned to Faragó as Gyuri was in no hurry to go back in and be the victim of further largesse; he was curious about Faragó's track record. 'I hear he did some appalling things during the war?'

'You don't want to know, sir. Some things should never be repeated, just forgotten. Satan himself is his coach.'

Gyuri waited outside as long as he could without triggering a search party and re-entered to find Ladányi and Faragó crossing the ten kilo mark, Faragó in discomfort, Ladányi still emitting a lean, keen look. A barrel of pigs' trotters in aspic was dumped in front of Gyuri and he wondered how on earth he was going to eat any. 'You didn't like the smoked goose, did you?' asked one woman accusingly and woundedly, although Gyuri estimated he had had six respectable helpings. Neumann next to him wasn't saying much, but he wasn't demonstrating any signs of suffering (however, he had sixteen stone to upkeep). The village must have gathered every bit of food for ten miles around. Gyuri could only regret that his stomach wasn't up to it, that it had left its office, put up the 'out to lunch' sign and wasn't doing any more business.

To round off his other distasteful qualities, Faragó had a bad cold and as he handed over his handkerchief to the deputy Party secretary to place on the stove to dry, Gyuri felt another surge of sympathy for the villagers. They had a straightforward, soily existence which if you liked that sort of thing could be quite pleasant. No wonder they were filled with hatred for Faragó; bewildered by their misfortune, it was like having a plague of locusts or a dragon deciding to set up home with you. 'Why us?' the elderly peasant had implored. 'A whole world to be a stinking horseprick in and he's never lost sight of Hálás. Why?'

The eating had now long since left pleasure behind. It was no longer a question of appetite, but a question of will, which was why Gyuri knew Ladányi would win, and knowing Ladányi, would end up recruiting Faragó as an altar boy. Conversion. It was funny how people could, while changing completely, remain the same. Fodor, at school, for example, for whom getting into trouble had not been a by-product of his activity but his sole activity, who had been almost as much of a nuisance as Keresztes, had, without warning, got a bad attack of the Holy Ghost. At first there was a suspicion that it was an elaborate and unfunny stunt, but Fodor was so unswerving in handing out leaflets to remind how Jesus wanted a word, that everyone realised that he had gone evangelist for real: preaching was his latest irritation tool. Fodor caught Gyuri hanging around in a corridor one day. 'Jesus Christ came to be your saviour, He died for your sins. You must acclaim Him and surrender to His teachings,' Fodor urged, and then continued, more quietly, really savouring the next bit, 'you've been warned now. You've had the message, you've got no excuse. If you ignore it, you'll burn. In hell. For eternity.' Fodor had then marched off with a satisfied air. This was the appealing part of the job for Fodor, going around with a sawn-off version of the scriptures and looking forward to the infidels being infinitely ignited. Gyuri had also seen

Fodor in the Körút, on a soap-box, giving a sermon to the unheeding passers-by, a glint of delight in his eye at the prospect of the mass fry-up that was coming. Fodor didn't want anyone to be able to reach for some mitigation when they stood in the pearly dock, saying no one had explained the Nazarene contract to them. Then Fodor could chime out: 'Liar! Liar! I told him, I told him. Let him burrrnnnn.'

What had befallen Fodor in the end, whether he had grown weary of his sadistic evangelism, Gyuri didn't know. Gyuri had last seen him at a school trip to the cinema where they had been locked in. You could tell it was a Soviet film when they locked you in. The school had taken over an enormous balcony in the cinema which descended in a series of plateaus. Fodor had vaulted over what he had thought was the edge of one of these sections, in fact the end of the balcony. Just before he disappeared from view, there had been a nanosecond's worth of expression on his face: why isn't there any balcony here?

Along with a couple of others, Gyuri had selflessly volunteered to take Fodor and his broken legs to hospital, thereby avoiding the feats of Sergei, who single-handedly repulsed the invading Germans in between repairing his tractor to produce a bumper harvest. Either for fear of ridicule or in pursuit of fresh souls, Fodor never returned.

'You don't say much, do you?' Faragó observed to Ladányi, with the implication that Ladányi was unfairly reserving energy for eating. Even if Faragó had had more fight, the switch to chocolate ice cream was the end. A large chicken's weight behind Ladányi, Faragó had chosen the sweet to which Ladányi was most partial; Ladányi's nickname in the troop, 'Iceman', came from his mythical disposal of chocolate ice cream, in the days before he had signed up with Jesus. Gyuri wondered whether Ladányi had mentioned to anyone back at Jesuit headquarters that he was popping down to the countryside to out-eat a Party Secretary. However laudable the goal, in an atmosphere of austerity where quips such as

'Isn't that the second meal you've had this week, Father?' abounded, this sort of indecorous gourmandise, however much a part of Christian soldiering, must have run the risk of some gruelling rosary work.

'What would you like me to say?' inquired Ladányi politely, keeping a spoon full of ice cream from its destination. The whole village was craning forward now, as Faragó was visibly floundering, gazing with resentment at his bowl of ice cream.

'As the saying goes,' said Faragó fighting for air, 'there isn't room for two bagpipe players in the same inn. We, the working class... we, the instrument of the international proletariat... we will defend the gains of the people...' Here Faragó jammed, fell off his chair and as if gagging on his propaganda, spilled his stomach on the floor. It looked very much to Gyuri like a job for the last rites.

Ladányi didn't seemed worried. 'There are some documents Father Orsó has ready for you to sign, I believe,' he said. The village priest crouched down and offered a pen to Faragó who was sprawled on the floor as if he were thinking about doing a push-up. Saturninely he scrawled a mark on the paper, and, supine, was lugged out inexpertly by the rest of the party cell, limbs lolling.

During their post-micturition conversation, the elderly peasant had also told Gyuri: 'Take the most rotten individual imaginable and there will always be someone, usually very stupid, but not always, who'll say no, no, he's simply misunderstood. Misquoted. Even with murderers, when they write about them in the newspapers, they have a wife or a mother who says he's not bad, he's a lovely boy when you get to know him. You ask anyone here to say anything in favour of Faragó; ask people who've known him all their lives to say one thing to his credit, just one courtesy, one thank you, one favour – you'll find the people of this village as quiet as melons in long grass. His own mother, if Faragó was waiting to be executed, would only say things like "Make that noose tighter" or "Is it permissible to tip the hangman?"'

Wiping his mouth with an embroidered napkin, Ladányi stood up briskly as if he had been having a quick snack between important engagements. 'Well, we have to go now. God bless you all.' Another hour of hand-kissing and loading up gifts onto the cart followed, but Ladányi resolutely insisted that they should depart since they had an opportunity of catching a train which would get them to Budapest in the morning.

By moonlight, Ladányi looked remarkably thin. Gyuri felt somewhat queasy during the bumpy cart-ride and he was astonished that Ladányi didn't have any inclination to deswallow. It would be months, Gyuri was convinced, before he would want to eat again. Neumann broke the peregrinational hush: 'Does that agreement really mean anything? Forgive me for saying so but Faragó looks as if he would roger his grandmother for the price of a drink, or even for free.'

'Look,' replied Ladányi, 'what we did tonight was to act out a morality play. I was asked to come. I couldn't refuse. I doubt if it will make any difference, not because of Comrade Faragó being probity-free, but because of everything else in the country. This was one night of miniature victory in what will be long years of defeat. I hope it will have some importance for the people in Hálás.'

'How long do you think this will last?' asked Gyuri, not sure that he actually wanted to hear the answer.

'Not long,' pronounced Ladányi. 'I'd say about forty years or so. You have to wait for the barbarians to get old, to become soft barbarians.'

This wasn't an answer Gyuri wanted to hear, particularly coming from Ladányi. 'Time to leave the country.'

'Not at all. Firstly, as I'm sure you know, it's not easy to get out any more, and secondly, and I should point out this is not an idea patented by the Church, matter doesn't matter. It's not physical conditions that count, but your opinion of them. Take the farmer in the small village in the middle of China who is the happiest man in the world because he has two pigs and no one else in the village has got one. Living isn't like basketball, it's not a question of points, but what's here.' Gyuri saw Ladányi touch his forehead with his forefinger. 'You only lose if you give up – and if you give up you deserve to lose. In basketball, you can be beaten. Otherwise you can only be beaten if you agree to it. You're lucky, you're very lucky. We're living in testing circumstances; unless you're very dull, you should want to be stretched.'

Thanks for the totalitarianism, Stalin. Gyuri doubted that he would enjoy a prison cell as much as Ladányi. 'A ticket to Paris would be more fun,' he retorted 'Couldn't I book a few prayers for that?'

'I'll be delighted to forward your request, but don't be too specific, or you might get it. One should pray for the best. Maybe you'll be happier here than in Paris.'

'I'm prepared to take that risk. Anything to escape from record-breaking lathe-operators.'

'Yes, this cult of the worker is a bit wearing. Ironic that it sprang chiefly from a fat, free-loading German academic who never had a job in his life, but just sponged off his acquaintances and who indulged in such very bourgeois practices as impregnating the chamber-maid. And so boring. People often overlook the work of a poor carpenter who chose fishermen as his company.'

They rattled on in the cart for a while.

'The greatest irony about Marx's influence is that his books are unreadable,' Ladányi mused. 'Perhaps his appeal lies in his unintelligibility, a sort of mysticism through statistics and the wages of textile workers. People will have a good laugh about it one day. But, unfortunately, there are people who believe it, not the ones who've joined now, but those who joined before the war, when the movement was illegal. They believe in it and as Church history amply shows crazy ideas can take a long time to die out.'

'I think it's a process I'd like to watch closely from a café in New York. I might even find it funny from that distance.'

'Me too,' chorused Neumann.

'The desire to travel is part of your age. You've never been out of Hungary, have you? Be careful, people can become very fond of their prisons, you know.'

They arrived at the station in the nick of time to catch the train back to Budapest. Neumann, who had the priceless gift of being able to sleep on trains, bedded down in another compartment on some unclaimed seats, while Ladányi took out a book – the *Analects* of Confucius. 'Is it any good?' Gyuri questioned. 'Life is too short for good books,' said Ladányi, 'one should only read great books.' 'How can you tell if it's great?' 'If it's been around for a couple of thousand years, that's usually a good sign. This isn't bad. Some of us younger ones have been told to study Chinese. Our superiors think it's a growing market. Every year a Jesuit gets a letter containing his orders. I have a feeling they may be getting us out of the country. I think that's wrong, but that's where the vow of obedience comes in.'

Gyuri hadn't been to church since he was fourteen when his mother dragged him to the Easter Mass. Naturally, he had attempted to get in touch with God on several subsequent occasions when he had thought he was going to die but always on the spot, away from church precincts. This was surely the real boon of a religious upbringing: it gave you a number to ring in emergencies, which was some consolation, even if no one answered. Gyuri had met with the various arguments for God's existence from his partisans, proof through design ('that's what I call a well-made universe'), the craftsmanship of the universe (it did seem to be an awful lot of trouble for a practical joke) or Pascal's way of looking at it, a hundred francs on God each way. But, all in all, the best argument he had come across for taking Jesus's shilling was that the sharpest razor, Ladányi believed it.

When they reached Budapest, Ladányi thanked Gyuri and Neumann for their support. It was the last time Gyuri would see Ladányi. Gyuri had no inkling of that, but years afterwards, re-examining the scene, he suspected that Ladányi knew. 'Don't forget what I said about good books. And read the Bible occasionally. It's had some good reviews, you know.' Ladányi's tone in this farewell admonition was not that of a salesman, or a friend recommending a good read, but rather that of a visitor handing a prisoner a loaf of bread with a file in it.

September 1949

It was as the tram was on the last stretch of the Margit Bridge that, from the corner of his eye, Gyuri logged the girl sitting on the edge of the railings, and then, the girl that wasn't sitting there. There was nothing he and the others on the tram who had spotted the suicide bid could do. By the time the tram had stopped and they could have got back to the bridge, the young lady's fate would be, one way or another, cleared up. It seemed a bit heartless to say 'Well, there goes another one' and to shrug one's shoulders but apart from forming an audience, nothing could have been contributed by returning. People down by the river bank would be doing whatever samaritaning could be done. Besides, Gyuri was late.

Having a suicide dropped in his lap, would of course, be typical of his luck, especially when he was late for work. On the other hand, it would at least be an honourable excuse for tardiness. A sharp picture of the girl stayed with him – eerie how quickly a detailed portrait could imprint. She looked like a country girl, seeking a populous conurbation for taking the exitless exit and not really attractive enough to encourage diving in after her but then if she had been attractive enough to have hordes of men diving in after her, she wouldn't have had to jump in the first place.

Also, one had to respect suicide as the national pastime, as the vice Hungarian. Gyuri wasn't up to date on how suicide was progressing under socialism, it could well have been abolished but the popularity of doing-it-yourself couldn't entirely be laid at the door of Rákosi & Co. For centuries, Hungarians of quality and quantity, who hadn't managed to be part of Hungarian armies that got wiped out, had been blowing their brains out or uncaging their souls in other ways. Yes, a few idle minutes, some melancholy music and a Hungarian would be trying to unplug himself. And not just the nobility – Hungarian maids in Vienna had been notorious for their fondness for bleaching their entrails.

The tram deposited Gyuri in front of the monstrous Ganz Electrical Works but he was the only one the tram off-loaded who made his way through the entrance of Ganz; all the other workers had arrived much earlier, before the shift had started.

Of course, Gyuri thought, the Hungarian propensity for suicide might stem from their other great proclivity: their love of complaining. Who better to complain to than the chief architect? Go to the top, go meet your maker and give him an earful about the shortcomings of the universe. There was probably a dirty great queue of Hungarians outside God's office ready to remonstrate.

As Gyuri entered the main yard, he passed a board which was bedecked with amateurish red decorations and which had a heading 'Socialist Brigades'. Underneath were lesser signs such as 'Guernica', 'Dimitrov' and 'Béla Kun', presiding over wonderful production figures and grainy black and white photographs of sheepishly pleased and self-conscious lathe-operators lathe-operating. These photographs didn't change. Alongside these displays was an elegantly penned scroll, 'Hungarian-Soviet Friendship Society', heading a series of ailing black and white photographs of Soviet lathe-operators watching Hungarian lathe-operators lathe-operate with avuncular, elder-brotherly encouragement, and photographs of Hungarian lathe-operators watching Soviet lathe-operators lathe-operate, with younger-brother wide-eyed admiration. There was no seasonal variation in these pictures either.

Not far from these displays, but diametrically opposed to them, on the other side of the yard, was an enormous caricature of US President Harry Truman made out of card. At the foot of this caricature was a board with the inscription 'FRIENDS OF TRUMAN' in wobbly calligraphy, and in less bold lettering *'I'm out to destroy the gains of the people of democratic Hungary, please help me by taking it easy. My thanks.'* On the board, which looked like an old situations vacant notice that used to be hung outside the factory, various names had been inserted. There wasn't much seasonal variation in this either. Top of the list was Pataki, Tibor, followed by Fischer, György (Gyuri could never fathom how Pataki had managed to get top billing once again) with one or two other more mutable names, Németh, Sándor or Kövrig, Lászlo. Unknown but agreeable figures to Gyuri.

This pillorying was attributable chiefly to the reluctance of Pataki and himself to come to work any earlier than was truly necessary to avoid dismissal. Gyuri didn't care too much about President Truman's friendship (though he did wonder if he ever got to the United States whether the amity would stand him in good stead there), largely because there were few additional penalties to having your name publicly associated with the President of the United States (and Gombás could deal with them). The juxtaposition of names was clearly deemed by the agit-prop department to be sufficiently shameful to obviate the need for further reprimand.

Being class-x, being a class alien, Gyuri really couldn't be much worse off; he was starting from the back of the queue for the goodies (had there been any in the first place). Apart from the obvious problems of having class-x stamped on the moral credentials you had to produce every time you wanted a job, a place at university or more or less anything, what was so grossly unfair and infuriating about being labelled as the son of a bourgeois family, was that Elek was so profoundly, all-round unbourgeois. Aside from the profession of bookmaking not being the most highly regarded of careers in canapé circles, there was the whole weight of the old morphinist's behaviour: molesting widows and chambermaids, carrying a cosh, shooting up. He had always instructed his employees to call him Elek (which in itself had been tantamount to membership of the Communist Party in the eyes of his fellow capitalists) and gave them afternoons off if the weather had been outstandingly good or if he felt like treating his torticollis with some morphine (although it had been evident for years that the dope didn't do his neck any good – just as the hypnotist had failed but Elek had only given him one go. The hypnotist had brandished his pendulum and chanted 'You are in a deep, deep sleep' for ten minutes after which Elek had said 'No, I'm not. Are you planning to charge for this?'). And then, when he lost all his money, instead of trying to recoup his losses, going out to toil dutifully in the respectable bourgeois way, Elek just sat around contentedly in his armchair, wearing his lacunar pullover, his neck cricked, grappling with the theoretical questions of how to get a cigarette. Bourgeois and Elek didn't mix. Agreed: he had some money at one point, but that had been a long time ago, before Gyuri was old enough to use it.

'What I'm giving you is priceless,' Elek had said, holding court in his armchair that morning. 'I'm giving you your independence. You're making your own way. You owe me nothing. Whatever you achieve you can say "I made it on my own". You're not weighed down by an over-solicitous father. You have no towering figure of paternal success to intimidate you. How many people can say that? You're a talented acorn that can grow without fear of the shade of a great oak.'

The curious thing about Elek was that the less active he became, the less he slept, thus ensuring his availability to give Gyuri the benefit of his thoughts as Gyuri got ready to go to work. 'You see, István, for example, will always have the disadvantages of everything that money could buy.' István, in practice, was bearing up beneath that burden rather well. He had returned at the end of '45, with a dozen chums who disembarked from the prisoner of war camp in Denmark where they had been guarding themselves, carrying two thousand cigarettes and fluent in fifteen languages. Before things grimmed up, István had managed to get a job in the Ministry of Agriculture where he had got to know everything there was to know about sugar. Because he was unobtrusively junior and because they had to retain some people at the Ministry who knew something about agriculture, he had been magnanimously tolerated.

István had laughed about it all, as he did about everything. Always of a jovial disposition, he had returned from his years on the Russian front, with one important souvenir: the inability to get worked up about things that weren't three years on the Russian front. You could tell István things like, you had gone to a restaurant and contracted hepatitis, you were going to be conscripted into the army, you had just been jilted by the girl who was more important to you at that moment than life and that you wanted to fold up and die, and István would just chuckle or if you looked really miserable, guffaw loudly.

István had reappeared in Budapest the day after they had been burgled. There hadn't been much left to steal after the Red Army had manoeuvred back and forth across the flat a couple of times and furniture had been traded for food. István had walked in as if he had just returned from the corner-shop to find Gyuri dazed by the inexhaustibility of their misfortune. István immediately went out again, and the next morning all the missing items were piled up outside the front door with a note apologising that the dust pan left wasn't the original but hoping the replacement would live up to expectations and wishing the family good health. The only other survivor from István's artillery unit it turned out, was one of the master burglars of Budapest who had been greatly peeved to hear that his commanding officer's family should have suffered such an indignity. There was only one question that István asked when you started to reconstruct some tribulation: 'What did you do about it?'

It was what you did about it, not the blubbering, that interested István. István came back for the peace, got married, got a job, got a flat. His most annoying habit was his way of making life look easy. His application and down-to-earthness were such that it was hard to believe he was related in any way to Elek. Where had he got it from? Why didn't he have any? Gyuri pondered. István was capable of sorting out anything, of making the best of the worst, which was why Gyuri couldn't understand what had made him come back to Hungary and what had made him stay there. István seemed capable of anything, except perhaps getting Elek a proper job.

'Have you just given up then?' Gyuri had demanded of Elek.

'Given up? Given up what? Tennis? Smoking? Horse-racing? My studies in Sanskrit? I'm an old fart, you know,' Elek remarked checking the length of each bristle of his moustache in a pocket mirror. 'You can't expect too much. You, the healthy, vigorous son with his whole life ahead of him should be thinking of supporting his valetudinarian father.'

'Doesn't it bother you?'

'Does it bother me? Yes. No. You may be surprised to hear that when I was growing up it wasn't the summit of my ambitions to end up in an armchair wearing a grey pullover with holes in it. I confess I was thinking more in terms of excessive luxury. But I do enjoy disappointing people by not being suicidally miserable.'

Elek should have considered a post as a Party secretary, Gyuri reflected, with his gift of the gab and his inclination for doing nothing. After the war they would have taken anyone. Not now. Now, they were hanging the Communists they already had.

Sulyok, the foreman, was doing one of his readings to Gyuri's workmates when Gyuri finally arrived to do his day's work. This discovery made Gyuri very pleased that he had arrived late. The main reason that Gyuri had such a surfeit of nonchalance about tardiness was that he and Pataki had been given jobs at the factory by Gombás himself, the deputy director of the works, and people knew this. An Olympic medallist, a weight-lifter whose efforts had been rewarded with a tasty sinecure at the Ganz works, Gombás was keen to build up the works' basketball team, to propel them into the first division. Thus Pataki and Gyuri, as Pataki's personal ball-passer, were invited to join the team and to spend a little time at the works. Gyuri got on well with Gombás and liked him, not just because he had provided Gyuri with the job and evasion of the army but also because Gombás was an affable type and Gyuri rather admired his open-handed perversion. What Gyuri rather admired was that, while other men would have been vein-openingly ashamed of their peccadillo, Gombás was charmingly frank and unrepentant about his penchant for girls teetering on pubescence. His office was spacious, sequestered and complete with shower. There, girls hand-picked by Gombás on his travels in the provinces and brought to Budapest for 'intensive training' received his 'personal tuition'. Gyuri was always expecting to see some enraged parent or the police march into Gombás's office, but so far it seemed the arrangement had upset no one and there was always the possibility, as Pataki had pointed out, that if fellatio ever became an Olympic event, Hungary would clean up.

Every now and then, Sulyok would feel obliged to give a reading from the Party newspaper which of course had the same content as the other papers but there were some fascinating variations in the punctuation. Considering how boring 'Free People' was on the page, and how people would only think about reading it in the most desperate circumstances of tedium, it was hard to see why it was thought that having Sulyok crawl through a passage, adding new layers of dullness, would render it more memorable.

The extract that morning was from 'Party Worker', a fortnightly journal that was even more tightly controlled by boredom than 'Free People'. It was as if they specially selected the dreariest bits from 'Free People', excised any microscopically colourful vestiges, and then published the whole thing as 'Party Worker'.

Sulyok was just finishing an article by Révai on the executions of Rajk and his band. Rajk had been convicted of working on behalf of not only the British and American intelligence services (in addition to a distinguished career as a police informer when the Communist Party had been proscribed) but also doing a bit of moonlighting for Marshall Tito and his filthy Yugoslav deviationists. Why wasn't he working for Walt Disney as well? Gyuri was tempted to ask. Probably because being Minister of the Interior had taken up too much of his time, Gyuri answered himself. It had been rather amusing to see Rajk hang, there was a shapely irony in the Minister of the Interior, the man who had so lovingly built up the Communist state, who had nourished the secret police, being the first to jig on air when they ran short of non-Communists.

Gyuri had no idea what the true facts of the hangings were but there could be no doubt that what was in the papers was a load of absolute bollocks, since it came from the people who specialised in absolute bollocks, the Hungarian Working People's Party.

'But with the disposal of the conspirators, our considerable victory will augment our strength and decisiveness, in order to finish the tasks waiting ahead for us,' Révai's article concluded. The only joke Gyuri could remember about Rajk was that he had been appointed to the government because they needed someone at hand in case documents needed to be signed on a Saturday. Rákosi, Gerő, Farkas and Révai, the quartet imported from Moscow to run Hungary were all Jews, or at least were considered to be Jews, since as far as Gyuri was aware no one had caught them at the synagogue. The Moscow quartet was giving the chosen people the sort of publicity they hadn't had since they voted to nail Christ to some bits of wood.

When he had started his readings, Sulyok had sometimes

tried to initiate discussion about the exciting articles he read out, since discussion, as long as it concurred with the party line, looked more democratic. 'There's nothing as fucking democratic as a good discussion, comrades,' Sulyok had insisted. The problem that he faced was that most of his audience was on piece-rates, and although the money was contemptible, especially for someone with a family, contemptible money was still better than no money. Others might have shared Gyuri's editorial doubts but the upshot was that no one wanted to engage Sulyok in debate. Today, Sulyok didn't try to elicit comment, but reached for a thin red paperback entitled 'They Were Heroes', evidently a collection of biographies of the people whose names were rapidly appearing throughout Budapest and elsewhere as streets: Communist martyrs. There was an inaudible, invisible gasp of horror from Sulyok's audience who had assumed their ordeal over. Obviously Sulyok was making a point for someone's benefit. This was real ideological overtime. But for whose benefit? Everyone gathered around was well below Sulyok on the ladder of advancement, so he couldn't be currying favour from anyone there, but perhaps he had deduced that someone present was informing to someone upstairs. The bonus martyr did seem a bit overindulgent. Nevertheless, it didn't make that much difference to Gyuri if he was standing there listening to Sulyok, doing nothing, instead of standing at his job, doing nothing there.

'Thus, Ferenc Rózsa, one of the outstanding leaders of the Communist Party, finally perished heroically in the torture-chamber,' Sulyok terminated his reading with a note of finality of the sort reserved for the end of a children's bedtime story.

'Sorry,' said Pataki interrupting the respectful silence, 'this was last week, was it?'

'No,' said Sulyok, shocked. 'It was 1942.'

'Oh. I see. It was the *fascists* who killed him. Listen, could you read that passage about him being tortured to death again? It's worth hearing one more time.' Gyuri wished Pataki didn't have to be so Pataki all the time. Pataki had said all this with the seemingly straight face of someone curious to learn more about the setbacks of the workers' movement, but Gyuri couldn't believe that Pataki's luck would be everlasting. The first day at work, Pataki had helped himself to a long length of copper wiring. 'The State owes me,' he asserted. Anyone else would have waited a few days to familiarise himself with the layout before sticking something to their fingers. And it wasn't as if Pataki was in abject need – he always had supper waiting for him at home.

'No, regrettably, comrades, we don't have the time,' Sulyok apologised, 'The imperialists don't rest; remember we have to harden our work discipline.'

'Why not harden a horseprick up your arse?' commented Tamás, not too softly, as he and Gyuri strolled back to the electrical engines. Loud enough to be heard, but quiet enough for Sulyok to be able to ignore it. Tamás could get away with this – who wanted to die? Tamás was incredibly good at killing people; he had a couple of Iron Crosses and an Order of Lenin to prove it.

He had been a great hit during the war, in a number of armies, starting with the Hungarians. He didn't mind being dropped alone behind enemy lines, not eating anything but the odd rat whose head he had to bite off, sitting in puddles that were thinking about becoming ice (the little finger on his left hand had been peeled off by frostbite) and killing Russians until the cows came home. He was an enthusiast of the knife. 'You know,' he confided to Gyuri, 'people don't like being stabbed.' After one mission, when he had spent two months dodging around behind Russian lines without resupply, he had been captured (no ammunition) and offered a job on the spot. 'Killing Russians or killing Germans, you think I give a toss?'

Tamás was, Gyuri guessed, heading for forty, but he still had the sort of hard, well-defined muscles that would have socialist realist painters fighting for space. He was in charge of insulating the parts of the electrical engines that needed insulating. Gyuri didn't understand it really, but since he really didn't do anything, it didn't matter. Tamás hauled the heavy parts up by chain and then immersed them in a vat full of chemicals which insulated the copper. Despite having been in attendance for months, Gyuri had no idea what the chemicals were or how the process worked. This was because Tamás did everything, while Gyuri watched him intently. It was supposed to be dangerous work and was by the standards of Ganz, well paid; i.e: you had change in your pocket after you had eaten.

What Gyuri was paid for boiled down to listening to Tamás's adventures, recent and ancient, which Tamás would recount without a break as he hauled electrical engines up and down. Tamás had a lot of adventures, chiefly because he didn't seem to sleep very much. He had no fixed abode and looked on renting a room as a waste of money. He slept the three or four hours he needed in some only very noisy part of the factory (as opposed to an unbearably noisy part) curled up on the floor, springing out of his slumber fresh and zestful. Most evenings, however, he didn't need to sleep at the factory because of an amorous entanglement or transnocturnal carousing.

Tamás had a unique view of Budapest in terms of the women he had slept with and of the kocsmas he drank in; this topography he would share with Gyuri during their work. A routine Tamás monologue: 'Yeah, I was over by "The Blind Drunk Blindman", they do a great Czech beer there. Anyway, I hadn't been there since I was giving cock to the French Ambassador's wife's maid, and it's just opposite to where I was delivering my dick to the wife of the gypsy violinist who used to play in "The Overflowing Ashtray", that was the violinist I had to stab, not the one who tried to pay me to keep his wife; she was the one I met behind the "You Can Even Make Wine From Grapes". That was a great place, you know, I had a marvellous evening there with a Bulgarian girl. I didn't speak any Bulgarian, she didn't speak any Hungarian. But then you don't need to, do you? She had a place that was

almost above the "Why Is The Floor Pressing On My Nose?".
I didn't get out for days.

'So, I was in "The Blind Drunk Blindman", they were
giving me some of the under the counter pálinka, they say the
Germans wanted it for their rocket program, when I noticed
some really small bloke in there with a good-looking woman.
They were sitting next to this group of dockers. Anyway, this
bloke leans over to the dockers who are mothering this and
mothering that, and says very professor-like "Would you mind
not swearing in front of my wife?" You have to admire his
bottle but getting upset about swearing in "The Blind Drunk
Blindman" is a bit like going into a grocer's and being shocked
by the vegetables. I can see the guy is going to get more kicked
around than a football at Ferencváros on a Saturday afternoon,
so I tell the barman to hide away a bottle of the special pig-
trough pálinka for me because there isn't going to be any
unshattered glass in a moment and I get over at the right
moment to wish one of the dockers the best of health with the
boot as he's giving the guy's wife's tits a courtesy squeeze.'

This episode was representative of Tamás's evenings,
leaving behind five unconscious dockers and two others
earnestly searching for their earlobes. 'They weren't going to
find them, because I swallowed them. Good protein – learned
that behind the Don. The police turned up. Think they were
thinking about charging me, because the guy I was helping out
suddenly choruses up: "That's him, I saw the whole thing.
He's the ruffian who started it." Still, the police knew they'd
look good and stupid in court explaining how I'd attacked ten
dockers. 'Course they took me in for questioning, but they
only asked one question: "Where's the pig-trough pálinka?"'

Perhaps for Gyuri's benefit, Tamás was always fastidiously
precise about the location of the women with whom he was
consorting.

Thus, Gyuri knew as well as his own address that Tamás's
separated wife lived halfway up Kossuth út in Kóbánya,
between the 'Short Dipsomaniac' and the 'Tall Dipsomaniac'.

Tamás also went to great pains to underline that his son, who was ten, got 'the best pocket money' in Budapest. Tamás did the work of three people and was remunerated accordingly. As he calculated his pay packet (an hourly event) he would include the information about the superlative status of his son's pocket money. Tamás's herculean exertions were a further reason why Gyuri didn't need to do much (although Pataki who was employed in the section where the copper wire was spun out had absolutely nothing to do but remark: 'Hey, look at that wire getting stretched').

But, from time to time, Tamás would create a task for Gyuri.

'Get a new blade for this hacksaw,' Tamás requested, which pleased Gyuri as that would fill up the time until lunch. He set off for the stores as slowly as he could to make the most of the trip. When he got there, he was surprised to see a 'Do not disturb' sign which looked as if it had been borrowed thirty years previously from a luxury hotel. Inside, the storemaster, who was the Party Secretary of that section of Ganz, was playing cards with three confederates. Gyuri had barely got his foot across the threshold when, without looking at him or noticeably moving his lips, the storemaster said firmly but without rancour: 'fuckyourmother'. This was said as such an aside, so mechanically, that Gyuri felt it couldn't have been related to his entry. So he asked: 'Sorry to interrupt, but...'

The storemaster wheeled on him: 'May God and all his holy saints fuck you!' he exclaimed in what seemed a deplorable lapse for an avowed atheist and a historical materialist. 'What's your name?'

'Fischer.'

'Okay, you're fired and on your way out stick a horseprick up your arse,' said the storemaster dismissing him in an enraged tone before turning back to his comrades in cards. 'Can you believe this? You can't get a minute's peace in this place.'

Returning to his electrical engines, Gyuri pondered the question of whether Gombás, his protector, was in a stronger position than Lakatos, the wing Party Secretary, and if he were fired, did he care that much? He tried to kid himself, but then realised that he did care. Ganz might be bad, but it wasn't Army bad.

Tamás was surprised to see Gyuri returning empty-handed. 'He said that he was too busy and that I'm fired,' Gyuri reported.

'He does have a cruel sense of humour, that Lakatos,' said Tamás setting off with the blunted hacksaw. Continuing to meditate on his predicament, Gyuri resolved to alert Gombás immediately to the threat to his employment and went up to Gombás's office.

Gombás's secretary wasn't there. Neither was Gombás. After repeated polite and clear knocking in order to ensure that he didn't accidentally spoil a 'training session', Gyuri found Gombás's office to be vacated. He stared at Gombás's black telephone. The idea of picking up the receiver and putting a call through to abroad, somewhere, anywhere West, sneaked into his mind. He toyed with the idea of just doing it, of placing a call, just to hear them say 'Hello' or 'Good morning', just to hear the sound of abroad, the crackle of free air, the ineffable language of out. The prospect xylophoned excitement along his spine.

He enjoyed toying with the idea for a few minutes, knowing for a variety of reasons, first and foremost, a lack of guts, he wouldn't attempt it but he fully savoured the opportunity. He imagined picking up the receiver and asking in a Gombás-like voice for New York, Paris, London, Berlin even Cleveland, Ohio. It was five of the best minutes he had spent for a very long time.

Then he restarted his worries on getting the sack. Where was Gombás? Had he embarked on a talent-scouting tour? Would he be in the army before Gombás paid another visit to his office? Going back to the shopfloor, Gyuri bumped into Pataki sauntering down a corridor, bouncing a basketball on the floor and off the walls, wearing his sunglasses. Presumably he had run out of wire to watch. Gyuri recounted his problems while Pataki bounced the ball furiously around a portrait of Rákosi. 'I always envisaged you as a military man,' said Pataki with the total lack of sympathy only a close friend could muster. 'No, don't laugh. I've never seen anyone who can rival your genius for digging trenches. In recognition of your trench-digging alone you should make General. And I hear military service is being extended to three years, that should give you plenty of time.' Pataki then moved off into the offices to dazzle dazzleable young women with his dribbling skills.

Even though he was highly exercised about his own perils, Gyuri couldn't suppress a pang of anxiety about Pataki who wasn't slowing down his disregard. He had always been the one to get them into trouble, the self-evident, self-incriminating trouble such as the scout camp where they had drunk all the communion wine, *all* the communion wine at Pataki's suggestion. There had been no hope of getting away with it. Father Jenik had been justifiably furious, but since there had only been three days of the camp left, there had only been three days of real wrath and punishment. This camp could be longer...

Bearing two new blades, Tamás reappeared. 'I told you he was pulling your leg. He's a good lad, old Lakatos. He wouldn't let me leave without giving me this carton of cigarettes. I didn't want to take them, but he really pressed me.' Tamás gave Gyuri two packets.

Then it was lunch. The weather was a muscular sunshine so most employees went out into the yard to eat whatever they had managed to lay their hands on. Zsigmond and Pártos, the two priests, were sitting next to each other, dealing with their bread and cheese, conversing in Latin, polishing their only remaining Catholic weapon. No one paid any attention to them any more. The workers were quite accustomed to the strange workfellows that had descended on them. Priests, accountants, diplomats, cartographers, nobility, all undextrous to a man. There was a great campaign going on for 'sharing working methods'. Posters, films, exhortations in print and in person were undodgeable. One of the newsreel versions of this appeal that Gyuri had seen featured a seasoned old worker, complete with the beret that was the hallmark of proletarianness, who having ignored the frustrated bunglings of the fresh-faced youth on the lathe next to him, reads the 'Free People' editorial on the imperativeness of sharing working methods. The old worker is forthwith struck down with shame at his laxness. Instantly, he rushes over to introduce the boy to the delights of advanced lathe-turning.

This was essentially the Party saying: you'd better train each other because we're not going to spare the time or cash to do so. While everyone in the works would rather have been dead than carrying out what the Party had urged, if for no other reason than not wanting to waste valuable earning-time, they had provided guiding help and encouragement to the newcomers who had been dropped into the midst of the factory without knowing how to do the job, and often not even knowing what the job was. They were silently acknowledged as domestic exiles.

Gyuri was warmly greeted by Csokonai, who was sitting scribbling away furiously on a mess of sheets on his lap. Csokonai had been a lecturer at the University, an expert on international law, a decent man, if tiresome in anything but the smallest doses, who looked on Gyuri as an ally. Having noted that Csokonai had a bulging bag of crisp apples, Gyuri sat down next to him, amazed at what he would do for a good bite. Csokonai was in a incessant state of fury with only slight adjustments in the volume. He had explained to Gyuri several times, firmly gripping him by the wrist (with prodigious force for a skinny lawyer): 'They replaced me with an idiot. An *idiot*. An *idiot*. A man who knew nothing, nothing. You must believe me.' Csokonai would repeat this just to leave no doubt that he wasn't using idiot as a figure of speech, but as a purely technical term. Gyuri always agreed adamantly, because he wanted his wrist released and because he found it plausible that some cadre who had flicked through the paperback edition of Lenin on International Law had got Csokonai's job. Over sixty, Csokonai was too old to take it; he couldn't even attempt to roll with the punches. Most of his lunchbreak was spent compiling further violations of national and international law and principles. 'I've really got them now,' he snarled. 'They'll pay, they'll pay. This nonsense can't last forever and then they'll pay.'

What Csokonai was doing was extremely dangerous and Gyuri had no intention of frequenting him any longer than was necessary to obtain an apple or two. The other week, a worker who had either too much pálinka or hardship had suddenly burst out with: 'They say that under Horthy, Hungary was the land of two million beggars. Well at least under Horthy it was just the beggars who were beggars and not the whole sodding country. I can't feed my family on this.' A black car had been waiting for him outside the gates. 'We have a few questions. It'll only take five minutes.' No one had seen him since, but then no one had ever seen again those people whom the Russians had invited for 'malenky robot,' a little work five years ago.

Being an old-world courtesy fiend, Csokonai handed over three apples which Gyuri could only bring himself to refuse once. Mulling over how egg-shell thin dignity was when your belly was yelling, Gyuri returned to work to find Sulyok talking to Tamás: 'Listen, Tamás, we need a little favour, we're having some comradely difficulties.' It took Sulyok some time to spit it out, but the problem was this: there was only one place manufacturing the machine tools Ganz needed and for some reason – enmity, superior bribery, incompetence, kinship, the machine tools were being shipped to other factories, not to where they were needed at Ganz, where despite Stakhanovite book-cooking, the Three Year Plan was not being fulfilled. 'Tamás, could you go over there and explain in a constructive, fraternal and socialist manner the absolute dire necessity for some urgent supplies to aid the intensification of the Three Year Plan fulfilment situation?'

'You want me to hijack one of their deliveries, right?' asked Tamás.

Taken aback by this uncomradely language, Sulyok winced, but didn't blab anymore. 'Yes,' he said, handing over a set of lorry keys. 'Take Gyuri and some of the other lads if you need.' It's all about having the right skills for the right task, Gyuri thought. You can read Lenin on International Law, but no amount of reading Lenin on ambushing and highway robbery could help you if you didn't know the business.

Tamás picked up Pálinkas, another well-known pugilist, and an apprentice jaw-breaker, Bód. As they were pulling out by the front gates, Gyuri noticed Pataki, apprehended by two security men who were unwinding a long length of copper wire from underneath his shirt. Smiling, Gyuri waved, looking forward with keen anticipation to hearing how Pataki could talk his way out of that one.

Tamás dropped everyone off, one by one, wherever they wanted to go, before putting his foot down on the accelerator to head off to the Zugló where the machine tool factory was located. 'Don't worry, I can take care of it on my own,' he said to Gyuri with an expectant grin on his face, slipping his knife in between his teeth.

At home, Gyuri found Elek still parked in his armchair, but entertaining Szócs, his former doorman who came monthly to pay his respects. Szócs was the only one of Elek's old staff who made the effort to seek him out and he was made welcome because of that and also, more saliently, because he always brought a package of food from his farming cousins. His mother had always complained that Elek showered his staff with holidays and bonuses, though as Gyuri recalled, Szócs, who had been on duty outside Elek's office, had never copped any of the goodies.

Szócs was inescapably stuck in cheerfulness but went up a jubilation or two when he saw a younger Fischer. 'How are you, Gyuri? Settling down yet? Thinking about getting married?' Gyuri knew he was at the age when everyone was immensely inquisitive as to what he was doing with his willy, so he was prepared for this sort of inquiry from his seniors; he was as keen to be castrated as to get married but he laughingly denied major romance with good grace. Someone who had come halfway across Budapest to deliver food was entitled to question away. Gyuri discerned an opened package of goose crackling, and started to make arrangements digestively.

Looking down the finger he was pointing at Gyuri as if down the barrel of a gun, Szócs remarked: 'You'll know when you find the right one, you'll know.' Gyuri nodded concurringly as one does towards someone who has mustered goose crackling. 'I knew the moment I saw my wife,' he said chuckling. This surprised Gyuri because he had only seen Mrs Szócs once, and his first, last and lasting impression was of consummate ugliness; he had always imagined that Szócs married her out of charity, or that their wedlock was a further symptom of Szócs's chronic misfortune rather than elective affinities. Szócs's life was one of round-the-clock calamity: an orphan, he had been shipwrecked as a cabin-boy, lost the use of one eye from an infection, lost his toes from frostbite in a Russian prisoner of war camp, lost both his children in the great dysentery epidemic of 1919. You just had to laugh. There was surely more disaster in his past, but unusually for a Hungarian with such promising material to draw on, Szócs was very niggardly in passing out the details of his years.

'The Party secretary catches Kovács,' said Szócs changing tack. '"Comrade Kovács, why weren't you at the last Party meeting?" "The last Party meeting?" replies Kovács. "If I'd known it was the last Party meeting, I'd have brought the whole family."' Szócs was now, in an odd way, a successful figure, now that poverty and misery had been generally distributed; he was a tycoon of jollity. In the land of the blind, Gyuri thought, the man who knows how to use the white stick is king.

The only irritating aspect to Szócs was that his whistling in totalitarianism rather invalidated one's licence for self-pity.

Gyuri could never enjoy his resentment for quite a while after Szócs had left. Szócs's presence made him lose that acute sense of accumulated injustice and aggrievedness that he had been so carefully working on. Elek, for example, might be sitting comfortably in the back of adversity's big black car, but Szócs seemed to thrive on hardship like a slap up meal.

To his shame, Gyuri was glad when Szócs left and he didn't have to pretend any more that he didn't want to throw himself on the goose crackling. Elek had ventured out earlier to get some fresh bread and this in combination with the goose crackling yielded a profound sense of well-being, an undispersable glow of plenitude that would linger on for the minimum of an evening or until Gyuri went to do some training.

The two packets of cigarettes (French) had been part of a great plan Gyuri had been hatching to do some profitable bartering – but Elek looked so deformed, so unnatural without a cigarette that Gyuri handed them over and watched Elek's face become an amalgam of joy and reflection on how to apportion the cigarettes chronologically

One strove to be hard, to be tough, dangerous and independent (Gyuri weighed up the effects of the pile of goose crackling) but self-discipline is such a delicate thing, a plant that wilts on either side of a narrow temperature band. In mitigation, it had been exceptionally adipose, unquestionably hastened to the capital that morning, wrapped before darkness had been dispelled, possessed of an evanescent crispness and a tang that had to be captured by taste buds within twelve hours or it would abscond to the limbo of fabulous flavour.

The glut of cigarettes and goose crackling engendered a pliancy and a conversation between the two of them. Of late, Pataki had been the top recipient of Elek's locutions, a hunched, cigaretted dialogue running through Elek's lewd material. Gyuri made a point of ostentatiously going for a run or loudly doing some housework while they were thus engaged, but it didn't have any dampening effect.

He decided to press Elek on abroad.

'What was it like in Vienna?'

Elek had spent a couple of years stationed outside Vienna as an Austro–Hungarian officer and gentleman before the Big One that had vaporised the Strudel Empire.

'I don't remember much now,' said Elek. 'It was a long time ago. I remember the sex but that's about it. That's the odd thing about Vienna: all that culture, all those libraries, piano recitals, all that learning, all that Mozart was here, all the elaborate chocolate and patisserie and the women were interested in only one thing. If I hadn't been twenty it would have killed me.

'There was one lady, the wife of a distinguished geologist, who was still vigorous enough to carry out his conjugal duties. I timed myself one day. From ten in the morning to three in the afternoon: five hours. I thought she might say stop or ask for an intermission, but no. We only abandoned the mission because her husband was coming back with some very gripping granite. When I got out into the street I had to call for a taxi because my body had gone on strike. Then I found out that someone else from the regiment was leaving his calling cards there as well – the husband challenged him to a duel and I had to act as his second. You would have thought she could have read a book or gone to a museum every now and then.'

'I don't think I'll be getting to Vienna for a while,' Gyuri remarked.

'Oh, I'm sure you will. This can't go on much longer. You realise you and István are my last hopes.'

'What do you mean?'

'The only sort of success I can anticipate now is sitting in a café regaling my cronies with tales of my sons' successes. I'm counting on you for some reflected glory and a modest income. You don't want your old father to be stuck in a café with nothing to boast about?'

'So you're going into sitting around full-time?'

'I'm working up to it. But don't forget you have no excuses: you're at the perfect age for disaster. Physical peak. Flexible. Durable. A good reservoir of optimism. Nineteen is the ideal age for misfortune. You can fight back. And things change. Nothing lasts forever. Hungary has had some bizarre moments in its history. Mongols, Turks wandering in and out. Our friend Horthy, a regent without a king, an admiral without a sea. But *Rákosi*. The one thing I can confidently predict as a non-starter in Hungary is a Jewish King. I'm willing to bet that you won't last long at Ganz, and that you will have a good laugh about all this.'

'How much are you willing to bet?' Gyuri asked, sensing easy money.

'We can negotiate a figure.' At this point Elek was racked by a caravan of coughs of lung-ripping ferocity. 'The trouble is,' he continued weakly, 'I'm not going to be around to collect at this rate. But you still have no excuse for not achieving stupendous prosperity. Think of all that bringing-up your mother lavished on you.'

Gyuri decided to tackle some of the housework. Nothing substantial, but tossing a coin to domesticity, Gyuri entered the waiting-room for washing-up and exposed some plates to running water. Considering how little they had to eat, there was an alarming quantity of dirty crockery.

'I told her for months to go to the doctor. For months. You know what she said, "I can't go. I haven't got a slip." I don't suppose it would have made a lot of difference,' Elek volunteered.

Suddenly, Gyuri wished they hadn't started to converse.

August 1950

They estivated outside Tatabánya.

The peasants out in the fields, on account of what they had endured or because of some innate earthiness, evinced no great surprise to see half a dozen naked and tanned figures strolling through their sunflowers. 'Basketball players,' they muttered.

Pataki was in the lead, wearing his sunglasses, striding out in his basketball boots, a map neatly folded under his arm. Although they got plenty of exercise at the training camp where Locomotive had been invited to act as resident sparring partner for the National team, they were full of kicks, and at Pataki's instigation had gone out for an afternoon constitutional in order to ascertain that the surrounding countryside was as boring as it looked. So far it was.

Most of the vicinity was flat and obvious, but Pataki steered them to a distant clump of greenery, a copse on a series of mounds, with a huge patch of baldness on top. The view from this hillock corroborated their worst fears: the total absence of anything that could be loosely accounted exciting or notable in the neighbourhood. 'So, gentlemen, there it is: the countryside. The place for those fond of vegetable antics. The abode of bucolic delights as celebrated by millennia of illustrious poets, who, in my opinion, were either heavily bribed by wealthy farmers eager to boost their standing, or gibberingly demented,' concluded Pataki.

There was a rectangular stone some four feet high on the summit, which Pataki, having consulted the map, announced was an object of significant trigonometrical value. If it hadn't been on the map, they probably wouldn't have bothered; but how often do you get a chance to destroy a landmark? The stone was recalcitrant and astonishingly heavy, but with the help of a few sturdy branches as levers, they eventually up-ended it and had the pleasure of watching it robustly tumble down a good way. Feeling satisfied with their afternoon's work sabotaging the Hungarian state, they headed back to the camp.

'Has the new Hungary overcome the old three-layered class system of workers, bourgeoisie and nobility?' Róka asked, swiftly providing the answer (before anyone thought he was posing a serious question). 'Not quite. There are still three classes in the new Hungary: those who have been to prison, those who are in prison and those who are going to prison.'

On their way back, Pataki saluted with the map a young peasant girl whose face would have been ugly on a young peasant boy. Joke civility, Gyuri noted, but another week of the camp and the gauche, sack-wrapped girls would start looking like beauty queens.

***

Usually, tired after the day's training, Gyuri would plunge into blackness as soon as he made contact with his mattress despite its high ranking in intractability. The training was demanding, and as always, Gyuri had to do twice as much as anyone else. Some people have athleticism handed to them on a tray, others have to sweat to get up to scratch. Hitting sixty push-ups had caused him dreadful suffering while Pataki could do it on demand while conducting a conversation on any theme you'd care to name. He had been born with explosives in his muscles, even his tongue.

When Gyuri returned from the first instalment of the morning's training, a run around the lake, gasping from the blow of such a brutal introduction to the day, Pataki would be lazily bestirring himself, often having a contemplative cigarette on the porch of their hut. Pataki could get away with this, because he could always deliver on court. 'I know life is unfair, I don't dispute that,' Gyuri would gasp, 'but does it really have to be this sort of industrial strength unfair?'

Pataki's rightful place was in the National team, not playing opposite them to give them a good workout. He had been invited to play with the junior squad years earlier when still at school, but was turfed out after a few months. Not for slackness in training or for any other basketballing deficiency but thanks to the light in Hármati's eye. 'She's the light of my eye,' Hármati would say in an exaggerated, overparental manner of his daughter, Piroska. Pataki's falling out with Hármati, the coach of the National team, had its root in Hármati walking in when Pataki was deflowering Piroska on a horrifically valuable Louis Quinze chaise-longue that Hármati had personally plundered from the debris of a neighbouring and deceased family's bombed flat. 'It was the mess on the sofa that did it,' Pataki maintained. However, Pataki's charm and undeniable talents would have boomeranged him back after a nominal banishment had it not been for Hármati walking in again to discover Pataki having a foam bath with some highly-prized bath crystals brought back, by hand, from a trip to Italy, and with Hármati's other daughter, Noémi. Fortunately for Pataki it was a flat designed with two doors to every room, and his speed enabled him to stay ahead of Hármati for six circuits of the premises, before he could gather up his garb and exit. 'It's bad enough being caught with your trousers down but when you have to dry yourself first...' Pataki reflected later, adding, 'I think it was the bath crystals that really upset him.'

Pataki had just found out about his speed one day and found it there whenever he needed it. If Gyuri didn't run every day, he'd slow up and balloon; if he didn't play ball every day, his edge would blunt but Pataki could wander onto court after a month in a Parisian restaurant and still be able to whizz down infallibly to dunk the ball in the basket. There had to be a good reason for Pataki to stir and training wasn't one of them. 'We're not paid to train, we're paid to win,' was his reaction to Hepp's supplications to hone his abilities. Hepp had no real choice but to put up with Pataki; he usually didn't keep a close eye on him during training, so that his non-cooperation wouldn't grate. On the other hand, Hepp had managed on one unforgettable occasion to persuade Pataki to run the 1500. Pataki must have had his mind on something else when Hepp had explained that the Locomotive athletics team was runnerless for the 1500 metres at an upcoming meet and had pleaded with Pataki to run it to avoid the ignominy of a no-show.

Gyuri was there on the day which introduced Pataki to effort. He could remember the uncomprehending shock that had appeared on Pataki's face after the first lap and a half when it gradually became apparent to Pataki, that unlike shooting the length of a basketball court, the 1500 would involve that most daunting of things, labour. He came in fifth in a field of six, arriving at the finishing line with his customary collected features exploded into a morass of leering agony. After minutes of gasping for breath on the dearly-embraced ground, Pataki finally announced: 'I thought I was going to die. These runners are out of their minds, how can they do this for a living? My track career is over.'

Gyuri had been very glad to witness Pataki stumble on a new world of experience, to see him dust off his will-power. Money, however, always got him going. The sprinters at the camp had already lost the more interesting portion of their worldly goods to Pataki as they always did when they challenged him. The sprinters, the 100 boys who trained with zealotic fervour, who stretched, bent, and twanged muscles for hours, who ran everywhere, lifted weights, ate carefully, and went to bed early and did nothing that didn't further their aim of doing the 100 faster, couldn't believe that Pataki could best them in a dash.

But he could, by challenging them to 50 metres. Sprinters who didn't know Pataki joyfully stumped up the cash for the bet (and those who did know him stumped up petulantly) and then saw nothing but Pataki's back. Over thirty metres he was so explosive, so swift, so straight out of the jungle, that no one could get close. By fifty, the professionals would have closed with him but they'd still be a sternum behind. The pattern, when Pataki, for amusement and not forints, had been dared to run the full hundred, was that before sixty the sprinters would have a nose ahead, by eighty they were clear and by the hundred Pataki could see their soles.

Rónai, an Olympic 100-metre bronze winner, was the one least able to come to grips with Pataki's kick start. Year after year, he had been vanquished by Pataki at training sessions, at meets, on Margit Island and once inside the bar at the Opera. Fanatical, even by the whole-hearted standards of the sprinters, Rónai had the obsessive nature of a marathon runner. At the camps, he was a largely solitary figure who seemed to regard conversation as, at best, impinging on his training program or, at worst, blatant sabotage, and he could, to anyone not directly involved in the perfection of his leg movements, begrudge even a 'good morning'. He would, even if waiting at a bus stop or in a queue for the cinema (not that he went very often), be bending and flexing muscles, or if refraining from using them would be plotting new techniques to lick them into shape.

Rónai was up before everyone else, in clement and inclement weather, trotting around, relishing the extra time he was putting in, that was putting him ahead of the others still in bed in Budapest and elsewhere, pushing himself and thinking about the next exertion. The world for Rónai was a conglomeration of various training possibilities that could enable him to load more ammunition into his legs in time for the '52 Olympics in Helsinki. Some of his mattress partners, miffed by his monomania, had let slip that when it came to bed, Rónai was less concerned with the merchant of pleasure knocking on his door, than in disciplining sets of muscles through a series of awkward and convoluted couplings that would last until he had counted out the required number of muscular contractions, the signal for a different constellation of brawn to come into service. 'It's so moving,' one netball player recounted, 'having gluteus maximus whispered in your ear.'

Rónai had lost heavily to Pataki, money, various edibles and a magnetic pocket-chess set he had obtained in London during the '48 Olympics. He couldn't leave Pataki alone; the very sight of Pataki lounging around made him twitch. He had come close to Pataki, very close, losing a number of runs by the breadth of a vest, and one even ended in a dead heat according to the adjudicators. But parity wasn't good enough for Rónai. It wasn't acceptable for him that a mere basketball player, who wasn't even in the National team to boot, who was regularly to be found loafing around, gassing, playing cards, drinking Czech beer and being hunted by his coach, that such a ramshackle athlete could best a sprinter who hadn't drunk a Czech beer since 1946. 'Beer,' he had pronounced publicly, 'is for the weak. There are seven people around a campfire, they all put a hand into the flames. One by one, they pull back. The one who leaves his hand in the longest is the world champion.' A man who never failed to exercise his ears before he went to sleep didn't give up easily.

'Quick, give me some cigarettes,' Pataki would say when he saw Rónai approaching, lighting up two together to compose the veritable picture of the prodigal sportsman. Two weeks into the camp, Rónai had lost all his money and any objects of value, including a pair of remarkable German toe-nail clippers and a less remarkable phial of Bulgarian rose-water, though the judging of the races had been made more difficult, as after the first few defeats Rónai insisted on running after dark when no one else was likely to be about. It was always tight, Rónai at Pataki's heels like a fleshed-out shadow, but the nipple-length losses were an awful gulf to Rónai, an abyss that became progressively more uncrossable.

One night Gyuri and Pataki entered the camp canteen to find Rónai entombed by empty Czech beer bottles, shouting out as if to the human race: 'It's too unfair. There's no point. It's all fixed.' It had never occurred to Rónai that there were people who couldn't be bothered to put a hand into the fire. It made Gyuri feel a lot better, and perhaps Rónai too, though he still kept losing to Pataki.

Predestination was not something to which Hepp subscribed. He was out to humble and humiliate Hármati's National team and he had a suitcase full of plans to bring this about. 'You're probably too young to understand this,' said Hepp addressing the team, 'but the real tragedy of life, the most appalling fact you will have to face in this existence is that there is no substitute for hard work' – and flourishing rolls of documents – 'and using the right plan.'

The sight of Hepp threatening a Stalin shift of training threw a panic through the team – they had been counting on a month of sunbathing and exploring the plentiful cuisine prepared for the sportsmen and women representing the Hungarian nation. Pataki took Hepp aside: 'Look, we get the message: you want to do the National boys?' 'Yes,' conceded Hepp. 'Okay, here's the proposition,' urged Pataki, 'We'll train hard, but, and the boys have asked me to approach you on their behalf, but if we can forego the above-the-call-of-duty stuff, we guarantee, *I* guarantee that at the last match of the camp, at the display when all the big cheeses are there, I guarantee that we'll beat them. But, believe me, the team will fray if we overdo it. Remember what the water-polo player said at the brothel after he paid for eight girls, but only employed five, "This is ridiculous. I managed all eight this morning."'

To universal surprise, Hepp entered into the Pataki pact. Pataki could be persuasive, of course. Aside from the effortlessness of his lying, he knew which key could open which person; he was the master locksmith of character. Take the way he had wriggled out of the copper wire fiasco at Ganz by claiming he had been *borrowing* some for a Lieutenant-

Colonel in the AVO who had discreetly asked him to acquire some for various secret projects. 'They're conducting electrical experiments.' The security people might well have caught a whiff of bullshit but who was going to take the risk of vexing a Lieutenant-Colonel, however infinitesimal the risk, over a bit of rotten wire? Pataki had walked away with a stern injunction to stick to proper channels.

Gyuri suspected that Hepp may have had other reasons, apart from Pataki's cajolery, for acquiescing but Pataki had unwound Hepp, and given the rest of the team a summary level of activity (except for Gyuri who couldn't afford to let any hour pass without exploiting it).

Gyuri was ushered out of sleep's antechamber by a procession of loud bumps, which his ejected senses slowly situated as emanating from the bunk above him. Craning out of his bed, he realised that unless Pataki had suddenly developed a brilliant ventriloquist act and grown a large pale bottom, he had enticed some female company back to their hut. It was outrageous – here they were in a Communist dictatorship, on the verge of World War Three, in the middle of the night and Pataki had the gall to enjoy himself and invade his sleep.

'God's dick,' was about all Gyuri could think of in his irate daze, not fully reconnected to his imaginative facilities.

'There's really no need to be polite,' insisted Pataki, not missing a beat. 'Don't pay the slightest attention to us. Pretend we aren't here. Feel free to carry on with your sleep.'

Not confident in the resilience of the bunkbeds in the face of love's vibrations Gyuri threw his mattress onto the floor, where he would be a safe distance from any collapsing reposery. 'If you tie a torch to it, you'll be able to see what you're doing,' he counselled.

At dawn's entry, Gyuri awoke, feeling more sleepy than when he had started. It was a morning he immediately recognised as one he wanted nothing to do with, a day that revealed itself, that flagrantly exposed itself as a day which wouldn't allow him to get anywhere. Gyuri found himself thinking, without any side-dish of shame, about why he hadn't joined the Communist Party. That was where his life had taken the wrong turn, he decided. Deciding where his life had gone wrong was something that took up a lot of his leisure time and he was convinced that he had pinpointed the chairman of the error board. If only he could send back a message to his younger self to sign up, if only he had accidentally walked into a Party office and inadvertently dropped his signature on an application form.

Now, of course, apart from the bad taste it would leave in his soul, his participation in the Communist movement would be as welcome as a bonfire in an ammunition dump. He had as much chance of joining as a blue whale had, assuming it could make its way to Budapest. But back in '45 or '46, things were different. Hitler could have got a membership card then – the more the merrier. He could have got in, denounced his family background, vituperating Elek as a decadent bourgeois (which would have been fun), and with a bit of Lenin-spouting, the odd weekend being chummy with coal miners down a pit somewhere, he could have ended up with a comfortable, well-paid workfree job as a funksh somewhere, and with the accelerating rate of arrests and hangings, promotion couldn't be avoided.

* * *

The Chinaman had stunned them all.

Gyuri had tried to get to know him, still curious about Red China. This was shortly after the thwarted visit to the Chinese Embassy. The visit to the Chinese Embassy had come a few weeks after the thwarted visit to the Ministry of the Interior, where he and Pataki had tried to get into the police. Getting into the police had originally been Pataki's idea, but Gyuri warmed to it, thinking about all the people he could be rude to while in uniform. The police had a second-division basketball team and Pataki had the belief they could work themselves a niche there. All those policeman jokes were a deterrent but after deliberation, Gyuri felt the list of people he had prepared for harassment was worth it, and the prime factor was dodging military service, since they had got wind of a rumour that suggested Ganz's workforce would no longer qualify for strategic exemption. No one had spelled out why they were turned down; they could only guess the police had found another source of first-division players or maybe the crippled and deformed status of their moral credentials had done in their prospects.

While he and Pataki were negotiating their transfer to Locomotive and wangling their places in the evening classes at the College of Accountancy, Gyuri, reviewing the options in case of severe emergency, had managed to find something preferable to self-mutilation to stay out of the Army: going Chinese. He had been thinking about Ladányi. He never had the chance to see Ladányi again after the feeding frenzy in Hálás, but he heard that he had been posted to China as predicted, just before the Communists had come into their own there. The only bulletin after that was that Ladányi was in Shanghai. He couldn't have been there for long. The Chinese had got a bad case of socialism, but at least they didn't have too many Russians. Not enough rice to go around.

Reviewing the state of China and speculating on Ladányi's whereabouts (celebrating one-man mass in gaol, running a restaurant, correcting some mandarin's ideograms?) Gyuri lighted on the idea of going to China. Red China was the first stop for the journalistic imagination; it was always getting slapped on the back every time you opened a paper or switched on the radio.

'Let's go con the Chinese,' Gyuri proposed to Pataki. 'If we get out there, it might lead to other things. And if it's awful, well, it's awful here and at least it'll be Chinese misery.' Anything seemed superior to homegrown misery. Gyuri argued they should go along in the guise of ardent admirers of the Chinese Revolution, avid to learn more about the achievements of people's power in China and eager to start Chinese lessons. 'With a border that big, it'll be no problem walking out,' Gyuri reasoned. Pataki had a look that alluded to the excellent rowing weather, but why not roll the dice?

The Chinese Embassy was in a quiet, elegant street just off Andrássy út, in what was the diplomatic quarter. Huge, ornate, opulent buildings that spoke of an unhurried lifestyle. How do you enlist for the diplomatic game? Gyuri wondered as he inspected the serenity and evident absence of work in the embassies. They had ruled out writing a letter or phoning: that left space for prevarication or refusal. The best would be to go along and put their feet in the door. The time of their approach had also been intensely debated, and they came to the conclusion that early afternoon would be most suitable.

The Embassy's door was black and enormous and didn't look like the sort of door that cared to be disturbed. It was a door that was meant to be seen but not knocked on, a door you walked past at a path's distance. Unlike the Western embassies there wasn't a policeman on guard outside, but the whole tenor of the facade was discouragement.

A sizeable bell was on duty at the side of the door. Gyuri pushed it once, manfully, for a very polite duration but didn't hear any corresponding ringing inside. He waited for a very polite duration, hoping for signs of life. This process was repeated twice as passers-by passed by wondering what two young, smartly-dressed Hungarians were doing outside the Chinese Embassy. The bell obviously hadn't been designed to be rung, so Gyuri gave a curt rap on the door, stinging his finger joints (there was no knocker provided). He continued lengthy intervals of polite waiting with painful knocking bouts. They were beginning to infer that the building was abandoned, when they noticed, from a first-floor window, an oriental visage peering out at them, having shunted aside a substantial lace curtain. Pataki and Gyuri acknowledged the watcher by switching on exemplarily polite and radiant smiles.

Nothing happened after this first contact for several minutes. 'They're busy learning Hungarian,' offered Pataki, free to amuse himself since it hadn't been his idea. 'They're scanning the phrase book for "Drop dead".' After an unreasonable length of time, the door was opened by a young Chinese man in a wearied suit, who greeted them in mechanical but correct Hungarian. 'We're fans of the Chinese Revolution,' said Gyuri, 'my friend and I have been stunned by the feats of the Communist Party of China. Could we come in to express our admiration?'

They were escorted to a luxurious reception room which only confirmed Gyuri's respect for the diplomatic life. Another Chinese official joined them. He seemed to have rudimentary or no knowledge of Hungarian, since the door-opener kept handing him chunks of the conversation in Chinese. 'We have been inspired by the example of the Chinese Revolution,' proclaimed Gyuri, 'as Mao Tse-Tung has said: "the Communist Party of China has brought a new style of work to the Chinese people, a style of work which essentially entails integrating theory with practice, forging close links with the masses and practising self-criticism." It is this new style that in an internationalist, fraternal and scientific spirit we would like to study, first-hand for ourselves, in order to aid the development of a peace-loving socialism on a global basis.'

Oddly enough, no one laughed when Gyuri finished – Pataki must have been biting the insides of his mouth. Gyuri had done his homework. Pataki hadn't. But this didn't stop him: 'Yes, as Comrade Mao said, "Hungary and China are closely bound by common interests and common ideals."' The good thing about Mao, like Marx, and in particular Lenin and Stalin, was that at some point or other, he had written or said everything from 'I ordered the steak medium rare' to 'Ontogeny recapitulates phylogeny' to 'Chattanooga Choo-Choo'. Everything had passed their lips, so you couldn't go wrong quoting from imagination.

Gyuri took the ball again, and reiterated their fervent desire to go to China, learn the language and study the newing of China. The two Chinese listened very soberly to the proposal, then the non-Hungarian-speaking one who exuded an air of seniority, spoke to the other briefly, and his words stumbled out through the other in clunking Hungarian:

'Comrades, your ardour is highly commendable and we are greatly touched that our achievements in China have proved such an example to you. But as Comrade Mao has also said, as he has so aptly phrased it, building socialism must start in front of your neighbours, and it is better for you to carry on the struggle here in Hungary in your own way.' There could be no doubt that in China the science of horseshit detection was not neglected or unknown.

Gyuri and Pataki were given a copy each of Mao's poetry on their way out. They thanked their hosts profusely. They had spent no more than twenty minutes on Chinese soil. 'I suppose if nothing else I can say I've been to China,' Gyuri said. Out but in.

The Korean War had seemed promising too. Pataki actually phoned the Ministry of Defence, pseudonymously, from a public phone, to inquire whether there was any chance of being able to 'go and fight those imperialist bastards'. The authorities, guessing the magnitude of these volunteers' numbers, deduced that they would most likely be the fastest-surrendering soldiers in the history of warfare. Pataki was carefully given details of an anti-American demonstration where, he was assured, he would be allowed to uncork his righteous wrath.

'Why are they fighting Communism in Korea, but not here?' asked Pataki irascibly. 'Are the hotels much better in Korea? Is it the superiority of the local cuisine? My only objection to the war is that it should be here and not in some rice-paddy in Korea. What have we done not to be invaded by the Americans?'

With this background in Far Eastern Studies, they were intrigued by the arrival of a Chinese basketball player at the camp. Hármati had presented him with great fanfare and to bursts of admiring applause. This first period of Hungarian-Chinese basketballing relations went well, but after that, despite the undeniable warmth, cordiality and curiosity on both sides, things slowed down somewhat, because whoever had arranged for him to attend the camp had either overlooked or forgotten that Wu, as he seemed to be called, spoke no Hungarian, no English, no German, no Russian or any other language of which anyone in the camp had a smattering. No one, of course, spoke any Chinese.

'He probably thinks he's in Moscow,' observed Róka as Wu trotted about dribbling the ball respectably but unbrilliantly. No one had seen him arrive, and the purpose of his presence remained rather mysterious. Hármati, under questioning, denied having any foreknowledge of Wu's provenance. 'He's Chinese, right? Or maybe Korean. Can you tell the difference? Or maybe he's a Cambodian who likes long walks. Anyway, if he's Chinese, we salute him as a member of the heroic Chinese people. If he's Korean, we salute him as a member of the heroic Korean people. This is a sports camp, blown by the breeze of progress, we fraternally give him a basketball and let him run around in a correct, scientific and socialist manner on our court. If nothing else he's going to learn that you've got to be a bit taller to play basketball.' Wu could have easily fitted into five foot six.

Everyone liked Wu because, despite his virtually trappist existence, he was extraordinarily polite and cheery. He was the only person in the camp who energetically thanked the cooks for the meals they provided, giving vigorous bows of gratitude every time. 'Things must be really bad back home,' Gyuri remarked, since the only thing you could say in favour of the camp food was that it was there, and you could have as much as you wanted. Wu's courtesy extended to the basketball court, where on those rare occasions when he unwittingly managed to get hold of the ball, he was too civil to refuse to hand it over to whoever approached him.

The sportswomen had invited all the sportsmen over to their half of the camp for an egg and nokedli evening. Despite the more important attractions, Pataki spent most of the evening launching strictures on the texture of the nokedli, how the wrong kind of flour had been used (which was strange since Pataki knew as well as anyone there was only one kind of flour available, flour flour, since Hungarian shops had adopted a philosophy of not taxing their customers with choice), that the water temperature had wavered, that the nokedli had been swimming for too long and the eggs applied at an inappropriate point, and generally indulging in a molecular appraisal of the method. Sensing scepticism at his culinary authority, Pataki then promulgated loudly that he would return the sportswomen's hospitality by preparing a true fish soup, a genuine fish soup, the following week.

'Why a genuine fish soup?' queried Róka, 'why not a sham one?'

'I mean,' Pataki responded superciliously, 'a traditional fish soup, prepared in the proper way, as Hungarians have prepared it since time immemorial.'

'But you can't cook,' Gyuri pointed out.

'There are certain things that every man should be able to do and cooking a fish soup is one of them. It might be tricky getting some of the ingredients, but I will endeavour to do my best.'

'Will it have some potatoes?' enquired Katona.

'No,' replied Pataki.

'But I like potatoes,' remonstrated Katona.

'So do I,' retorted Pataki with one foot on the ladder of petulance, 'I also like my basketball boots, but I wouldn't put them in a fish soup. Potatoes don't belong in a genuine fish soup.'

The day of the reception came near and Pataki, beseeched twenty-four hours a day to include potatoes, was getting truculent and also, although Gyuri could only suspect it, worried about his ability to cook fish soup. Fish soup would be something very difficult for Pataki to talk his way out of, since fish soup was either there or it wasn't. But, somehow, Pataki had managed to round up the ingredients, so that as a minimum he had something to attempt to cook

'Where are the potatoes?' asked Gyuri.

'There aren't any,' said Pataki, trying to look expertly at the fish he held, overdosed on air.

'That's not carp, is it?' asked Gyuri.

'No, it's not,' said Pataki, 'it's perch.'

'Oh,' said Gyuri exiting, 'I didn't know you could make fish soup with perch.'

In came Gyurkovics. 'Where are the potatoes?' he asked.

'There aren't any,' reaffirmed Pataki, still working hard to give the appearance of preparing fish soup.

'That's not carp, is it?' asked Gyurkovics.

'No, it's perch,' was the terse response.

'Oh,' said Gyurkovics walking out of the kitchen, 'I didn't know you could make fish soup with perch.'

When Hepp came in and asked about the potatoes, Pataki calmly replaced on the cutting board the perch he had been considering, and enunciated forcefully: 'I know what's going on. I know what you're trying to do. You're trying to get me worked up, but,' he continued in a determined but un-irate tone, 'I'm not going to let you.'

'Okay,' said Hepp, 'but where are the potatoes?'

It was Demeter who won the bottle of reserve pálinka, when Pataki, at the fifteenth questioning, answered by attacking Demeter with a brace of perch. Having fired off his perch at the swiftly retreating Demeter, Pataki stormed off into the countryside.

When Pataki returned to the camp (some hours later, Gyuri noticed; too late to make another stab at the fish soup) he found everyone gathering in the marquee as if for a fish soup soirée.

'Come on,' said Katona, 'you've got to see this. I've managed to persuade Wu to do it.'

'Do what?' asked Pataki puzzled.

'His numbers. It's quite amazing, I caught him playing along with the radio the other day.' Pataki followed Katona into the marquee where the entire camp seemed to be in attendance. Katona appointed himself master of ceremonies:

'Ladies and gentlemen, we are very privileged tonight to witness a performer who has travelled thousands of kilometres to be with us. First of all, can I ask for some discreet lighting.' The flaps of the marquee were closed to produce a fair penumbra. A stretcher was carried in with a figure hidden under a blanket. The blanket was lifted up to reveal a pair of Chinese buttocks. 'Secondly, may I ask you to maintain absolute silence during the recital. Over to you, Mr Wu.'

The sounds commenced and though it took a few moments for the audience to latch on, they soon realised that Wu was farting out the Internationale. The audience, distinguished by its ideological unsoundness, despite the recent injunction for quiet, burst into spontaneous applause. Wu's phrasing and stamina were astonishing and the Internationale was only the beginning. As the audience wondered what on earth he had been eating, Wu launched into a medley of tunes, concluding with 'The Blue Danube'. There was a standing ovation.

Then the fish soup was served. Gyuri and the others could see that Pataki was itching to remonstrate about the salination or some other aspect of the soup, but he realised that his reputation could be irrevocably marred and he had to sit and take it. 'It's really rather good, considering where it came from,' remarked Hepp to Gyuri. The origins of the soup were never revealed to Pataki: it had been tinned at the behest of an official at the Ministry of Agriculture who thought it would make a good export product to Britain, until someone reminded him that Britain was a capitalist country and as such couldn't be the recipient of Hungarian fish soup. Indeed it transpired that all the countries likely to pay for tins of fish soup were capitalist, whereas their trading partners, the socialist countries, wouldn't cough up a mouldy kopek. It was decided to divvy up the fish soup within the Ministry, so all the families of the staff experienced a fish soup bonanza. István had dumped ten tins with Elek, who would eat anything – except fish.

Playing for the railways had some benefits, including free deliveries.

* * *

Gyuri was looking forward to the end of the camp, since he was becoming preoccupied with seeing Zsuzsa again, and he was also looking forward to the end of the camp because Pataki wasn't. Pataki wasn't because he knew he had promised Hepp that Locomotive would win the match against the National team. Pataki didn't show this, but his exuberance was steadily deflating as the day drew nearer.

As the Locomotive players sparred with them, it was a constant reminder to Pataki that the National team was the National team because it had the best players, drawn from the Army and the Technical University. Thoughtfulness clouded Pataki's brow as he studied the opportunities for winning. The others had been quite content for Pataki to parley a truce with Hepp, for while losing the match would bring a certain general retribution, for Pataki it was going to bring intensely specific retaliation from Hepp, of whom it was said he bore grudges thirty years old.

Worrying about things wasn't Pataki's forte, so after a couple of introspections which didn't hand over a solution, he chose to leave the action to the day.

The only thing in Locomotive's favour was that the National team didn't have much to lose. Although the supremos of the sports world would be at hand, no one was going to pay any attention to the result. In the outside world it wouldn't count. 'Why aren't any of the buggers injured?' Pataki lamented as he changed for the match, clearly having prayed for some disability since nothing else could provide victory.

The first half went well for Locomotive. At half-time, they were in the lead 32 to 26. It had been a lively session, played with one of Locomotive's favourite leather balls, Vladimir. As one of the National team remarked to the referee, 'Couldn't we have another ball please? Pataki won't let us play with this one.' Gyuri had never seen Pataki run around court like that before. It was as if he were playing on his own, charging after the ball like a lunatic, in top gear all the time. His relentless acceleration paid dividends – he got the ball where others wouldn't have, but Gyuri could see it was at a cost. Pataki was looking fully drained when the half time whistle blew.

'Angyal!' Pataki called out to Gyuri's co-worker in Locomotive's dirty tricks department. Angyal, who had been sitting it out on the bench, trotted over. His talent was to neutralise players in the opposing teams who demonstrated too great a facility at scoring baskets, by using a variety of techniques, never recommended by coaches, but extraordinarily effective – the backhand testicle-grab or the airborne elbow-jab to the face. Angyal was injured, he had sprained his ankle after administering a particularly devastating elbow to Demény, Hungary's leading scorer, turning on the crimson nostril-taps. Leaning close, Pataki poured some words into Angyal's ear, who then sauntered off.

'What are we going to do?' Gyuri asked Pataki. 'You look a wreck. You're not going to last the second half.'

Pataki smiled. 'We just have to soldier on.'

The second half showed that Pataki had expended his fuel and lost his magical ability to corner the ball. Hepp remained impassively on the bench, aware as anyone else that the points were starting to snub Locomotive. The score was 33 to 32 to Locomotive when the shouts of 'Fire' were heard and someone ran in to call for help in carrying buckets of water to put out the blaze that was consuming the quarters of the National team. Hearing this, the National team to a man dashed out to save their hard-earned toiletries. They had been due to leave the camp that afternoon, and what with sifting through the ashes to find French shampoo and Italian soap, the match never resumed.

Hepp didn't look happy about this, but more importantly, to everyone's relief, he didn't look very unhappy; he did also look as if he wouldn't be listening to Pataki much in the future.

Boarding the bus that was to take them to the railway station, Pataki and Gyuri noticed Wu sitting beside the running track, looking as affable and out of touch as ever. 'I don't suppose anyone has told him the camp is over, or if they have, I don't suppose he knows,' Gyuri said. They collected Wu, since, if nothing else, they knew exactly where to leave him in Budapest...

* * *

He had met Zsuzsa a fortnight before the camp. She represented a change of tactic for Gyuri. He had been pursuing a number of attractive women, who far from considering docking had recoiled from his greetings as if his hello were a wielded knife. 'Communism *and* celibacy, that's too much,' Gyuri had moaned. Rather like an injured player seeking a fixture in the division below to repair his pride, Gyuri had met Zsuzsa at a dance. Gangs of hormones, supported by a sense of desperation, had unearthed beauty from an unpromising surface. Even though they had only met three times, Gyuri had been unpacking the equipment, setting up the furnishings of affection and a good part of his time in Tatabánya was spent contemplating the ransacking of her fleshy treasures.

Gyuri went back home only long enough to spruce up and to verify his summered, youthful looks in the mirror. Staring at himself, he really couldn't understand why women weren't climbing in through the windows. He didn't mind about totalitarianism at all as he sauntered over to Zsuzsa. 'All you need is something to look forward to,' he said to himself.

Zsuzsa's flat had a phone but he felt like reappearing in person.

Zsuzsa was in, but was showing out a guest. In his initial shock, Gyuri couldn't decide which was worse, that the caller was a strapping gentleman, the holder, probably, of a jaunty dong, or that he was also owner of a blue-flash AVO uniform. A professional, not like the poor green sods conscripted to tramp around the borders and shoot any decamping capitalists, foreign spies or general bad lots seeking to flee the gains of the people. Even without the blue uniform, they would still have looked at each other as if they were being introduced to a dog log.

What further incensed Gyuri was that Zsuzsa was unaware of the monstrosity of inviting a blueboy home, even when he pointed it out to her. 'Elemér is sweet,' was about all Zsuzsa would say as Gyuri fulminated about the iniquities of the AVO. Under interrogation, Zsuzsa explained that Elemér had entered the scene by apprehending Bodri, Zsuzsa's dog, when Bodri had inexplicably succumbed to the call of the wild in the park and spurned Zsuzsa's implorings to return. 'He ought to be good at collaring,' riposted Gyuri.

The other great disappointment he suffered that evening was the realisation that Zsuzsa was heavily involved with stupidity. Her occupation (florist) should have warned him but Zsusza, although she inhabited Hungary, didn't seem to live there. She didn't understand what was going on, she hadn't noticed what was going on and couldn't grasp what Gyuri was saying. Gyuri also noticed that her nose was looking too large that evening but on the other hand he couldn't help being envious of her total lack of contact with 1950. She had an air-tight insulation of dimness.

'Have some tea,' Zsuzsa insisted. She was still pleased to see Gyuri and didn't pay any heed to his ravings and didn't comprehend what upset him on either the masculine or ethical plane. Gyuri enumerated the AVO's privileges, their special supplies.

'That's not true, Elemér was just saying he has to work very long hours and he needs to earn extra money by translating articles from *Pravda* to help look after his mother.' Gyuri realised it was like trying to demolish a house by throwing a glass of water at it and a strong sense of familiar futility descended on him like a cage. He had a good look at what was on his plate and he didn't find his appetite stirred. This was going to be, he sensed, another fine addition to his collection of failures. He could see the title of his autobiography: *Women I almost slept with*. Not kissing and telling. '1950 was a good year, I almost slept with four women: a heroic production increase, under strict Marxist–Leninist principles, from 1949, when I almost slept with two women.'

He had an expired affair on his hands, but he was going to have to prop up the cadaver, as troops might do in a trench with fallen comrades to dupe their enemy into thinking they still had greater numbers to fight. The complication was that the following Friday, Locomotive was having its annual party, the summit of its social gatherings, and Gyuri knew that he would sooner face a firing squad than attend without a companion, and unfortunately Zsuzsa was the only representative of her sex willing to even talk with Gyuri. If Zsuzsa didn't go with him, no one would.

Elemér was removed from the conversation but this eviscerated their badinage severely and with a reminder about the Locomotive festivity, Gyuri took his leave and reflected deeply on the absurdity of living in a country more than half full of women (demography being on his side since the erasure of the Hungarian Second Army in 1944) and being unable to transact some romantic commerce. Standing in the tram, with the passengers packed as tightly as cigarettes in a carton, centuplets in the oblong womb of the tram, even with the backs of three other citizens coupling with him, Gyuri felt sappingly lonely. Crushed, but lonely. How do you find people you can talk to? There should be a shop. And once you've found people you can talk to, how do you hang on to them?

He devoted a lot of his spare time over the next few days to internal lamentation and some deft self-pity, cassandraing about the flat, looking at himself in the mirror and asking: 'Ever had one of those lives where nothing goes right?' But on the Tuesday night he found himself awake. Mental eructations growled up clearly from the cerebral digestion. It was three o' clock in the morning, the hour favoured by the back-seat drivers in his cranium for interrupting his sleep. Whatever was bothering him would be thrust up, and although he couldn't name the issue, a strong discontent was emanating from his cerebral colon.

Switching on the light, Gyuri referred to his watch. Three minutes after three. Why was it when he wanted to wake up with punctuality he couldn't but the seething rage inside always popped out at its self-appointed seething hour and why was it that when he wanted to feel awakened in the mornings he could never feel as fresh as he did now? He switched off the light and hoped for sleep to creep up on him. His freshness was undiminished when he heard the doorbell ring. His first thought was Hepp, but it was too early and too outrageous even for Hepp and he was in the clear with Hepp so there could be no justification for a dawn raid. Such a ring could only herald a really interesting misfortune amongst the neighbours. Murder? Rape? Cardiac arrest? Or was it the AVO? he thought sarcastically. His curiosity rubbing its hands with glee, Gyuri went to the door to find four plainclothes AVO men there. The plainclothes usually made them stick out as much as the uniforms since no one but the AVO could get proper clothes.

Everyone knew about the bell-shock, sweating away with the fear of arrest, but Gyuri had never felt important enough to be arrested. For an instant he believed they must be looking for someone else or that they had the wrong address; until they explained, not that they were arresting him, but that they had a few questions waiting for him.

Gyuri got dressed and left a note for Elek who was nowhere in evidence (warming up a widow somewhere no doubt).

Kovács the concierge, an inveterate arsehead, was waiting, deeply disgruntled, to let them out and to lock up. Gyuri did manage to pick up a very faint sensation of satisfaction as he saw Kovács fuming in his moth-eaten, cigarette-ventilated dressing gown, his hair floating in all directions.

The car wasn't black, as tradition dictated, but a sort of pukey brown. This was a little disappointing since it was going to spoil the story he could relate when he got out in five, six, seven, ten years time, whenever. It was a short drive through empty streets. Gyuri was surprised in a way that something he had been fearing for so long should have come so inexplicably out of the black. Was he going to be coached for a show trial? Who was being stored in the clink these days? They seemed keener on Communists these days but there was always the need for a supporting cast.

Curiously, there was an element of relief. Now he had touched bottom. There was no need to fear being arrested when you're arrested. What was the charge going to be? As far as Gyuri knew, considering the government to be a bunch of wankers wasn't on the statute books. Why hadn't they arrested him in '45, in November, after the elections when he hadn't anything to eat but did have a loaded revolver and had gone out into the streets in Elek's overcoat to shout 'Fifty-seven per cent' with lots of other people? Why the Smallholders, a crowd of people with moustaches who liked going to church and waving loaves of bread, should have got fifty-seven per cent of the vote would have been a mystery if it hadn't been for the Russians and baldy Rákosi's party on the other side. Rákosi's Communist Party, which only scored seventeen per cent, despite all sorts of largesse from Moscow and regular deliveries of prisoners of war to demonstrate Rákosi's diplomatic skills. Rákosi had messed up that election, partly, because like everyone else in the Communist Party he couldn't believe how disliked he was and partly because he'd only just unpacked the 'build a Communist state' kit that had been posted to him from the Soviet Union and was still reading the manual. 'Fifty-seven per cent' was a rather witless thing to shout in the streets, but it had been great, and the slogan was a portmanteau, replete with sesquipedalian imprecations and oaths against the Communists.

As Gyuri was led into the elegant interior of 60 Andrássy út, for some reason, the rumour about the head of the AVO's wife came to his mind: Gábor Pétér's wife was bruited to be lesbian with a strong penchant for triadic trysts. This salacious aside stepped aside as a young AVO officer (presumably the junior members and recruits got the night shift) who was Gyuri's age, opened a folder and muttered 'Fischer' as if he were taking receipt of a consignment of desk lamps. The officer flipped through the file in a moderately annoyed fashion because it seemed to be virtually empty and lacking the crucial items he was searching for. Gyuri studied him and thought: if only I hadn't been born with moral vertebrae, with intelligence, with dignity, I could be sitting there comfortably.

'Your confession doesn't seem to be here,' remarked the officer with the clear implication that he was the only person in the building who dealt conscientiously with paperwork.

'It had better be good, I'm not signing any rubbish,' said Gyuri diving into the silence. On account of the dearth of menace in the proceedings (it was rather like a dentist's waiting room without the magazines) and because he had the feeling it would be his last chance to crack a joke for a long while, he took the initiative. It would be the sort of story that would tickle everyone in prison.

The receptionist looked at Gyuri as if he had fouled the carpet, not stupid or boorish, but simply sad. He called to a colleague in an adjoining room. 'One more. Fischer.' The colleague came in with a clipboard he was consulting closely, professionally. He spent rather longer than one could expect it would take to scrutinise a single sheet of paper, even with very small print. Finally he pronounced, 'There's no Fischer.'

'Can I go home, then?' asked Gyuri, feeling he had nothing to lose.

Both of them turned to him with a look that said it would be extremely unwise, *extremely* unwise to open his mouth again. The receptionist gestured at Gyuri. 'What do you think he's doing here? Waiting for a bus?'

'I don't care what he's doing here. He's not on the list. I've told people about this before, you know. We're not the Hotel Britannia. Your name's Fischer?' he asked, addressing Gyuri.

'Yes.'

He looked lengthily at the list again. 'You don't have any aliases or nicknames do you?'

'No.'

The list was regarded again in the hope it would suddenly divulge a Fischer. 'You are Hungarian, I take it?' he asked scanning a violet piece of paper evidently intended for foreigners. Gyuri confirmed his nationality. 'Well, I've got a Fodor, but that's it, and there aren't even any Fs on the foreigners' list.'

'It doesn't matter,' said the receptionist, 'just stick him downstairs.'

'It does matter. What's the point of having a fucking list if people's fucking names aren't on it.'

The receptionist seized the clipboard and eyeballed the list with an air of doubting the other's ability to spot a Fischer even when there was one there. 'Okay, just take him down.'

'But we're full up. I've only got the double left.'

Gyuri was led underground and shown into a cell which had a feeble member of the bulb family lighting it and which was predominantly full of gypsy. There were two benches in the cell, both of which were covered by the largest gypsy Gyuri had ever seen, in fact one of the largest people he had ever seen. Like Neumann, but with three or four pillows tied to him. How could anyone get that fat in Hungary? Apart from his striking collection of collops, the gypsy's left fist had 'bang' tattooed b-a-n-g on the topmost phalanges of his fingers and his jowly face had a grid marked on the left side as if someone had been playing noughts and crosses with an exceptionally sharp knife. Gyuri wondered if the gypsy had ever contemplated a career in water-polo.

'Hello,' said the gypsy, withdrawing a division of thigh to expose some bench and stretching out a hand. 'I'm Noughts.' Then he added beamingly, 'Pimp.'

Gyuri shook hands and introduced himself. He admired Noughts's clarity of identity. How should he depict himself: basketball player? Railway employee? Student of life? 'Fischer, György, class alien.'

'What have they got you in for?' Noughts inquired.

Gyuri reflected. 'Nothing really.'

'If it's nothing, they're going to throw the book at you. I reckon they have a quota of ten-year sentences they need to fill. One of my mates in Nyíregyháza got taken in a few weeks ago. "Nothing personal, Bognár," they said, "but we have to put someone down for a ten-year stretch, and we know you wouldn't mind too much, being a stinking gyppo and that. Just sign the confession so we can go home."'

Noughts was in for obstructing the course of justice. Two AVO men were chasing a kid who had let down the tyres on their car, when they tripped over Noughts who had been recumbent in a stairwell dead drunk after a protracted wedding celebration. Noughts's lack of consciousness was why he hadn't been able to implement his usual escape technique: 'The policemen these days aren't as well made as they used to be. You just have to sit on them to hear them snapping.' The terriblest threats of retribution had been issued to Noughts because it had required two arrest teams and a butcher's van to bring him in.

'I can't say I'm looking forward to a stretch. The prisons have really gone downhill,' complained Noughts. He had been, he elucidated, in most of Hungary's penal institutions, including the infamous 'Star' prison in Szeged, where Rákosi once spent fifteen years. Rákosi had had a satisfactory library, a cell to himself and an international campaign to obtain his release. Progressive intellectuals from all over Europe had sent telegrams of protest to Hungarian Consuls. Gyuri had seen one from the West Hull Branch of the Friends of the Soviet Union in an exhibition about Rákosi's life. The telegram had spoken of their 'emphatic disgust' at Rákosi's conviction. Gyuri had reflected that he might well feel more friendly towards the Soviet Union if he lived in West Hull. He had also looked up 'emphatic' in his English dictionary, since it was a word he hadn't come across before. Odd that the progressive intellectuals were so silent about the abounding convictions in Hungary now. Gyuri also had the presentment that progressive intellectuals in West Hull, or anywhere else, wouldn't be sending any telegrams on his behalf but then Gyuri was ill-disposed towards them anyhow for saving Rákosi from the death-penalty.

'The bread and dripping were outstanding,' said Noughts continuing his reminiscences about the 'Star' prison. 'It was worth it for the bread and dripping alone.'

Noughts's soliloquy went on, encompassing other gaol delights, which were punctuated with an exhortation to Gyuri that whenever he got out, one year, two years, ten years, he should hasten without delay to Noughts's sister who could habitually be found around Rákóczi tér. 'There's nothing like it for getting it out of your system.'

The main difference between prison and being out in Hungary, Gyuri ruminated, was that in prison there was less room. That was about it. Less room and a strong smell of unbathed gypsy. As compensation for the ammoniac tentacles growing from Noughts, there was, at least, no portrait of Rákosi in the hall.

Still enjoying a burst of aplomb, Gyuri couldn't help reviewing the various outcomes of his incarceration, all of which contained generous helpings of more incarceration, pain and pain's subsidiaries. Gyuri liked to think of himself as quite tough and self-reliant which was why he didn't like to find himself in circumstances which might amply demonstrate that he wasn't.

On the wall, someone had scraped 'I am a member of parliament': this statement didn't seem to be worth the trouble on its own – presumably it was an aposiopesis, produced by the author's untimely removal from the cell. Underneath, in a different style, with a different sharpish instrument, someone had inscribed, 'I am a member of Újpest football club.' There was also in faded pencil (remarkable since Gyuri had had all his portable personal and impersonal items removed, as well as his belt and shoelaces) 'If you can read this, you're in trouble.'

Well, thought Gyuri, here I am under the frog's arse. Under the coal-mining frog's arse indeed, at the very bottom of existence. Nothing could make things worse. Was he going to be entitled to any of those things in life that were accounted as worthwhile or enjoyable? He was twenty. Was he going to get out in time to grab any of the things worth grabbing? Without great satisfaction, he inspected the ledgers of his years. When the venerable poet Arany had reached eighty, according to Pataki, he was asked how he viewed the peaks of his celebrated life, a legend-creating poet, revolutionary, seer, national hero and ornament! 'A bit more tupping would have been nice' he replied. This pronouncement hadn't made it into Arany's biography. The prospect of having his willy in dry dock for a decade was only marginally less alarming than having all his bones broken or dying unpleasantly, or indeed, pleasantly.

Noughts got tired of his discourse on penal cuisine and the merits of his sister and reclined for some sleep. 'This can't go on much longer,' was revealed on the wall behind him, underneath which, with the true Hungarian desire to have the last word, someone had written 'It already has'. Would there ever be a new round of Nuremberg trials? Gyuri wondered. Would he be around to see them? What would the AVO say in their defence? 'We were only obeying ideals.'

It was hard to judge the passage of time, but it seemed to Gyuri that a day had gone without any change or incursion into their cell, apart from the odd commotion at the judas-hole when they were scoped by the guards. There was no sign of food although Gyuri's appetite had scarpered. 'It's my fault they're not giving us anything to eat,' apologised Noughts, 'they can't bear the sight of a fat gypsy.'

Having got to the point where he was strapped in, mentally steeled, ready to look a ten-year sentence in the face with equanimity, Gyuri was released.

Judging by the light outside, it was the following morning. No one had said anything in the way of explanation. He had been summoned, given back a portion of his personal effects (not his shoelaces or small change). Gyuri hadn't taken the trouble of inquiring about the whereabouts of the missing items or the wherefore of his manumittance. Outside, he felt so pleased to see Budapest, Budapest looked so effervescently active, that he half-wished he could be arrested more often.

He was coming to terms with his deliverance when he noticed Elemér, the dogcatching mailed fist of the proletariat, step up to him. Elemér, who was smoking a dawdling cigarette, had clearly been expecting him. 'Any time,' was all he said before he walked off. The shock was such that Gyuri had no time to kill him before he vanished. His anger expanded steadily and so intensely he thought the rage was going to pop his skull. Trembling with anger, he made his way home on the tram, and if anyone had so much as brushed against him by accident it would have resulted in an instantaneous, furious, bone-crushing, onslaught.

At home, he discovered the note he had left on the kitchen table for Elek, looking unread. Where was the old goat? he wondered as he ripped up the note. Elek entered at that moment, sniffed and commented ebulliently on Gyuri's malodorous condition after the AVO's cold sauna: 'Communism doesn't prevent washing, you know.' Gyuri never told anyone.

August 1952

It had only been a month but if he never achieved anything else in his life, that month would be achievement enough.

The camp had been at Böhönye but they had been met at Pécs railway station by the sergeant-major who had been specially selected to shape up the university students during the four weeks he had charge of them, to mould them into lusty officers. The sergeant-major was in no way perturbed by the centuries-old tradition of sergeant-majors being sadistic, aggressive and very loud. From the start, he was out to prove he could be far worse than anything they might have imagined.

'We're going to be fighting World War Three soon,' was his opening gambit. Like all soldiers he wasn't too enamoured of peace – it didn't give the military the respect and resources it considered it so richly deserved. But a peace which was simply a build-up to a world conflict was something the sergeant-major could stomach.

'You are turds. Unspeakable turds ... whom I am obliged to transmogrify into barely useful turds. My philosophy: my philosophy is to make life for you so unpleasant you will find war an agreeable recreation, a bit of light relief, and that you will die in a manner that will not disgrace the fine traditions of the Hungarian Army.' (Which is about all Hungarian armies have ever managed to do, Gyuri thought.)

'I expect some of you will be committing suicide. Indeed I will consider my work a failure if some of you turds don't try a bit of wrist-slashing. And if you don't do the job properly, we're willing to help; attempted suicide is punishable by death.' To be fair to the sergeant-major, he at least looked as if he knew something about soldiering: large, vigorous, confident, gnarled, the sort of person you were glad was on your side. A bastard but a competent bastard. 'It's all right, having a shaky officer when you're in barracks,' Tamás had told Gyuri at Ganz. 'It's not important there if it takes him two hours to find out which way up the map should be, but when you get to the front, you need someone good, or you get jacked. We had one officer called Kocsis. The funny thing was he had always wanted to be an officer, he came from a military family but even after going through the Ludovika, he couldn't direct piss into a bucket, let alone direct a military operation. Within an hour of getting us to the front, he got us pinned down, and he was killed straight away by some Soviet who got through our defences, infiltrating brilliantly in a Hungarian uniform, speaking fluent Hungarian and having lived in Budapest for thirty years.'

The sergeant-major's first threat: 'When we get to our base, you will become acquainted with the parade ground. You will become so well-acquainted that if by some unheard-of miracle you survive, you'll remember every crack when you're ninety.' Here, the sergeant who had been delegated as assistant, whispered into the SM's ear, what they were to learn later, that Böhönye didn't have a parade ground. 'There'll be plenty of drill,' the SM continued, 'so that, from a great distance the Imperialists might accidentally mistake you for soldiers.'

The military had not lost its fondness for cow pats. What Böhönye did have was meadows, so they practised their ceremonial march, with bayonets fixed and resting on the shoulder of the person in front. On a level parade ground, this could have been an impressive sight of co-ordination and martial display. In a meadow full of cow dung and hollows it was a massive exercise in ear-removal. The first to lose his aural equilibrium was Gyöngyösi, a lawyer, who being a lawyer deserved it. He wasn't going to be produced in any show trials after that.

The month was bad, very bad. But a month only being a month as such, it couldn't be unbearably bad. Most of the time was spent on the usual military tricks of making you try and do half an hour's worth of doing in five minutes. And Dohányi, the SM, who never told them his name ('I don't want you to think of me as a person, just as a fucking bastard') was very keen on making people run around in full gear, with twenty pounds of kit, wearing a gas mask. The odd thing about gas masks, Gyuri reflected, when you thought about how they were designed for you to breathe through, was that they were virtually impossible for you to breathe through, particularly when doing anything more arduous than standing still.

The bulk of the agony revolved around unending physical exertion. Even for Gyuri, as a professional amateur athlete, it was demanding. For the students who had been more sedentary, it produced the effect Dohányi was after: intense pain, shock, disbelief at how much physical punishment the body could take in twenty-four hours. 'Sleep is bourgeois,' pronounced Dohányi, before sending them out on all-night manoeuvres with the sergeant. Most of the group developed an air of aghastness after the second day, as if they were permanently being punched in the stomach. At moments of excruciating physical effort, running with a stretcherful of hypothetically wounded soldiers for example, Gyuri recalled a painting he had recently seen of a soldier lying down in a comfortable field, reading pensively, surrounded by comatosely relaxed brothers-in-arms. The painting was entitled: 'Soldier reading, surrounded by his brothers-in-arms.' Dohányi would have shot anyone he found lying around pensively or reading.

Despite Dohányi doing his best to make things as horrific as possible, he was cruelly let down by the weather which was regulation summer issue, warm and invigorating. The heat was sometimes cumbersome but the summer didn't permit suicidal misery. Dohányi's torments which would have been unsupportable and shattering in a cold muddy winter were kept digestible. He became visibly frustrated by the lack of breakdown. Standing by Bencze, the architect, who had collapsed in a meadow under a rucksack full of ammunition and who was floundering on the grass, rather as if he were feebly trying to swim across the meadow, incapable of getting to his feet, Dohányi shouted sympathetically: 'Had enough? Want a rest? Desert! Then I can have you shot.' Dohányi kept on counselling desertion, to no avail, but he always repeated the punchline: 'I'll have you shot. Why should you waste the Imperialists' time?'

The Imperialists were another classic Dohányi theme, from a man whose knowledge of world affairs was based on the few months when he had travelled out of Hungary to kill people. 'The Imperialists are coming. Any day now, we're going to have number three. Third time lucky. Of course, you barely uniformed turds won't make any difference but we don't want you wetting yourselves in civilian shelters, distressing the populace. The best thing you can do when the war starts is dig a hole, jump in, and fill it up.'

So where were the American Imperialists? The British Imperialists? Or even the German ones? They had been promised Imperialists for years on end, Gyuri thought angrily. What were the Imperialists playing at? He had carefully rehearsed the phrase with which he would greet the American invaders: 'What kept you? Let me take you to many interesting Communists I am sure you will be eager to shoot.'

The whole camp and the idea of the camp was a complete waste of time courtesy of the people who had given Hungary such impressive ideas as the centrally-controlled economy where you had to work your way through dozens of barriers to find the man at the ministry who was responsible for getting you some extra bolts only to find he was on holiday. Apart from confirming their suspicions about which end of a rifle the bullet emerged from, the heroic sons of democratic Hungary had learned only one other thing: a formative hatred of the Army. The futility of the training was doubled in Gyuri's case: although the camp was devised to render them sturdy leaders of men, Gyuri, being class-x, wouldn't be allowed to be an officer, so the most he could ever be was the best-trained corporal in the People's Army.

The political classes were for once extremely welcome although they were raw tedium. Everyone looked forward to them because you could sit down, not be shouted at and not have to worry about donning a gas mask. Dohányi would stand to one side, fuming conspicuously at this respite from his meticulously conceived diet of ordeal.

The political officer was called Lieutenant-Colonel Tibor Pataki, a fact that Gyuri fully intended to tease Pataki about when he returned to Budapest, away from the military and the countryside where all you had was a choice of grass and excrement served up in a variety of styles. Lt.-Col. Pataki obviously did a lot of this sort of instruction – he had been chauffeured into the camp hot from another engagement, and his monotonous, unfaltering flow suggested regular practice.

'It is, of course, Generalissimo Stalin, who has given us life, that we salute, and the triumph of Stalinian strategy in the Great Patriotic War that we take as our guiding precept but it is above all the Hungarian edition of the works of Stalin, a new invincible weapon in our hands, that will enable us to model ourselves on the glorious Stalinian Soviet Army.' This was all without a breath, and in front of a mounted, hazy photograph of a Soviet officer looking knowingly and professionally down the gun barrel proffered by a Soviet infantryman, smirkingly proud and confident of the unbesmirched state of his rifling. That photograph was to the left of Lieutenant-Colonel Pataki. To his right was a grey, hard-to-distinguish photograph of small figures in a line, carrying banners with indecipherable slogans. This picture was bottomed: 'Peace Demonstration, London.'

Lt.-Col. Pataki took up Dohányi's theme of Communism getting ready to put its boot on the throat of decadent bourgeois countries, to stick the bayonet in and twist it about, but in much more refined and dull language for fifteen minutes or so, before expounding further about Stalin, leader of the Peace Front.

If the Lieutenant-Colonel took this seriously, if he believed what he was saying, Gyuri pondered, it was sad. If he didn't believe the nonsense he was spouting, like a parrot or a khaki gramophone player, that was sad too. Which was sadder? Or maybe you could take the whole scene, all of them assembled in the hut pretending to imbibe the wisdom that the Lt.-Col. was pretending to impart, as an enormously elaborate practical joke. Perhaps one day everyone in Hungary, in Poland, Czechoslovakia, Germany, Rumania, the Soviet Union and even Albania would wake up one day to hear Stalin shrieking with laughter in the Kremlin: 'You didn't think I was serious, did you?'

Living according to bolshevik principles: the idea was as absurd as walking around all day with two fingers stuck up your nose. At least the Church only expected you to turn up once a week, but otherwise was prepared to keep out of your hair. If people's power only meant a weekly hour-long lecture, Gyuri thought, I could live with it.

Scrutinising the Lieutenant-Colonel, Gyuri inclined to categorising him as a true believer, a moral cripple, ethically stillborn. This would surely be seen as the most lasting, the most magisterial accomplishment of the Hungarian Workers' Movement: unearthing, rounding up, nurturing so many prize shits. How many supershits could a small country like Hungary yield? A few hundred? A few thousand? No, the Hungarian Working People's Party's talent scouts had offered contracts to hundreds of thousands of manshaped turds. Admittedly not all of them would be truly first division brigands, and who knows, maybe there were even people who joined by mistake, thinking they could do some good.

But for the conscripted audience, the ostensibly dull lecture had, in fact, been garnished with the tang of corporeal détente; numerous limbs and muscle installations had had an opportunity of resting, and as they filed away from the political instruction, they wondered if they would be treated to another session.

At the end of the four weeks, everyone was so glad to leave that they couldn't find the energy to really hate Dohányi as he gave them some parting abuse: 'I'm sorry to see you barely biped turds leaving. It would have been a better deal for humanity if you had died here, but I don't suppose you self-propelled dicks will get very far. There's no need to thank me.' Gyuri and some of the others vacillated over giving Dohányi some obscenity, but you never could be sure how far military jurisdiction stretched. They settled for some sloppy salutes and ran to the railway station.

Returning to Budapest, Gyuri felt older, wiser, proud of having taken his four weeks without falling to his knees, begging for mercy. The sight of Budapest brought a torrent of excitement and gratitude. A desire to kiss the ground lasted for several seconds when he stepped off the train and the delight in being capitalised lasted until he got to Thököly út, by which time the crowded tram had pressed the last drops of rejoicing out of him.

It was as he strolled down the last section of Thököly út to turn into Dózsa György út, that a figure in a heavily-peopled delicatessen caught his eye. His subconscious elbowed his conscious, and he noticed Pataki in a queue at the counter. He gazed through the window at this spectacle for a few moments, and then, excited and fearful of missing the continuation, he ran into the shop.

There was Pataki, sandwiched between resolute housewives, carrying a shopping basket, a large wicker construction that Gyuri didn't recognise as an official Pataki family household object.

Pataki's awareness latched on to Gyuri as he approached. Just for a shaving of a second, there was a general alarm, a call to action, a glimpse of consternation bolting around the corner. If Gyuri hadn't known Pataki from the age of four, these fleeting, mostly subcutaneous movements couldn't have been noticed. As it takes a trained expert to judge a counterfeit banknote, so it took a Pataki expert to detect the counterfeit cool, to detect the thinnest recoil, a proton of shame, as if he had been caught extracting his dick from a herbivore.

The reason for Gyuri's amazement was that Pataki never went shopping. Never. For certain masculine accessories such as clothes etc., yes, but then that sort of shopping wasn't done in a shop but by cajoling acquaintances to produce the required item through barter, bribery, blackmail or begging. Even when Pataki was at a more malleable age, at six or seven, he had stubbornly refused to run out to the shops, no matter what the incentives or threats. Though Pataki had never publicly proclaimed it as a policy decision, there was a clear implication that going to the shops was one of the things you didn't do, that it was an infringement of rowing time, a blight on male dignity. When Gyuri went off to collect the dress from Angyalföld, Pataki had said nothing, but his silence was eloquent: *you're my friend, so I won't dwell on this deplorable lapse, this sad weakness.*

Pataki was the chief exponent of 'snatch the snatch', of amatory hitting and running for the rowing-boat. Gyuri didn't have the black and white evidence yet, but he had the feeling that Pataki's waiting for some cheese was a sign of doctrinal collapse, that his mulierosity had got him distaffed.

'How was the Army?' Pataki greeted him, impeccably casual, as if they were meeting in the sports hall and not at the cheese-counter. 'I hope they offered you a generalship?'

'It was everything you'd expect,' said Gyuri unable to contain himself and going for the jugular question. 'Doing some errands for your mother, are you?'

'No. Bea asked me to get a few things for lunch,' replied Pataki. It was Pataki, in one way, at his greatest. The flawless tones of mundane, routine queuing, as if he were simply standing in a queue talking about standing in a queue and not utter capitulation, the unbridled massacre of a young lifetime's precepts.

So it was Bea.

When Pataki had been thrown out of the College of Accountancy it hadn't come as a surprise to anyone concerned. He had only found out about the exams by accident. He was walking past the College when he had been overcome by the need for a leak and he had fortuitously discovered the exam lists on his way to the gents. He had pleaded with Gyuri to remind him of the subjects he was supposed to be studying – was it the light industrial inventory course or the advanced cost analysis? He was so far gone, even cheating couldn't have helped him.

Pataki had then rapidly obtained a place at the College for Theatrical and Cinematic Arts. Ironically, this hadn't been for the outstanding performance that freed him from the clutches of the Army, which had snapped him up the minute he had been jettisoned by the College of Accountancy. He had feigned a dud cartilage which required him to walk around with an inflexible leg, all the time, for six weeks, a marathon acting feat that demanded rigorous verisimilitude twenty-four hours a day, thespianism without respite – though it was true that the potential savagery of the non-commissioned critics was a great encouragement in maintaining a correct impaired cartilage posture. A friendly doctor whom István had lined up removed a healthy cartilage from Pataki's right knee and he got his discharge from the Army. Before his knee had time to heal properly Pataki was in at the College of Theatrical and Cinematic Arts to study photography and thus exempt once again from military service.

Bea's existence had been gradually revealed, more by Pataki's absences than her presence. But Pataki was finally caught, having informed everyone that he was going to get some developing agents, in tandem with Bea on a bench overlooking the Danube.

Gyuri and Róka spotted them as they were completing a run around Margit Island.

The vigour of her hello, the choreography of Bea's movements, the mellifluousness of her voice that made every syllable stand on its own feet, the projection of her posture would have convicted Bea of being an apprentice actress, without the production of her student identity card. Discovering Bea and Pataki on the bench was rather startling because Pataki's stated policy was that sitting around on park benches was for simpletons or failures.

'You don't mind if we join you?' said Gyuri sitting down on the grass next to the bench. He and Róka fastened onto Pataki and Bea, surmising that this would be of some hindrance, embarrassment or annoyance to Pataki, whose demeanour was one of affability as if there could be nothing more natural and agreeable than all of them sitting there watching the Danube. 'Been saving up for my present, have you?' asked Gyuri, taking advantage of Pataki's corneredness to remind him about the non-appearance of his birthday present, then ten days overdue. Pataki writhed, too briefly for anyone but a seasoned Pataki-watcher to behold, and then handed over, to Gyuri's surprise, a neatly wrapped volume (it must have been wrapped by someone else). 'We were just out shopping for it,' said Pataki. There was no doubt it was intended as Gyuri's birthday present but Pataki's reluctance in handing it over soon became understandable.

The present was a book, *Hungarian Writers on Mátyás Rákosi*, a volume issued to commemorate Rákosi's sixtieth birthday in March. 'It's what I always wanted,' said Gyuri, using one of his subtlest sarcasms, since only minimal irony was called for. The anthology was self-evidently not only something Gyuri didn't have the slightest interest in, it was a gift that he had no more intention of taking home than he had of sticking a serrated blade through his palm. Pataki had probably bought it to read himself and catch up on the latest in literary goings-on.

The book was a collection of pieces by leading Hungarian writers which might as well have been titled *Arse-Licking in*

35 Variations. The only real literary ability called into action was to minimise the degradation and shame in composing a panegyric on the bald orang-utan who happened to be Prime Minister and the First Secretary of the Hungarian Working People's Party. You could imagine them sitting around in the comforts of the Writers' Union saying to each other: 'No, no, Zoli, I'm not distinguished enough to make a contribution to the book. I'm sure Józsi or Laci can knock out something.'

Bea was attractive, though by no means the fairest to be Patakied, and her theatrical nature prompted Gyuri to read out the first work from the book, a poem by Zoltán Zelk. Zelk at his best was well, appalling. Curiously, Pataki, normally merciless in his critical judgements on poetry, always went easy on Zelk, although he had claimed he could train any reasonably intelligent dog to compose better verses than Zelk, by picking out words from a hat.

'*Comrade Rákosi is sixty,*
No other words required,
If I write it down,
You'll know instantly,
Comrade Rákosi is sixty.'

Perhaps because of Gyuri's skilful inflections in reading, Róka started to cry with laughter. Mastering his mirth, he was handed a stanza by his muse: 'Comrade Rákosi is an arse, no other words required, if I write it down, you'll know instantly, Comrade Rákosi is an arse.'

'Oh, don't be unfair,' chided Bea gently 'Rákosi's a good old soul, he's why I joined the Party.' This only added fuel to the fire. Both Gyuri and Róka laughed to the point of pain, doubled up on the ground, much to Bea's puzzlement, since she hadn't intended to be funny, since she wasn't joking.

Pataki made good their escape before any offence occurred. 'We're going to the cinema. We'd better be off.' He and Bea sauntered away to the bus stop. Bea's parting words made it clear however that she was quite genuine in her admiration for Rákosi. 'He's done a lot of good for this country.' Róka was quite shocked – although he was indiscriminate in assisting women with their orgasms, this bounty was coupled with an austere, petrous morality that forbade any form of intercourse with the Party. Bea struck Gyuri as someone who hadn't thought too much about Rákosi & Co. – as someone who hadn't thought too much about anything. For her the Party meant social occasions, meetings, songs, speeches, set texts.

'*What* is he doing?' Róka asked persistently, largely rhetorically.

'Isn't it about time the Party showed him a good time?' replied Gyuri, flicking through the homage to Rákosi, wondering whether he could find anyone stupid enough to barter something for the book. There was only one bona fide cadre in Locomotive – Péter, a peasant lad from Kecskemét, who was bullishly in favour of the new order as well anyone might be who had been rescued from a region where the most dramatic event was the sluggish production of oxygen by the local verdure. Péter was always attending courses, radiating optimism and socialist zest for life. He would have been ideal for one of those photographs where young Hungarians look on proudly and wistfully at the brand new achievements of people's power. Moreover, Péter was always ferrying around books such as *Stalin: A Short Biography* ('not short enough', others would remark) and in moments of leisure he would work his way through ponderously underlining passages that he deemed to contain bonus significance. Might Péter be willing to exchange some of those delightfully tasty objects that he received from his solicitous relatives for this outstanding literary work?

'But,' said Róka, 'what is he *doing*?'

Róka's bewilderment might have been greater if he had known that Pataki's father, an accountant who had wandered into social democracy, had spent 1951 tied up in an AVO basement. Pataki's father had only told Pataki and Pataki had only told Gyuri. Gáspár had been picked up in the regulation fashion in January, asked to come to Andrássy út as a witness.

His suspicions had been aroused when they tied him up from shoulder to toe in a sort of all-encompassing rope strait-jacket, a hemp cocoon, and deposited him in an unlit basement for what was probably a week. After that he was unwrapped in an interrogation suite, punched in the mouth and admonished:

'Confess something. Surprise us. Entertain us.'

All Gáspár could do was to say there must have been some mistake and then emit a few ouches as they tried to punch-start him into admission. He was thrown back into the basement with the verdict: 'Who arrested that boring bastard?' He stayed there for the rest of the year, eating by pushing his face into the billy-can that was introduced from time to time into the cell. He felt like an envelope waiting to be opened in someone's in-tray. There were dribs and drabs of conversation he heard emanating from outside: 'Don't you need a social democrat, Jenö?' 'What do you think this is, 1950?' 'What about an accountant?' 'Well, I certainly don't need one. You've been greedy again, haven't you? Remember what Belkin said, never arrest more than you need, it just creates paperwork.'

Every six weeks or so, Gáspár was taken for a wash. On one occasion he shared a shower with someone who looked remarkably like János Kádár, the former Communist Minister of the Interior. He even sounded like Kádár. 'How much longer can this go on?' asked the Kádár lookalike. Gáspár hadn't been able to think of anything to say in the circumstances.

Finally, just before Christmas, someone came into the basement, untied him and said, 'Piss off, we need this cell.' Luckily for Gáspár one of Budapest's five taxis was passing outside ('I get most of my trade here,' the driver had informed him), as the walk from the basement to the street had bankrupted his muscles.

Never an outgoing fellow in the first place, Gáspár had become even more armchair-bound than Elek, flattened by the physical ordeal, by the shame of imprisonment and the additional humiliation of having been adjudged too dull to be stuck into a conspiracy.

To the boys, Pataki presented his relations with Bea with a bluff 'The Party has screwed me, now I'm screwing the Party', but now, as he waited with Pataki for three decas of Anikó cheese, Gyuri realised it was all over. On the one hand, he wished he had his diary with him so he could pencil in whole months' worth of vilification, mockery and needling. The quality of the material that he had struck in finding Pataki with a shopping basket promised an almost unlimited quantity of ridicule, from one-liners to epic-length denunciations. 'There I was, walking down Thököly út...'. On the other hand however, Gyuri felt sorrowful. Pataki had assumed heroic status in the battle of the sexes, invincible, unconquerable, immune to the ailments that floored others, and here was the mighty mightily fallen, ozymandiased with a shopping-basket. Pataki had become a mortal.

Huge jars of pickled gherkins lined the walls of the shop, lording it over smaller jars of apricot conserve. Any level surface in the shop had these crammed glass jars. They were what you could find all over Hungary, in all the one-room shops: pickled gherkins and apricot conserve. If you liked pickled gherkins and apricot conserve a lot, you were in the right country. Abundant pickled gherkins and apricot conserve were quite an accomplishment, Gyuri mused, as Hungary got on with the second half of the twentieth century.

That was the sort of organic stagnation, displayed stasis, obedience under clear glass that they would like from people, stacked in their homes, products that didn't require attention, that wouldn't be troubled by the languors of the system of distribution, that would just exist docilely on the shelf until needed.

July 1954

Fuming at the injustice of a regime that was turning him into an accountant, Gyuri went along to his English lesson.

Makkai's flat was off the Üllői út and – unusually for someone Gyuri visited regularly – only on the second floor. It wasn't a very spacious flat but as a pre-war diplomat and current incurable bourgeois, Makkai had a son of the soil, a toiler for international peace, a student at the Party's College, billeted legally, forcibly, permanently in his home.

Makkai usually let his pet complaint off the leash the moment he opened the door, berating his lodger as he ushered Gyuri inside.

'I don't mind that he's a Communist. I don't mind that he leaves Rákosi's speeches all over the place. I don't mind that he's an oafish imbecile – after all one should hesitate to pass judgement on others – but what I can't stand is that he stinks. It's unforgivable. Unforgivable. We had an SS officer dumped on us during the war, a mass murderer, torturer of infants and so on, one assumes. I could stomach that, but not this. And don't think I'm being harsh. It's not the didn't-have-time-this-morning-I-was-in-such-a-rush unwashedness, no, no. This is the unmistakable reek of a body that doesn't even have childhood memories of soap. You can shake hands with the smell.

'I've tried subtlety: daily eulogies on the joys of running

water, leaving fresh towels prominently in his room, detailing at length the trouble I had purchasing and installing a new shower-head. Relating a fictitious newspaper account of how washing regularly could extend your life expectancy by twenty years. Relating another fictitious newspaper article reporting Comrade Rákosi stressing the urgency of all good Communists scrubbing their armpits with the slogan Cleanliness is Next to Sovietness. Nothing. I even tried presenting him with two superb bars of soap on May Day.'

Makkai seemed a trifle indiscreet for someone who had to cohabit with a cadre, or perhaps he saved up his indiscretion for Gyuri. Last year, when Stalin had died, Gyuri left the College of Accountancy to find Comrade Kompán kneeling in front of the bust of Stalin in the hallway, weeping quite uncontrollably, in the way one does when a close family member has died. She had been quite decent to Gyuri when he had enrolled at the College, pointing out that since he was class-x, 'We have our eye on you, Fischer. You'll have to work twice as hard as everyone else to make amends for your background.' She hadn't meant this in a malevolent, hectoring fashion, but rather in a forgiving, encouraging way and she had been only voicing what any Party functionary would have thought after reading the file that always followed Gyuri around – his moral credentials.

Comrade Kompán had been so distraught that Gyuri thought perhaps he ought to offer some solace out of courtesy, but he sensed it wouldn't work. He had continued on to his English lesson.

On reaching Makkai's flat, he had found Makkai dancing on the table – something, he divulged to Gyuri, he hadn't done for over forty years, which was why he looked so out of practice. He went to the larder and produced a bottle of champagne. 'It's Soviet, sadly – I've been keeping it cool for years so I'd be ready to celebrate.' The lesson that day had consisted of toasts to the late, unlamented Joseph Vissarionovich and selecting pejorative epithets. 'You're lucky, you're young. This can't go on much longer now,' said Makkai. 'And you'll be able to make the pilgrimage to pass water on Stalin's grave. But by the time you get to the front of the queue you'll be an old man.' It was the first time Gyuri had seen Makkai smile, in the four years of his tuition he had never glimpsed the woebegotten Makkai enjoying anything. He thought he knew the whole Makkai, childless widower, glum scholar, whose erudition – far from earning him esteem and fortune or securing him a comfortable position – was a handicap, as if he were chained to the decomposing carcass of an elephant. The smile made Gyuri realise there were whole departments of Makkai he had never glimpsed; it was like turning a dusty vase stationed on top of a wardrobe for years to discover the reverse has an unseen design.

When he heard the news of Stalin's death, from the radio, Gyuri was shampooing his hair. Apart from experiencing an intense well-being, his first thought was whether the whole system would collapse in time for him not to have to take the exam in Marxism–Leninism he was due to sit the following week. Could he count on the downfall of Communism or was he actually going to have to read some Marx?

His second thought was how to achieve maximum disrespect during the ten minutes' silence that had been decreed for the next day. When he later saw in the cinema the film tribute of Stalin's Budapest obsequies, the whole city coming to a halt, grim faced workers frozen on the edge of pavements, grimy railway workers easing off the steam on their engines, entire crowds steeped in black making their way to the enormous statue of Stalin by Hősök Square – when he saw all this, Gyuri regretted that he hadn't been able to invite a film crew up to his flat to record for posterity the only part of him that was standing to attention, as it was readily interred and disinterred in an old girlfriend, married now but still eager to reminisce.

Gyuri watched that newsreel several times, because there was one wide shot of the crowds around the Stalin statue which had microscopically featured his bedroom window, enabling him, with some imagination, to relive the joy of his only-just-off-camera mourning.

But Stalin's death, although derangingly enjoyable, hadn't changed things much. Rákosi was a little less cocky and Nagy became Prime Minister. Gyuri heard rumours that people were being cleared out of the prisons, but Stalin stood monumentally on. The eight metre bronze statue, planted on the site of a church that had been demolished at the end of the war, was the main feature visible from Gyuri's bedroom window and he had taken the positioning of the statue as a personal horseprick from Fate. Nagy, of course, was different to Rákosi. He had a moustache. Rákosi didn't. Also, Nagy wasn't completely bald. But the Stalin statue statued on, sodomising the Budapest skyline, sundering any remaining dignity from a city still recovering from its postwar hangover.

This evening, Makkai appeared at the doorway of his flat without any doorbell prompting. 'Three–two to the Germans,' he said, 'it must be a fix.' Completely enraged by auditing, frustrated and bored with his accountancy course, in a stupor of fed-upness, Gyuri hadn't been paying attention to the World Cup Final that was engrossing everyone else, Hungary *vs*. West Germany. He certainly hadn't been in the mood for his English lesson but as Makkai had no phone he hadn't had any means of cancelling it, so he turned up so as not to offend Makkai, who was a connoisseur of courtesy and did enjoy giving language lessons. Makkai didn't charge very much for two hours although it was still a strain on Gyuri's resources. But Gyuri felt that for Makkai teaching had less to do with the money (although he certainly needed it) than with importing an audience into his flat and that for a while he was taken seriously. Out on the street he was another pensioner, an old fart with no position, no clout, no job, no money, but in the instructing chair he was a skilled keeper of deep intellectual treasures.

These infusions of esteem were vital to Makkai who would

shed a few years during the course of his revelations about English syntax, pronunciation and life in England where he had once worked at the Hungarian embassy. 'A marvellous building. We couldn't have afforded it, but it was an inheritance from the Habsburgs. We got the old Habsburg building in London, the Austrians got Paris and the Czechs were very pleased about getting the building in Berlin. That'll teach them.'

Gyuri sat down and waited for Pataki who had suddenly decided that he should start learning English as well. Pataki had also decided that the ideal method for him to learn would be to sit in on Gyuri's lessons. Gyuri had reminded Pataki that he was fairly advanced in his acquaintance with the English language but this hadn't deterred Pataki who had assured him he would pick up the gist easily.

'Three–two,' Makkai repeated, stunned by the result of the football match, dumbfounded as everyone else in Hungary was, apart from Gyuri who was too preoccupied with the misery of accountancy. Along with the rest of the football team, Puskás, the man with the unstoppable feet and the golden toes, was the sole repository of national pride. Hungary, in accounting terms, had only one thing to its credit – Puskás the footballing genius. He was tubby, he looked a joke (even more than Pataki he would have nothing to do with training) but once he was on a football pitch he saw things that no one else did and would end up unfailingly whacking the ball into the net. The rest of the team was talented but Puskás was the diminutive giant of the side. They had even destroyed the English five–one, so everyone had been confident that the Germans would be vanquished in the final.

'They must have been bought off. The Germans must have offered some bribe. They must have offered the government a loan or something. The team must have been ordered to lose,' said Makkai.

The lesson should have started five minutes previously but there was still no sign of Pataki. Makkai decided to indulge in a cup of coffee, Brazilian coffee routed into Budapest by a cousin living in Köln. 'I was lucky. The customs people only stole half of it, normally the whole package disappears,' commented Makkai. 'Of course, I may be unfair to the customs, perhaps it was the postman who stole it.' Gyuri's polite refusal only lasted as far as the second offer.

The English lessons had been going well. Gyuri had reached the point where he could boldly open a book and the page would hold no secrets for him. There might be murkiness and fleeting confusion but there would be no huge catch of meaning that could escape him. This rather pleased him: after all, his studies had been carried out on an intermittent basis, in the evenings when he was often half-dead from basketball. The main appeal of English was, he supposed, that it was only spoken by rotten imperialists, filthy bastards such as the bloated Wall Street Capitalists or the conniving British empire-builders. The appeal was that English was not only not compulsory like Russian, but that it was rather hard to study anywhere since it was viewed as lax, sullying, unsalubrious – unlike the bracing, cleansing cyrillic script.

Gyuri had taken a number of exams in Russian which consisted of having a firm grip on phrases such as 'Have the Steelworkers' Trade Union delegates arrived yet, Comrade?' or 'How is the hegemony of the proletariat today?' You could almost pass the exam by supplying a plethora of 'comrades' into the text or the conversation. Gyuri was proud of the fact that he had the lowest passes possible and that he had forgotten everything by the time he walked out from the exam, his self-collapsing knowledge gone.

His English had only really been put to the test once, when a basketball coach from Manchester University came to visit and Gyuri was nominated to transmit understanding between the guest and his hosts. He had been horrified to discover that he didn't understand a single word, not a single word the man was saying, so much so that he took aside the man from the Ministry and checked with him that the visitor really spoke

English. 'He should do,' came the reply, 'he's a Scot.' Gyuri resorted to inventing questions and statements approximately the length of the Scotsman's speaking. Both sides ended up satisfied.

'Here,' said Makkai, handing over the coffee; it was strong enough to encaffeinate at five paces, dark, aromatic with abroad. Brazil, thought Gyuri taking a sip, lots of coffee, beach, Hungarian fascists. Despite the Hungarians, Brazil wouldn't be such a bad destination.

There was still no sign of Pataki who had never taken much interest in time and its regulated passage. Even if he had been sovietised to the point of having a dozen wrist-watches on his arm he couldn't have kept an appointment. His lack of synchronisation with the rest of the country had become more pronounced since Bea had forsaken him. Pataki had never admitted it. He never conceded that Bea had dumped him, had dropped him from a great height, but Bea's opening a liaison with one of Hungary's most senior, most influential, most monied actors had coincided with Pataki staying in bed for three days, unable to muster enough courage to brush his teeth or even to join Elek for a tête-à-tête. 'Come on,' Gyuri urged after Pataki had remained connected to his bed for forty-eight hours, 'pull yourself together and let's go rowing.' Pataki turned over onto his other side so that his melancholy would be unblemished by Gyuri.

'Frankly, I can't see the point of being conscious. It's more trouble than it's worth,' Pataki had replied. 'Be a man,' Gyuri reiterated, 'look how often I get the elbow.'

'Yes, but you're used to it,' had been the response.

Even Hepp had been unable to persuade Pataki to get vertical but he rose on the third day and Gyuri spotted him bouncing down the street dribbling a basketball with an air of haste. 'What happened?' he had asked.

'I got an erection.'

Twenty minutes late, Pataki entered, saying 'Three–two to the Germans. It must have been fixed.' Pataki and Makkai traded indignation on the infamy and turpitude of the age, much to Gyuri's annoyance. However, once the lesson began, he regained his equilibrium and began to enjoy Pataki's absolute bafflement at a language of which he didn't understand a word, as Makkai yet again cruised the olfactory vocabulary of English, drawing on thirty adjectives to portray the miasmatic nature of his lodger's crannies. Gyuri could tell that Pataki wouldn't be back in a hurry.

Showing them out of the flat, Makkai returned to the theme of his flatmate. 'He's doing a three-year course at the Party College. Three years! I mean how long does it take to learn to say "Yes, comrade"?' He insisted on showing Pataki the interloper's room to give a more forceful illustration of the magnitude of the stench. 'What can I do? You don't know a place where I can buy some powdered glass?'

'Why not drop a letter to Andrássy út,' suggested Pataki, 'something on the lines of seeing him hanging around the American Embassy with a false moustache. If you could get a few dollars to slip under his pillowcase that would be a nice touch.'

Makkai had been preparing to laugh but then realised Pataki wasn't being facetious, and settled for a nod or two that could be interpreted any way you wanted.

The tram was empty apart from Gyuri and Pataki but still indisputably public when Pataki pulled a thin manila folder from the large hold-all he used for hauling around his photographic paraphernalia. He handed it over to Gyuri. 'It's this year's belated birthday present,' he said.

The file was marked with the AVH acronym, the latest rearrangement of the AVO's name, and lower down with a lower-case 'severely secret'. Inside was Gyuri's form, his Ministry of the Interior file, his civic, ideological profile and worth. His date of birth and name were typed. His date of birth was incorrect and his middle name was misspelt. The only entry on the file, in a rather flourishing hand, in blue ink was 'No particular remarks'. It was the most insulting assessment he had ever had, leaving the caustic remarks of his schoolteachers at the starting-line. The police state didn't think him worth policing, not interesting enough to merit further consideration.

'How did you get this?' asked Gyuri, feeling distinctly uneasy holding such an Interior document in his hands.

'Ágnes, the singing secret policewoman. If you know whom to ask and how to ask you can get anything you want.' Pataki, Gyuri knew, in the cursory way he was acquainted with the female figures that conveyor-belted their way through Pataki's bedroom, had had an affair with a typist in the AVO who was also a singer in the AVO's all-female choir brought out to croon on special occasions for the Soviet Ambassador. The reddest of Pataki's girlfriends, she was also taking a night-course in scriptwriting at the College of Theatrical and Cinematic Arts, 'to help crispen those confessions' as Pataki had observed.

'They didn't have much to say on the subject of me,' said Gyuri.

'Let's face it, you don't join the AVO because you want to work. Mind you, you should see my file,' said Pataki, pulling out a folder like a volume of an encyclopaedia. 'I never would have guessed they had so many women working for them, including one very sexy chimney sweep that I briefly met in '49. I haven't read it all,' Pataki paused to scan a few pages. 'But there's definitely someone grassing on us in Locomotive.' He fished into his pocket, and produced a card. 'But anyway, thanks to Ágnes, I'm well prepared.' He held an AVO identity card, with his picture and name.

Gyuri's lengthy astonishment had only started its journey into expression when, as the tram rumbled down the Muzeum Körút, they saw and heard the commotion of a large crowd around Bródy Sándor utca. 'It's not Lenin's mother's birthday or something, is it?' asked Pataki, although the gathering had an unfamiliarly unofficial air about it. They got off the tram to have a closer look.

Hundreds of people were crowded around the headquarters of Hungarian Radio. It quickly became clear that the crowd was there on account of its displeasure with the result of the World Cup Final. There were periodic bursts of rhythmic chants: 'We want justice, we want justice', and 'It's a swindle, swindle, swindle'.

More than anything else, Gyuri was shocked by the flagrant public expression of sentiment. It was something he hadn't seen for years, not since the '45 elections. 'Let's take a closer look,' said Pataki pushing through the people. The crowd was surging towards the entrance of the Radio where the AVO were out in a chain, armed and looking unhappy. Pataki was eager to get to the clashing point, and despite Gyuri's reservations, the motion of the crowd kept pushing him closer to the irascible, gun-toting defenders of state authority.

To add to Gyuri's discomfiture, they had arrived just at the moment when the commanding officer was about to lose his temper. What the crowd was after, Gyuri couldn't work out. Whether they considered the Radio a more tangible representative of power than the parliament and thus a target to vent their anger on, or whether they wanted to broadcast something, he couldn't discern. Perhaps it was the commentary on the match they objected to. The commanding officer of the AVO detachment was repeating very loudly, again and again: 'This is the last time. I'm telling you, move back and go home.'

'This is the last time I'm telling you, you're a wanker,' shouted a man squashed next to Gyuri. The crowd was very angry and surprisingly sure of itself, bearing in mind the AVO were carrying guns and the crowd had nothing but its fury, and the AVO men patently fell into the category of crowd-shooters.

The commanding officer kept telling everyone to disperse and those not immediately in front of him but well within earshot kept telling him he was a wanker. Gyuri, riding high on the crowd's sum, shouted profanities since it seemed the done thing. The AVO pressed forward. The crowd pressed back, three AVO men went down and there was a joyous shout of 'I've got him in the bollocks'. A stone shattered a window in the Radio building.

Then there was a burst of fire into the air. The entertainment was over. Gyuri and apparently lots of others thought that dying would be an over-reaction to the Hungarian goalie having fumbled one ball. He ran as fast as he could in the millimetre of space that he had between him and the person in front. The AVO was coming in with the rifle butts. It took a while to unclog the street, but people were soon running away full pelt from the Radio.

Gyuri, who had been monopolising all his concentration on leaving the vicinity as rapidly as possible, found that Pataki had disappeared. He wasn't worried that Pataki was one of those lying in the street trying to hold their heads together. He had probably picked up some comely rioter.

He got home to find Elek listening to the radio denouncing the hooligans who had been running wild in the streets of Budapest. It was nice to be famous.

'I learned something interesting tonight,' Gyuri recounted to Elek. 'Hungarians don't mind dictatorship, but they really hate losing a football match.'

November 1955

The man was snoring, snoring so loudly, so rattlingly, that even if one had been over-dosed with tolerance, it would have been too much. Gyuri and the other passengers, only equipped with everyday indulgence, found their forbearance crushed like an aphid under a sledgehammer.

The man had the look of an engineer, something lowly and civil, the pens in his shirtpocket spoke of a rudimentary learning and erudition; the adept way he blew his nose with the aid of his right hand and with one motion hustled the catarrh out of the open window spoke of too much time on building sites. He had got on the train at Budapest and placed his dowdy belongings on the overhead rack, sat down in one of the seats next to the door, leaned his head against the glass and turned on the sleep, instantly, without any preamble.

Within a few seconds the snoring had commenced, as if approaching them from a great distance, faint at first but growing steadily to a prodigious din erupting from the man's open mouth. Everyone else had looked at each other, first with a sort of tacit amusement that had progressed to bemusement and carried on to irritation. The odd thing about people behaving badly, Gyuri noticed, letting their boorishness slop out onto others, was that it was usually the victims who were embarrassed rather than the perpetrator.

The volume of the snoring was phenomenal. A mild,

intermittent rasping might have been bearable but the engineer's lungs pummelled everyone's eardrums mercilessly. Also, truthfully, it was most unwelcome to be privy to the detailed internal workings of a corpulent engineer – to have a ringside perspective on his respiratory adventures. There were sporadic lulls, producing an optimistic sense of relief, of the auditory siege being lifted, but these interludes of silence while the snoring caught its breath only made the restored gurgling more serrated.

Gyuri, at the opposite end of the compartment, had no contiguous opportunity to impede the snoring but those closer attempted to trip up the volume. Discreet coughs followed by indiscreet coughs, yells, proddings and shovings didn't succeed in making him miss a slumbering beat. The woman in the headscarf started clucking loudly, as if giving the traditional imitation of a chicken. The snoring faltered and disappeared under the onslaught of the clucking. 'It always works with my husband,' she said proudly but as she did the snoring pulled out into the fast lane again. The man opposite tried trailing a powerful garlic sausage under the sleeper's nose. Nothing. The engineer snored on blissfully.

The flawless repose, the effortless snoozing excited Gyuri's admiration as well as irritating him. He could never sleep on trains, or at best, could only achieve a disorientating stupor that was worse than being tired.

The sausage-waver was becoming edgy and aggressive towards the morpheused slob who was wholly indifferent to the implorings and digitings he was getting. If it hadn't been for the obvious passage of air in and out of his workings, the sleeper's lack of response would have been rather worrying, so loath was his body to do its job and pass on the complaints.

'My dear sir, you're snoring rather loudly,' said the bespectacled protester, giving another push to the snorer. To flee the palatal thunder, Gyuri left the compartment.

What a gift to be able to sleep like that, he thought. How

agreeable to sleep through the entire thing, to only wake up when everything had changed. That was one of the worst things: the boredom. Dictatorship of the proletariat, apart from the abrasive and brutal nature of its despotism, was terribly dull. It wasn't the sort of tyranny you'd want to invite to a party. Look at the great tyrannies of antiquity: Caligula, Nero, now there was tyranny for you, excess, colour, abundant fornication, stage management, excitement on the loose, *panem et circenses*. What have we got? brooded Gyuri. Hardly any *panem* and as for the *circenses*, only the sort involving people running around wearing red noses.

Not only do I get a dictatorship, fumed Gyuri, but I get a tatty dictatorship, a third rate, a boring dictatorship. I could have stayed in Budapest and watched *Boris Godunov*, he thought. He had only seen it four times. Another, somewhat unacknowledged triumph of the new order was that you could always watch *Boris Godunov* any time you wanted to. After all, there were only so many Russian operas to choose from. Róka, entwined with a singer, had acquired an unquenchable taste for opera and had invited Gyuri to accompany him to see his fiancée in action. It was amusing to see all the policemen and steelworkers packed into the front rows of the auditorium, whether they wanted to be there or not. (At Ganz the lathe-turners had drawn lots to allocate the tickets distributed to them by the Party secretary, many preferring to do an extra shift rather than having to face the music.) Gyuri had put in attendance at *Boris Godunov* the month before so he had decided to go down to Szeged to investigate the party for which Sólyom-Nagy had been acting as harbinger.

In the next compartment, a beautiful girl was talking animatedly to a female friend with the bounce of the attractive. With the right looks, a good stock of beauty, you were always going to come out on top, it was the life-belt that would keep you floating on the surface. Sadistically, she licked her lips and dangled her left calf, crossed over her right leg, energetically in a manner and in a brisk rhythm that even someone without Gyuri's unifilar mind would have found reminiscent of riding the unirail.

Why, lamented Gyuri, does the beautiful girl never sit in my compartment? Why am I always lumbered with the noisy oaf? Admitting to himself, as he returned to his compartment, as he was old enough to know, that if she had been sitting in the compartment he wouldn't have been able to craft any conversational grappling-hooks or have the nerve to use them.

The passenger who had been trying to stop the slob sleeping aloud had finally despaired of polite memos to the snorer's nervous system. He arranged the sleeper's hand into overhanging the doorway and then slammed shut the sliding door in a vigorous attempt to guillotine the fingers. The sleeper awoke but only with a mild grunt of surprise as if he had dropped off unexpectedly.

'So sorry,' apologised the door-slammer, 'I seem to have caught your fingers.' The slamee wasn't bothered at all. He proceeded to unwrap a rug-sized piece of paper from which he dug out three greasy fried chicken wings which he ate with such gusto and noise that everyone felt they had a molar eye's view of the mastication. The general relief that came when he had chomped the last of the chicken was promptly dispelled when, on the count of three, sleep was resumed and the slob carried on snoring from where he had left off. Szeged was still two hours away.

As a putative employee of the railways, Gyuri travelled free, but this didn't make the trip any less onerous. When you're eighteen, you'll travel to the other side of the earth for a party, he thought, sensing how he needed to talk himself into the pursuit of pleasure now.

'Don't worry,' Elek had said, struck by a wave of paternity. 'There is a season to these things. 1911 in my case. In 1911, I couldn't so much as say hello to a woman without her running away or calling the police. The whole year there was this great wall of China between them and me. Nations, individuals, they all have their ups and downs. Pussy shortage doesn't last.' This paternal wisdom might have been more consoling if Elek hadn't been coiffuring himself prior to some nocturnal escorting of one of his female acquaintances. Pataki had doubtless passed on gleefully to Elek the news of Gyuri's latest failure, an unprecedented hat trick of romantic flops.

On Andrássy út, Gyuri, having bumped into István's wife's youngest sister, had been introduced to two shapely netball players she had in tow. He had taken advantage of their fortuitous discussion of a new film to propose a joint outing. The film, like all Hungarian films, would be rubbish, but it might help to flush out the girls' evaluation of him. And the beauty of suggesting the film was that he hadn't, technically, asked the netball players out, so that a refusal would be a rejection of the film rather than his charms. This appeal to culture was necessary because: his self-confidence was pavement-high, and also, because from such a cursory reading of the netball players' interest meters he hadn't been able to ascertain how keen they were to admit him to the two-legged amusement park. Then there was the question of balancing their inclination towards him with his inclination to them; the blonde was more attractive, but on the other hand it would be foolish to pass up the brunette if she were unattached and itchy.

The invitation would act as a form of natural selection; the less eager being less likely to attend, it would be survival of the amorous. Determined to put his fist through his bad luck, Gyuri had also issued a third summons to another aspiring accountant, Ildikó, whom he had got to know in the library by fetching a book for her from a top shelf that she had been struggling to reach.

Standing outside the cinema, Gyuri congratulated himself on his blunderbussing his misfortune, overcoming his jinx by a concerted human wave attack. However, as the film started with no trace of the girls, so did his perplexity and the choking sensation that he had been stood up in triplicate. By trebling the odds, he had trebled his penalty And he had had no chance to sell the other three tickets. He had been skint and although Gyurkovics owed him a hundred forints, it was exactly because he had been so hard up that he hadn't been able to ask for it because it would have looked as if he had been extremely hard up which he didn't want.

Gazing out the train window, through the snoring, Gyuri could see peasants engaged in doing something autumnally agricultural. Too stupid to find the road to the city, Gyuri chuckled, confidently conurbational. Still, someone had to grow potatoes. And someone had to film them. As part of his acolyteship at the College of Theatrical and Cinematic Arts, Pataki had been out in the countryside, acting as tripod carrier for a newsreel crew he had been assigned to study in action.

They had gone to the village of Zsámbék, the closest representative of hamletness and unabashed bucolicality to Budapest, only an hour's drive away. The story the newsreel crew was covering was the fourth and a half anniversary of the collective farm which might have been connected with the need of the director, Gáti, to acquire some comradely crates of white wine for his garden parties.

Even in the artistic circles of Budapest, where the entry fee was egomania, Gáti had tantrummed his way to prominence. However, for some reason he had interpreted Pataki's presence as homage, as a tribute from one eager to learn the secrets of documentary filming from a master, and Gáti warmly took him under his wing although Pataki would far sooner have been rowing. 'It's a shithole, this place,' Gáti said, surveying Zsámbék. 'I think I voted here in '47. Mind you I voted everywhere in '47. How many people can say they voted sixty times in a general election? These three-duck hovels all look the same though. Me and the Second District Communist Youth Committee, we spent the whole day driving around, voting. Bloody tiring, democracy.' They were standing in the office of the collective farm. Feeling it was time to do some directing, Gáti shouted out of the window at the cameraman who was contemplating various angles: 'János, I want you to capture that feeling of historic achievement, okay?' Then he returned to glugging rows of local wines. 'Rule number one: know what you want. Rule number two: good casting. Good casting does all the work for you. I've already got the centre character, Uncle Feri. He's the village elder, as it were, who's been through decades of suffering, hunger, exploitation etc., etc., but who in his contented old age can comfortably beam on the gains of the people, happy in the knowledge that future generations will never know want or hardship, thanks to the application of scientific socialism etc., etc.' Gáti emptied the glasses of wine as if pouring them down a sink.

'Uncle Feri's the perfect candidate. I found him when I came down last week. Research ... research is everything. This yokel is perfect. He's got a moustache that must be half a metre long. He oozes earthy wit, rustic swagger. Everyone's Uncle Feri. He thinks he doesn't want to do it but I'll make a star of him.' There were only a couple of glasses left. 'And remember, rule four: you can never talk too much to your cameraman.' Gáti leaned out the window: 'János, you finished?' To Pataki: 'You'll go far. You know how to listen.' To the chairman of the collective farm: 'Great. We'll take the lot.'

His arm avuncularly around Pataki, Gáti went out to the fields for key shots. 'Where's our Uncle Feri?' he shouted.

'Uncle Feri is gravely ill,' explained the chairman. He had rounded up a selection of aged, gnarled peasants for Gáti to choose from. 'You see,' said Gáti to Pataki in what was probably a failed whisper, 'people always interfere. They all think they know best. They all think they're film directors. Come on, where's the coy old bugger?'

The chairman, the mayor and the Party secretary all explained in succession, very apologetically, that old Feri really was very ill and wouldn't he be satisfied with another, carefully approved, suitably decrepit codger? Gáti just laughed and ordered to be taken to Feri's abode where the priest was timidly administering the last rites.

'Cut that out, or we'll have you nicked,' said Gáti, who was joking, but it looked to Pataki as if the priest had shat himself. 'How are you, Uncle Feri?' said Gáti, giving him a hearty slap which produced no noticeable reaction since Feri was too busy dying. 'He looks fine to me,' Gáti pronounced, but the cameraman and Pataki had to laboriously carry Uncle Feri out because none of his body was in working order. Even if Uncle Feri had wanted to issue instructions to his legs, they wouldn't have paid any attention.

Gáti strode on to find a good spot while Pataki, the cameraman and the chairman transported Uncle Feri who was light as peasants went but still an uncomfortable burden. 'This is it,' said Gáti, surrounded by burgeoning husks of corn. 'This filmically says it all,' he announced as the peasant-porters struggled up.

'Yes,' interposed the chairman, 'but this doesn't belong to the collective. This belongs to Lévai. He jumped out of the window at the meeting when everyone had to sign over their land.'

Gáti wasn't bothered. Fortunately, there was a wooden gate they could leave Uncle Feri leaning against, since his legs wouldn't have supported him.

'Okay, roll,' called Gáti. 'Now, Uncle Feri, how old are you?'

Uncle Feri didn't say anything – he seemed to be concentrating on breathing.

'How old is he?' Gáti asked the chairman.

'I don't know. Seventy something.'

'Okay, so, Uncle Feri,' continued Gáti, 'how does it feel to see the achievements of the new Hungary?' Uncle Feri still failed to respond. Gáti tried another question: 'Uncle Feri, how do you feel gazing on the wonderful changes that have taken place here in Zsámbék?' Uncle Feri remained mute. Pataki had no doubt that if Uncle Feri had had the power of locomotion he would have walked off by now. But all he could manage to do was to cling onto the gate. Gáti patiently let the camera turn, waiting for Uncle Feri's views. After a minute or so, Uncle Feri started to cry.

'This is great,' exclaimed Gáti, 'he's moved to tears by the successes of people's democracy. Get a close-up. We can write into it.' Pataki found Gáti's explanation unconvincing and reasoned that Uncle Feri's weeping was caused by his dying in a field, on camera.

According to Pataki, Uncle Feri survived his moment of posterity but not for long. Well-mannered, he waited till he was returned home before pegging out while Gáti loaded up the van with crates of wine, reiterating 'Did you see that moustache?'

Knowing what you wanted helped a lot, reflected Gyuri.

What are your ambitions?' Makkai had asked him the first time he had gone to him for English lessons when he had revealed to Gyuri that, at the age of four, he had been placed on a bareback horse in (as Makkai claimed) the traditional Magyar fashion to test his fortune and fortitude. The question had made Gyuri realise that he didn't have any ambitions as such, just a wish – to get out. It seemed embarrassing somehow not to have ambitions, a sort of lack of social grace, an ignominious shortcoming. Something like billionaire or ruler of the planet would be nice though. He wouldn't refuse that. Perhaps his failure to have gone shopping amongst the stalls of ambition was due to Elek's forgetting to place him on a saddleless horse when he was four.

* * *

Gyuri had been hoping that the slob would remain asleep and overshoot Szeged, but with the same precision the driver of the train used to bring the carriages alongside the platform, the slob timed the moment to eject from sleep. By this stage, Gyuri was the only one left in the compartment, the others having fled under the relentless bombardment of zeds.

He didn't know much about Szeged but he knew enough, when the slob asked the way to the centre of town, to send him helpfully in the opposite direction.

Treasuring the miniature revenge, Gyuri set off to look for

Sólyom-Nagy to fill up the time until the party in the evening.

The search for Sólyom-Nagy meant a lot of crisscrossing the university, making repeated treks to his room and asking randomly for his whereabouts, of which everyone denied all knowledge. By a process of elimination, eventually, Gyuri made his way to the library.

The university library had a duly grave, library-like dumbness, still with the sediment of millennia. Most libraries with their accumulated letters gave Gyuri an oddly reassuring sentiment. It's okay, the books encouraged wordlessly, we're here. Out there it might be lunacy piled up to the heavens, rubbish on the rampage, the havoc of mediocrity but we have no truck with stultiloquence; in here, it's fathoms of culture, the best of the centuries. The Zelks sifted out, the poetasters and bores, the platitude-salesmen booted out. The invertebrates of the past, desiccated, powdered, crumbled, blown away, leaving only the bones of those with spines, those who were fortunate enough to have been backboned before Marx so they had no opportunity to cast aspersions on him and cast themselves into lectoral exile as a result.

The shelves served up the freedom to travel, thousands of escape hatches into countries, eras that Lenin had never heard of and that had never heard of Lenin ('What happened in 1874?' Róka had asked him the day before, coaching Gyuri for his Marxism-Leninism exam. '1874?' '1874!' 'No idea.' 'Lenin was four'). Entering a library was always cleansing (as long as you didn't tamper with anything published after 1945), though Gyuri could never settle down there because after a quarter of an hour or so he would break out into fidgeting, yearning to scratch his backside or stretch his legs, have a coffee, do anything but read. However vehemently he strove to immerse himself in his books, to hold his academic breath, he invariably had to come up for interludal air. When it came to studying he was a sprinter.

Then there was the trouser barking. The discipline and decorum of libraries were somehow great catalysts for the cultivation of amorous propensities. It was exactly because libraries weren't supposed to be about sex that they were. Gyuri would sit down, soak up a few lines, and then, there she would be. No matter how empty it was, every library seemed to be provided with a young lady. No matter how fascinating the accountancy textbook he was reading, the entire crowd in Gyuri's control-room would throng around the newcomer. The staid background of a library boosted the pulchritude of even the plainest girl to unbearable levels.

The speculation would begin. Would putting this in that affect the rest of her life? Would you need a machete to work your way through the sub-navel jungle? Density of the venereal grass was a tiresomely recurring theme, the irrigation of the delta, the borders of the areolae. The panel would raise the same questions again and again, until the curiosity made him ache and he was out of breath. If only he could have diverted some of this torrent, he would have been the president of a medium-sized country somewhere. It was perpetual motion. It might slow down but it never stopped. He would sit in the library and the quim styles would rotate: the doormat? the black sheep? the winter tree? the pom-pom? the paintbrush? the chainmail? His vision would tunnel down to mons size.

Ascending the various levels of Szeged University's library, Gyuri kept on not seeing Sólyom-Nagy. He remembered that Attila József had been a student there, this making the staircases fractionally more interesting. For some reason Pataki had been very angry about József. Gyuri had caught Pataki kicking a volume of his poetry about. József had been so insanely poor and insane that he had no choice but to become a poet. So poor he couldn't even afford to starve in a garret and so insane he had thrown himself under a train at a good age, thirty-two, though some might quibble that thirty-two was the outside limit for a young and tragic death, especially since his life had been so unremittingly awful it was hard to understand why he had waited that long.

József had also been the only person with any character,

and certainly the only one with any feeling for the Hungarian language, to join the Communist Party, which he had done, driven by an incurable loneliness, in the thirties when the Party was illegal. He had been expelled almost immediately for having the temerity to think, saving himself from iniquity and saving the Party's record of unblemished imbecility.

Sólyom-Nagy cast his absence all over the library. Passing one studious lady with a window-seat, Gyuri's gaze dovetailed with hers and he realised it was Jadwiga, the Polish girl he had met the week before, slightly obscured now by glasses. Having exchanged mute greetings Gyuri moved on to check a few remaining biblionooks, full of books, devoid of Sólyom-Nagy. Sólyom-Nagy wasn't such riveting company but what was he going to do until the evening?

He retraced his steps to where Jadwiga was reading behind fortifications of books, thinking that if nothing else Sólyom-Nagy and university life should provide enough conversational substance to cover a coffee. Jadwiga agreed to Gyuri's suggestion and spent a few moments packing away the paraphernalia of study with a thoroughness that caused Gyuri much envy. Bookmarks went into the books, pencils into a box, the books joined stacks and the notes were herded together into a pack, then all the academic utensils were brought together into a neat heap. Jadwiga took her coffee breaks seriously.

In the café, they split up, Jadwiga holding down a table while Gyuri went off to queue for the coffees. When he returned with them, the second chair had vanished from the table. 'I'm sorry,' said Jadwiga, as if waking from sleep, 'I didn't notice anyone take it.' The café was full and Gyuri had to wander around to filch a seat. Some pale fresher who was guarding a set of chairs lost one to Gyuri, who was looking sufficiently dangerous and violent as a result of his early rising not to meet with any protest.

'So, is Sólyom-Nagy a good friend of yours?' Gyuri inquired.

'No,' Jadwiga smiled mischievously, 'I don't have many good friends.'

She was studying Hungarian literature. She measured out the conversation, enough to cover politeness but no more. Gyuri had to squeeze inquisitorially to picture her background. Her Hungarian was frighteningly good, with only the slightest accent, almost deliberately maintained to give a little exotic charm; it was merely a reminder that she shouldn't be mistaken for a Hungarian. Because it was true and because praising women had never done up any buttons, Gyuri said:

'Your Hungarian is better than most Hungarians. I think you must also have the distinction of being the only non-Hungarian to learn Hungarian this century. What made you do it?'

'My father was here during the war. It's a family interest.' There had been hordes of Polish soldiers passing through Budapest during the war, Gyuri recalled, escaping from one front to go and fight on another. Hard, determined men, upset that they were momentarily unable to kill anyone and puzzling over who should be first on the slay-list, the Germans or the Russians. Oddly enough in a region where nations spent most of their time trying to figure out which of their neighbours they hated the most, the Poles and the Hungarians were centuries-deep friends. There was even a couplet, available in both languages, commemorating how much the two nations enjoyed putting the boot in and drinking together. It seemed a bizarre desire to go to Hungary to learn the language, but on the other hand, he had tried to get to China, and even Poland, red as it was, would have made a change. He had been chosen for the fixture in Gdansk the year before, his smiling face had been on the publicity poster but he had again been refused a passport. Even Hepp had been surprised by that. Still, Gyuri certainly felt that he could do something to further Hungarian–Polish relations. Mentioning the party that was being co-sponsored by Sólyom-Nagy, Gyuri asked Jadwiga if she would be going.

'I haven't been invited,' she said, adding to further extinguish Gyuri's overture, 'I'm not very keen on parties.' After allowing a seemly period to elapse after the consumption of her coffee, Jadwiga rose to resume her studies. Gyuri accompanied her, on the off-chance that Sólyom-Nagy had surfaced in the library, though this, he had to concede, was unlikely, unless it was a question of Sólyom-Nagy smuggling out a few valuable books to find new lives with fee-paying owners.

He left the building without Sólyom-Nagy but with Jadwiga's room number at the student hostel which she had imparted with only the slimmest hesitation. It never did any harm to know where intriguing Polish women were located. She was, he guessed, nineteen, twenty, but she had a spiritual weight well in advance of her years and a flirtation technique that was superb in handing out the sparsest of clues.

Gyuri wandered around Szeged, not seeing Sólyom-Nagy at all. Szeged, as Hungarian towns went, was quite large: it took five minutes to walk from one end to the other, but it was still peculiar that he hadn't bumped into Sólyom-Nagy. Had he got the date wrong? Was Sólyom-Nagy in Budapest? When in doubt, have lunch – which he did standing up in a butcher's, working his way through a csabai sausage with bread and a miserable mustard that marred his gusto. After lunch, he decided to have another lunch, after which he returned to the university to prowl for Sólyom-Nagy. He did the now familiar circuit of the dormitory, the grounds, the library.

He knocked on Jadwiga's door. He heard the sounds of occupancy. 'I missed you,' he said as she opened the door. She scrutinised him for a long second, then admitted him. 'I hope you like tea,' she said, 'because that's all I can offer you.' As a veteran of impecuniosity, Gyuri immediately read penury in her room. It was clinically smart, causing Gyuri to admire once again the miraculous ability women had to automatically instil order, having that morning stumbled through various items on his bedroom floor, items which had certainly been there when he had started his accountancy studies.

It was as Jadwiga picked up a kettle to boil the water that Gyuri received two co-nascent bulletins from the back-room boys. One thought, how elegant and graceful she was, how she made picking up a kettle touchingly, triumphantly erotic. Optically revisiting her bosom, arms and legs, he appreciated how lithe and athletic she was. Lucky: she had the sort of slender age-resistant frame that would provide the same conjugal scenery at forty as at sixteen.

The second thing that barged into Gyuri's attention was the certitude that he wanted to marry her. That was surprising. He had never felt wedlockish before; indeed the idea of an additional bond to Hungary, anything that would make his flight less streamlined, was anathema. So this was what it felt like. But here it was, unannounced, without any warning, no throat-clearing – the notion that he wanted to get married, as precisely defined and as urgent as a craving for chocolate cake. Was he going crazy? He pondered this development while Jadwiga boiled the water on the gas ring down the corridor. Old Szócs had been right.

On the wall was a roughly-hewn wooden crucifix, the sort of thing a pious peasant with time on his hands would do. Maybe Stalin was dead, maybe this was 1955 after all, but this was tantamount to having a two-metre marble horseprick deposited outside the Rector's office. Clearly, it wasn't just Jadwiga's breasts that were firm. Gyuri welcomed the audacity, but wondered whether there would be theological tape interfering with the expedition down south?

In a way, Gyuri regretted having the tea and the rather wretched biscuit that Jadwiga offered him since he had the feeling he was consuming half her worldly goods; the tea she had had to scoop out of the bottom of a tin and the biscuit, he suspected, had been stored up for a special occasion, which he wasn't. An offer of supper, as long as he could find a ridiculously cheap restaurant, was doubly required.

'Could you help me with the window?' she asked. 'It's a bit stuffy in here.' She was standing by the window, pushing against its stuckness. How did she do it? The request couldn't have been more exciting if she had asked him to take off all her clothes. The window didn't need that much persuading, but even if it had been nailed down, it would have been shooting open, Gyuri was experiencing such vigour.

Jadwiga still wouldn't relent on the party, or having supper. 'I'm behind with my work,' she said steadfastly. This refusal didn't bother Gyuri unduly. Intuitively, he sensed that it wasn't powered by a desire to extricate herself from his company. Her regimented books testified to her earnestness. Unusually for someone at university, she was interested in her studies. The biscuit, lone and sagging as it had been, prevented Gyuri from being discouraged. He felt their lines were converging, not staying parallel. This was love at the first cup of tea.

He withdrew to let her study for a while and to craft some advances. Sólyom-Nagy was now back in his room. He apologised for his absence owing to several trips to collect fluid supplies for the evening.

The party was held at the Theatre. Gyuri who had thought he had seen professionally debauched festivities in Budapest had anticipated a more provincial level of bacchanalia but he had to concede that that night in Szeged was nothing but arrestable and immoral behaviour. It was indisputably the fastest social event he had ever attended. There was a hip-bath on stage in which Sólyom-Nagy mixed what he billed as the largest cocktail ever fashioned in Hungary, a triumph of socialist planning involving Albanian brandy, ice cream, vodka and other things that no one could or would identify.

Within half an hour of the hipbath opening for business, there were people unable to prise themselves off the floor. Gyuri had only one small glass which he sipped pensively and he was very glad he hadn't emptied it down his neck like the others. It already seemed to him that the stage had grown a vicious slope.

Ágnes was there, whom Gyuri hadn't seen for years. That

was the problem with a small country: you were always walking into your past. Gyuri had heard that she had gone to Szeged to study. For a lengthy period of time Gyuri had asked her out. Pataki had been squiring her best friend, Elvira. Gyuri asked, Ágnes ducked. 'She always goes out with the friend of whoever's going out with Elvira,' Pataki had encouraged, insisting that Ágnes had already indicated her approval of Gyuri's merits.

However, whenever Gyuri proposed some social union, Ágnes always produced some excuse. There was no untreated refusal. She never gave the same excuse twice and they ranged from hair-washing to one twenty-minute apology featuring an escaped lion from Budapest Zoo where her brother was the deputy Party Secretary. Gyuri remembered that the plot began with an attempt to shift elephant shit in a more socialist and scientific manner, applying only the strictest of Marxist–Leninist principles. It was without doubt the longest alibi Gyuri had endured, and, since he doubted that Ágnes's imagination was up to it, probably true, but at the end of it she said that, sadly, she couldn't go to the cinema. Gyuri would have taken off his chasing shoes long before if it hadn't been for Pataki's protestations that he had approval from flight control. 'Just ask her out,' he censured impatiently.

Finally, after listening to dozens of instalments about Ágnes's crammed time, since she wasn't the sort to engender rabid desire, Gyuri had let it drop. After all, Gyuri had reasoned, if it was going to be unrequited love and regular humiliation, it might as well be unrequited love and regular humiliation at the hands of a prodigiously attractive female, which would be a shade less humiliating. 'You don't know how to ask. You just don't know how to ask,' Pataki had commented.

Ágnes seemed sorry about past misunderstandings, as she was crying, as indeed many people were. The acceleration from initial jocularity to maudlin impotence had been phenomenal. An hour after the kick-off at eight o'clock, there was already a three o'clock in the morning atmosphere.

'I'm so sorry, Gyuri,' she sobbed. Her contrition seemed genuine because she kept repeating this with her head slumped on Gyuri's chest. He assumed her grief was to do with her rejections of him, though it was hard to tell. At the behest of hormonal petition, Gyuri thought about a bareback waltz against a sequestered wall somewhere but discarded the idea. He didn't want to gain admission to the club because there was no one on duty at the door, and besides, although part of him was already working on self chastisement for not taking what was offered to him on the tray of his sternum, he realised that he'd rather be with Jadwiga. He'd rather be sitting with Jadwiga chatting about some Hungarian writer, than taking a tongue tour of Ágnes, or indeed any other highly acquiescent lady. You always get what you want when you don't want it, he concluded, dumping Ágnes into a more comfortable bit of aisle where she could continue her soliloquy.

He left and was braced by the cool night air which swept out some of the alcoholic debris left by Sólyom-Nagy's concoction. He learned later from Sólyom-Nagy that two actresses who had been dancing on a prop coffin, had, shortly after Gyuri's departure, taken off all their clothes. There had been no risk of them being voted the most beautiful women in Szeged, or indeed the most beautiful women at the party, but still, whoever got tired of naked actresses? Sólyom-Nagy had also reported the arrival of the police who were summoned because of a group jumping out of the theatre bar, a drop of twenty feet to the pavement below, as the result of some inebriated logic. The neighbours complained to the police because of the loud noise made by the jumpers as they laughed raucously about their broken ankles.

The police story was better. 'I left the party five minutes before the police arrived' made better narration than 'I left the party five minutes before two actresses stripped naked.'

As Gyuri approached the student hostel, he could see a light in what he surmised was Jadwiga's room. That was all you needed: a lit window in the distance, the knowledge that there was something there, something to work for. The company of a dwarfy hope.

He knocked civilisedly on Jadwiga's door. 'I have an important consignment of vernacular Hungarian for you,' he said as she opened up. She studied him thoughtfully with much-read eyes, then backed away in a silent invitation to enter. She closed the door. Gyuri sat down on the bed of her still absent room-mate, while Jadwiga sat opposite him. Tired from her studying, she appraised him as if she hadn't seen him before, slightly narrowing her eyes as if trying to focus better. Then she said with a half-smile: 'We must talk.' A pause. 'We can be friends ... but no more.'

'You have a boyfriend?' asked Gyuri, feeling exceptionally confident that any competition could be trampled underfoot, obliterated effortlessly. He was intoxicated with the certainty that he was on to a winner. He liked everything about her, the way she spoke, the way she sat, the way she handled him. Perfection. She paused again.

'No.' With the full smile. 'I have a husband.'

September 1956

Striding down Petőfi Sándor utca, Gyuri saw the sign in the window of the photolab: 'Lab Technician Required'. This, more than the phone call, brought home the fact that Pataki was gone.

The phone had rung and Gyuri had counted out the crackly silence. He had made it only forty-two seconds before the distant receiver was replaced but it could only have been the forty-five second signal agreed with Pataki. Pataki was out. He had gone to heaven and called from a pearly phone. As if it had been stitched there, Gyuri carried a smile so wide it hurt for the next day, a smile that completely cancelled the mild melancholy he felt at Pataki's escape: a mild melancholy because he hadn't wanted to dwell on the probability that he would never see him again.

Pataki was out. It was not only a stinking horseprick in the posterior of the authorities, it was a colossal stinking horseprick. It gave him so much pleasure that he tried not to think about it too much, to ration himself to a few hours' gloating a day. But this notice cut the floor out from under his satisfaction. Only a fortnight gone and he was missing Pataki acutely. There was no one else in the country who could call him an arsehead with quite the same authority, the authority of a lifetime's acquaintance.

When he got home, he was glad Elek wasn't manning the

armchair and that his nosiness wouldn't be snooping around. He was also glad Jadwiga had consented to come to Budapest and that he didn't have to trudge down to Szeged. Did other people really have to work this hard for happiness? You find world-class love but your beloved lives at the other end of the country. He peered out of the window and inspected the street although it was too early for her to appear. She had insisted that he shouldn't wait at the station – with her Polish disregard for the passage of clocks, she couldn't guarantee which train she would catch. But at least there was no more nonsense about her husband. When she returned from Poland after her summer visit, she had been full of news about the riots in her hometown of Poznan. Gyuri had got all the details about that but Jadwiga had been pleasingly reticent on the subject of her husband who seemed to have been airbrushed out of the picture, like Trotsky standing behind Lenin.

The news that Jadwiga was married had caused all his carefully handmade aspirations to shatter like the china in a porcelain shop crashed into by a well-fuelled bomber with a full payload. Gyuri had hoped that his facade indicated the manly resolve he was searching for but couldn't feel and not the widespread collapse that was dominoeing its way through the regions of his body. He should have expected something like this; it had gone far too smoothly. Jadwiga had talked proudly of her husband. 'My husband is a writer,' she said in a way that left no doubt this was the only thing for a quality husband to be. He was writing a book on Polish painting.

They had gone out for a walk anyway. It had been pitch black, cold and windy and there wasn't much to be seen in Szeged even in the best of daylight but Gyuri enjoyed the walk because despite having the someone-just-trod-on-my-throat sensation, the black environment had given them a duopoly. They were the movers of the universe, the animation in a depeopled darkness. Gyuri had generally considered walking to be one of the most inferior of amusements but that walk with Jadwiga had been infinitely preferable to doing anything else with say, Ágnes. Kissing her respectfully on the cheek, he bade her farewell.

On the train back to Budapest, he had juggled two main thoughts. Firstly, that he didn't care whether she was married or not and secondly (as a consolation prize for his floored morality) the conclusion that it was rather an odd sort of marriage, where you lived hundreds of kilometres, days of travel apart. It didn't look like a thriving marriage at all, it was a marriage stretched so thin that you couldn't really notice it.

He had determined to avoid Szeged for a fallow fortnight but the next weekend found himself dashing to the Nyugati station. He invented some nearby athletic activity to justify his presence and sought out Jadwiga. He found her dutiful in the library, asleep. He went out, bought a flower, and returned to leave it on her notebook and to wait for the study-fatigued student to rouse herself, which she did after ten minutes. She was surprised to see the flower and then, looking round, was surprised to see Gyuri. Despite the arguable propriety of the flower, she was pleased. 'You are a very keen friend,' she remarked.

This time supper was accepted and Gyuri didn't regret having to sleep on Sólyom Nagy's floor although its embrace lingered on his back for the next twenty-four hours. The conversation had been agreeable and unremarkable but as with the walk it had been intensely pleasurable. If Pataki had known that his friend had spent the better part of two days travelling in order to have a so-so meal with a side-serving of jejune dialogue, he would have been shocked and incredulous, but Gyuri felt it was time well used. Jadwiga's husband worked very hard, it turned out, though the admiration with which she wheeled out this information had been a trifle faltering, a little adulterated.

The next weekend saw Gyuri becoming a real expert on the Budapest–Szeged rail link. Individual haystacks and trees were recognised on the way down. Gyuri hadn't let Elek in on the reason for his travelling down to Szeged but it was obvious that it wasn't Gyuri's passion for the local architecture. 'Have fun,' Elek had said in the way that parents do, convinced that their offspring were engrossed in incessant debauchery the moment they set foot outside the front door.

Jadwiga was again surprised to see him. 'You take friendship very seriously indeed,' she observed. They went to supper and the cinema which vacuumed Gyuri's pockets clean. Posting a birthday card to her grandfather, Jadwiga asked Gyuri if his grandparents were still alive; this annoyed him slightly because she asked the same question during their first walk and thus it was obvious she didn't store away everything he said in the way that he noted down her words for future examination, building up a dossier on her. 'My grandfather was in what the Germans called Auschwitz. The Jews don't like to mention how many Poles died there. My grandfather survived, I think, because he's a persistent man: a very persistent man. He taught me the value of persistence too.'

Reviewing the proceedings, Gyuri was astonished how much pleasure could be had without taking off any clothes and with a moat of oxygen dividing him from the castle he wanted to storm. He had listened politely when she had made reference several times to her husband not writing dutifully enough to her, though this had been presented more as a general critique of men. The travel was a nuisance though. Gyuri wished they could provide a gymnasium in the train so he could do some athletic training. He opened an accountancy textbook and he and the print stared sullenly at each other for a while. The travel was eating up a lot of his time.

The next weekend he was spared the purgatory of hours of travel because Jadwiga came up to Budapest to visit some fellow Polish students, to whom in the end she barely said hello. It was an unusual situation for Gyuri. He had never shown anyone around Budapest before, indeed he had never had the inclination to do so. Jadwiga had only spent half-days in Budapest in transit to Szeged, so he had to shake his brains for an itinerary.

He took Jadwiga up to the Gellért Hill where there was the Statue of Liberty, a woman reaching out above herself with her arms at full stretch as if reaching for something on a top shelf. Into her grip had been lowered some amorphous burden, perhaps palm fronds, perhaps oversized laurels, certainly something of heavy significance weighing down on the sprightly dame, who nevertheless effected a transcendental expression.

You could see the statue from most parts of the city and from the statue's foot you had a panoramic view of Budapest. The Statue of Liberty had been originally intended as a memorial to Admiral Horthy's son, a fighter pilot who like most Hungarians of his age had died around the Don but before it had been erected there had been a change of government and of uniforms in the street. Purged of its dynastic and political past, charged up with the ideology of a new age, it had been stuck on top of the Gellért Hill to act as a spiritual beacon.

As a supplement to the Statue of Liberty, perhaps as an additional ideological boost to compensate for the statue's ignominious beginnings, was a smaller, clumsier statue of a Soviet soldier, known locally, Gyuri explained, as the Unknown Watch-Thief.

Situated underneath the Statue of Liberty, less visible and not tampering with the skyline, the rather morose Soviet soldier, scowling from being left on duty for so many years, had an inscription: 'From the grateful Hungarian people'.

'I assure you the Poles are far more grateful,' said Jadwiga.

Bánhegyi had, as always when he ran out of cash, dislocated his shoulder (he could dis- and relocate his joints at will), gone to the doctor, collected a cheque from the insurance company (despite the fact that he would be out on court bullying the ball the day after) and invited everyone to the restaurant at the Keleti railway station. Jadwiga impressed everyone with her Hungarian (Róka refused to believe she was Polish) and also with the way she dealt with an enormous plate of wienerschnitzel and a liberal portion of calf's brains. Gyuri caught glances of admiration from the team and Róka in a state of extreme perturbation had to leave twice for 'fresh air'.

Pataki had been quiet. His mutism amply expressed his high regard for Jadwiga. Gyuri would have been worried about the possibility of competition from Pataki were it not for his conviction that he was backed by destiny this time. 'I don't suppose you've drilled for the white oil yet?' Pataki inquired. Gyuri snorted as an all-purpose reaction which contained amusement, denial, confirmation and contempt, hoping that Pataki would select whichever element would shut him up. Everyone else was evidently assuming that he had full access and this had been quite satisfying, since reputation is only one step away from the real thing. 'I think you're going to make it this time,' Pataki appended.

As he railwayed down to Szeged the subsequent weekend, he tried to think of some good pretext to cover his trip, at the same time thanking providence that he worked for the railways which made such a long-distance liaison financially possible. Jadwiga didn't seem surprised to see him nor did she bother to ask for any explanation of his presence in Szeged.

Gyuri had still not met Jadwiga's room-mate Magda, but had developed a great affection for her solely on the strength of her absences. As they sat in the room, Gyuri wondered how to elegantly polevault from friendship into a more clasping form of love. He checked his watch. By six o' clock, he resolved, he would be entangled in her garments or out. He had put in the miles. This deadline kept shifting steadily like the horizon as time progressed and he remained frozen in a posture of warm cordiality opposite her.

A clock's far-off chiming entered quietly during a caesura in their conversation. 'It's eight o'clock and you haven't pounced,' she commented. 'You men are such frail creatures.'

They closed in to fit their urges together. The main thing, he pondered, hugging her thankfully was that she felt it too; if he had made no inroads on her heart, that would have been unbearable. They clung to each other as if they were tumbling through outer space. Two supplementary conclusions made themselves comfortable in his thoughts: that by holding her he had captured everything he wanted in life and that he had got to the end of pleasure. 'Switch off the light,' she breathed. Just before he alighted on her in the darkness, she halted him, and from the bed she reached up to draw back the curtain; her naked body was instantly coated with moonlight. How did she learn that?

They sweated out the loneliness and after the gasps of surprise and exertion, prostrated themselves on each other. That's something that can't be wrenched from your possession, Gyuri reflected. Money in the unrobbable bank. Whatever happens now, I've won.

Jadwiga's husband, it turned out, was a bastard.

* * *

On the orders of his ball-gripping lust, Gyuri kept looking out of the window, and just when he thought he was going to swoon with expectation, Jadwiga appeared. She was walking at a furious pace, he noted, a woman with a purpose, the weekly week-long separation eliciting the same concupiscent smouldering from her. One of her most endearing features was the way she would take her clothes off as if they were on fire, leaving them where they dropped, without a thought for any sartorial suffering that might occur, and plunging into bed as if it were a cool pond of water. The other women had, no matter how high the flame was under them, been fearful of creases and had taken time out to utilise a hanger or a chair to drape their attire.

Gyuri saw her shape through the smoked opaque glass of the front-door and he thought how lucky he was to have such a visitor. Virtually ignoring him, she made for the bedroom, casting off her dress and stumbling on her knickers, fell flat on her face on the bed. 'Come inside,' she commanded at the end of the crumpled clothes-trail.

A part-time god, Gyuri ruminated in a bout of lyricism, *I loosed off liquid lightning in my private thunderstorm.* Jadwiga rose to go to the bathroom, and Gyuri perceived a fructiferous droplet dash along her thigh towards her ankle. He wanted to make her pregnant. He wanted to make her pregnant. What was going on? He couldn't believe he felt like that but you can't beat biology, he concluded.

Furthermore, it was very, very unlikely that he would achieve anything more important or significant than this, making one person feel full happiness, manufacturing a roomful of ecstasy, even if it were only a bubble in a gloomy ocean. It seemed a mundane pinnacle for a life, a trite climax for a biography, a flippant line for a gravestone – 'did some worthwhile willying'. But was there anything else that had given him the same reward of joy and plenitude? The oldest trap had opened and snapped shut and he didn't mind at all.

'There goes the best moment of my life,' he said to the absent Jadwiga. Which story had it been where the devil offers a man the chance to stop time, to slam on the brakes at a point of his own choosing, but the man can't decide when to say when? Gyuri had had intimations of love before, but looking at Jadwiga, he realised that was a prospect that could last him for eternity, whatever went on outside the walls. He didn't care who the general-secretary of the Hungarian Working People's Party was or whether or not socialism was being built outside or whether people were swinging around in the trees. He had his portable universe, his mobile self-sufficiency. This sort of satisfaction could bog down a man with great aims, but since he had never got around to preparing any, Gyuri felt ready to sink back and enjoy it.

As Jadwiga started recovering her clothing, Elek returned and for some obscure reason (he only ever visited Gyuri's bedroom on average twice a year) wandered in to catch the whole story of her skin. Mumbling apologies from the other side of the door, Elek retreated to his armchair, like a parrot to its perch, as if that would render him inconspicuous and inoffensive.

Unhindered by Elek's entrance, Jadwiga carried on with her dressing. Her poise made a contrast with Tünde's hysterics when Elek had found her torso exhibited in the shower. She had yelled as if her life was in danger and threw her arms tightly over the regions acknowledged to be of most interest to men, to staunch the flow of libidinous material. Tünde's behaviour had been excessive; despite living in an age when the public baring of bodies was frowned on, her physique was as well-viewed as the Statue of Liberty and in particular the parts she was shielding with her hands, making fleshy fig leaves, had been as relentlessly fingered as the timetable at the Keleti railway station. But for some reason Tünde believed that all-lung hysterics was the pertinent reaction of a well-brought-up girl to an unannounced guest. Jadwiga's nakedness hadn't blinked.

Gyuri loved her alert breasts. He loved her runner's legs (she had dabbled in sprinting) paradisiac containers of aphrodisiac. He loved her sagacious buttocks that had settled the entire subject of good buttocking. He loved her lips, the well-marked borders of her mouth; he loved her felicitating soles and all on them. He couldn't see anything that let the view down. Perhaps that was the symptom of fully-defined love: like a great work of art, nothing could be docked, interjected or tampered with. If the Creator had come to him with a special offer of restyling, 'For you, Gyuri, I can change anything you'd like: a little more leg? another helping of breast? blonder hair? darker hair? more ear lobe? younger? older? wittier? graver? repainted eyes? American passported?' Gyuri realised that he would just reply: 'We'll stop here.' He wouldn't change a hair, not a pore, not one particle more, not one particle less, because then she wouldn't be she. And it was no use trying to make up his mind about which sector bested the others; he couldn't judge Jadwiga's beauties' contest, because her components kept leapfrogging over each other, grabbing his favour. Then he knew that he had jettisoned the world. That he was marooned on the planet Jadwiga.

Although not Jadwiga's first foray into the flat, it was the first time she had met Elek who had taken up employment as a night-watchman at the László hospital (an occupation that suited him since it involved a lot of sitting and doing nothing and gave him complete freedom to speculate on what he would do with the money he was counting on winning in the lottery). So, after the full-frontal introduction, time was set aside for a formal hand-kissing which Elek did with a snap of the heels.

In the kitchen, as Gyuri lined up the ingredients for an omelette, Elek sidled up to whisper his warm admiration: 'My congratulations.' Gyuri didn't want to register pleasure at Elek's approval but it was pleasing nevertheless. Elek watched Gyuri's egg-cracking with the admiration of the culinary illiterate. 'You haven't heard any more from young Pataki, have you?' he asked.

Gyuri shook his head.

The fastest motorcycle in Hungary had been the root of Pataki's departure. Or maybe one of the roots of it. Or maybe, Gyuri continued to reflect, really in the mood to push a metaphor around, just part of the foliage. Who knew?

The motorcycle had been a Motoguzzi, a mountain of a bike. Sándor Bokros had owned it originally. Bokros had, by a series of dazzling commercial speculations, starting in 1945, when there had been a widespread vogue for a really good wash, juggled a dozen bars of soap through ever-augmenting metamorphoses until he had half a dozen fur coats. Then Bokros left the country and went to Italy, where, according to reliable accounts, he had almost willied off his willy and bought the motorcycle. Suddenly, through some incomprehensible mental aberration, Bokros had returned to Hungary on his bike, just as the country's borders were being sealed so tightly they lost fifty kilometres. Even in Italy there had only been a handful of bikes like that one and for the citizens of Budapest it was like something from Mars. Bokros had two problems: having to cope with an epidemic of adulation and street-enquiry and finding a stretch of road on which he could get out of first gear.

By the time Bokros realised that he should have opted for a totalitarianism that went in for long stretches of immaculate tarmac, it was too late. Everyone assumed it would end in tragedy, either his bike being nationalised, or him dying as a result of not seeing eye to eye with a Hungarian bend but what happened was as unforeseen as you could get. As he was overtaking, on a country road, a tractor with a load of fixed, upturned scythe-fittings on the back, one of the blades slid down, decapitating Bokros. 'You don't need much in the way of brains to ride a bike,' Pataki had said at the funeral, mulling over the bike having carried on for half a kilometre without a head.

'You'll like Sándor, everyone does,' was the way Bokros was always described. His brother, Vilmos, was described as one of those people who was disliked by everyone. Indisputably, Mrs Bokros hadn't been eating enough affability when Vilmos was conceived. One of the most upsetting aspects about Sándor's death had been that it meant the fastest motorcycle in the country would be passing into the hands of the loathsome Vilmos.

Vilmos fulfilled a useful function on the Locomotive team: everyone could rally round their dislike of him. Instead of suffering from a selection of grudges and vendettas, Locomotive could use Vilmos as the dustbin of enmity. He hardly ever played in a match because he wasn't much good and because of one of the standard amusements on the way to a fixture – pushing Vilmos out onto a railway platform as the train was pulling away, ideally when he was wearing only his basketball boots. 'Where's Bokros?' Hepp would ask. 'We saw him going for a walk in Hatvan/Cegléd/Veszprém', someone would say. Vilmos discovered the only way of ensuring he wasn't exposed in rather dull parts of the country with poor transportational possibilities was to barricade himself in the toilet until they reached their destination.

It was the week after Gyuri had lost his bet with Bokros on the outcome of the Army *vs.* Ironworkers football match.

Gyuri had confidently bet on the Army, not understanding why Bokros was being ostensibly that stupid, because he didn't know as Bokros did that an international match had been fixed for the same day so that the Army was going to be stripped of all its best players. Gyuri was skint at the time but he had had his eye on a leather belt that had also formerly belonged to Sándor, so he had wagered in exchange for the belt, in an excess of colourful hyperbole, that Bokros could crap into his hands if the Ironworkers won. The Ironworkers did, but fortunately, out of the blue, Vilmos had grown a sense of humour.

Naturally, everyone gathered around for the show. Vilmos crouched down, and Gyuri obligingly hunkered down behind him ready to catch the fecal ball. 'No fumbling,' was the general exhortation. Honourably, Gyuri waited to settle his debt but Bokros, suddenly the centre of approval for devising such a wonderful entertainment, was laughing so much that he was incapable of invoking the muscular bailiffs to evict some tenants from his bowels.

'Give me a newspaper,' Bokros had instructed, hoping that reading some of Prime Minister Hegedus's speech on Hungarian–Soviet relations would induce a state of tranquillity and sphinctal détente but the crowd eventually had to disperse in disappointment.

The following week, Gyuri had missed the preamble of the argument but the bet between Pataki and Bokros had grown out of a furious abuse session. It happened on Margit Island, after a training session and Gyuri entered as Pataki, who had recently been extremely tetchy, was telling Bokros what trash he was. Pataki was angry, and he looked angry, which was unusual in that he didn't routinely hand out public bulletins on his feelings like that: Bokros, who you would have thought would have been quite used to being called a shit and so on, was greatly incensed.

'Who do you think *you* are?' he spat out. 'Do you think you're so great? That you're so *hard*?' Bokros almost ruptured himself getting the word out. 'You toe the line when it matters.'

'But I haven't licked the arse of everyone at the Ministry of Sport, including the doorman.'

'No, you're so independent, the changing-room rebel, the revolutionary who's going to bring everything down with some explosive whispered sarcasm ... you haven't got the guts to speak out. If you think it all stinks why don't you say so?'

'I'll show you,' said Pataki, pointing at the White House across the river. Why doesn't he just hit Bokros? Gyuri wondered. 'You'll have the chance to see what I think if you want. Let's have a bet. You put up your bike against half of my salary for a year and I'll run stark naked around the White House and give them a 360 degree view of my fine Hungarian bum.'

'Done,' said Bokros, made adamant by his anger and the certitude that Pataki wouldn't attempt it. But Pataki waved in Gyuri and Bánhegyi. 'Come on, I want witnesses.'

Gyuri had spent most of his life thinking that Pataki had gone too far, but he hadn't felt so strongly that his friend was on course to crash head-on with destiny since that time in '45 when Pataki had said to him: 'Of course we should try out that revolver. Your mother won't know. What do you think's going to happen? The Russians are going to arrest us and have us shot?'

The White House was nominally the headquarters of the Ministry of the Interior; it was mostly a haunt for the Hungarian Working People's Party and the AVO. Some said it was the headquarters of the AVO, but the AVO taking no chances, seemed to have several headquarters: Andrássy út for one, plus a number of villas up in the hills of Budapest where they could beat people up in comfort and tranquillity.

The White House, as the Ministry in its well-appointed riverside location was popularly known, had a marked resemblance to a shoebox. The story went thus: the architect who had been commissioned to design it (not because he was a Party member, but because of his family background – his father had been a dipsomaniac and a worker manqué, his mother a moderately successful prostitute, so he was valued as being suitably anti-bourgeois) had, in the recognised tradition of Hungarian architecture, namely boozing and gibbering excitedly, spent both the six months he had been allotted to create a plan and the commission fee, boozing and gibbering, telling everyone he met – building workers, shop assistants, proctologists, swimming pool attendants, paviours, percussion players and a man on the number two tram who was breeding leeches, waiting for their big comeback in medicine – that he had been commissioned to design the Ministry.

The architect was cruelly woken one morning by a phone call from Party headquarters saying they had been looking for him for a week and that he was expected that afternoon to display the model of the new building and that Rákosi wasn't in a very good mood. Luckily the architect didn't have a hangover, as he was still drunk, having only just got to bed after three days' revelling at a gypsy wedding in Mátészalka. He had enough clarity of mind to realise that he would be shot or if he were lucky he could spend the rest of a short life making uranium pies down a mineshaft under an unfashionable part of Hungary.

Desperately rummaging through his closet, he unearthed a model he had constructed years ago in his student days before the war, for a competition to build a luxury hotel in Lillafüred. The model was quite detailed, though the gothic towers weren't in keeping with the latest thinking from Moscow but while this model would finish his career as an architect, it might save his life and allow a possibility of further boozing and gibbering. Who knows, Rákosi might even have a thing about gothic towers?

As he was dreaming up some brazen lies to accompany the model, he didn't pay the necessary attention to pulling on his trousers and he keeled over, crushing the model beyond redemption and the most epic of his falsehoods.

Spotting a shoebox skulking in the closet, he remembered the words of his professor: 'All the best ideas are accidents.' (The professor had got the commission to build the Ethnography Museum because he had copied down the wrong address for a prospective client who wanted a layout for a cakeshop and had ended up on the doorstep of the head of the museum committee who had been won over by his gibbering.) Seizing the shoebox and drawing some windows on it, he started to improvise a speech making copious reference to the dictatorship of the proletariat. 'I could have brought an elaborate model but surely in an era when the working people dictate...'

Then there was the Széll story. Every time Gyuri looked at the White House he recalled it. Széll and his father specialised in food-processing equipment and he had insisted that they had received a decree to install two king-sized meat-grinders in the basement of the White House, obviously to mince up those particularly difficult corpses for the fishes. Of course, both Széll and his father were inveterate liars. If they were facing a firing squad and you were to ask them, 'Do you want your lives to be spared?' they'd be forced to answer 'No'. On the other hand, you could see how an ample meat grinder could come in handy and it was a good way of turning the blue Danube red.

Gyuri, Bánhegyi, Róka and even, in the end, Bokros, all tried to dissuade Pataki from executing the wager, but Pataki was, even in the bright sunshine, almost incandescent with anger. Bokros attempted to jolly down the situation, perhaps realising that the consequences of such an action might well injure even himself. 'No,' said Pataki walking off, 'tomorrow, at twelve.'

Worried, Gyuri pondered how to divert Pataki from taunting the White House with his buttocks. Talking him out of it directly wouldn't work and Gyuri was unsure which style of machination would have the desired effect. It was like lacking the right-sized spanner to undo a bolt; simple if you had the right tool, otherwise impossible. There was a formula of words that would make Pataki laugh and go rowing but Gyuri couldn't think of the combination.

So alarmed was Gyuri that he even took the step of talking to Elek about Pataki's planned run. Elek wasn't taken aback; he showed no consternation at the prospect of losing his partner in nicotine, indeed he maintained his armchair aloofness. 'I suppose you'll be getting arrested with him, will you? They say prison is character-forming. Mind you, my character was already formed when they put me inside in Bucharest.'

'You were in jail?'

'Only for a few days. Bribery'

'Bribery? Who did you bribe?'

'No, the problem was I hadn't bribed anyone. They were very upset.'

'Look, Pataki'll be in for more than few days.'

'It's very hard to work out why people do things. Back in Vienna, when I was in the Army, one of my friends ended up in a furious row over something trifling. The positioning of napkins in the officers' mess – something like that. But he challenged this other fellow to a duel. We all took turns trying to get them to call it off. Apart from the chance of someone getting killed, duelling was furiously prohibited and droves of careers could have dropped dead like flies. The thing everyone was terrified of was losing face, so I put my arm round him and said "József, this is a stupid misunderstanding. Grown men don't behave like this. Honour's honour, but you can't shoot a fellow officer over a napkin." I thought I was doing a good job when he looked at me and I can still remember this vividly, he was so passionate. "No," he said to me. "You don't understand. I *want* to blow his brains out." Nothing to do with the napkin, of course, just the usual traffic jam on the thigh of a Viennese fraülein.

'I'll talk to Pataki if you want but I don't think it'll make any difference. These lunacies-in-waiting are usually readied well in advance, like all the best off-the-cuff remarks. It was the same with me resigning my commission; it had all the appearance of an extempore fed-upness but it had been in training for a considerable while. That was my problem with the Army, I just couldn't take it seriously and that's what they couldn't forgive me for. I suppose people in any profession who don't carry the due reverence are in trouble. But the whole military was a joke. Every time they get something good going they throw it open to the amateurs anyway and then a natural soldier sticks out like an oak in a meadow.

'I'll talk to Pataki if you want. But I'll be surprised if he'll listen. You never did.'

But that evening Pataki was nowhere to be found for dissuasion, so, at the appointed time they gathered on the Margit Bridge. Bokros had a pale, posthumous look since he wasn't going to gain however the day went. He implored Pataki to refrain from his task. If he'd offered the bike, that might have tilted it, but he didn't. 'Better stay here' Pataki suggested, entrusting Gyuri to look after the shortly-to-be-forfeited motorcycle.

'This could take some time,' Pataki said, trotting off towards the White House with the ease of a ruthless athlete. He was wearing his black tracksuit, until he reached the embankment adjacent to the Ministry.

From their vantage point on the bridge, Gyuri and Bokros watched as Pataki reduced his attire to Locomotive-style basketball boots. He looked tanned, relaxed and even from hundreds of metres away his muscles had precise definition. A superb musculature, Gyuri thought, recalling how Pataki had been in line to be the model for the naked proletarian Adonis-figure on the back of the new twenty-forint note. They had been looking for a striking example of the new Hungarian might and the artist had gone for Neumann who made a much more towering symbol of resurgence, justice and truth, of socialist invincibility and grit, and perhaps because Pataki had asked for money. 'They're not getting my pecs for free.'

All around the building there were guards. People weren't exactly encouraged to walk past the Ministry. While on the one hand, the AVO felt it only right to have ostentatiously lavish headquarters by the Danube, the drawback to having a headquarters was that people knew where to find you, which obviously made the AVO slightly uneasy.

The guards were drowsy and clearly not accustomed to doing their job. Pataki had drawn up to the main entrance before they became noticeably stirred and perplexed by this challenge to workers' power. Then one of the guards had the idea of chasing Pataki and the others thought this might be worth trying and followed his example. The guards were well armed, but not well legged. By judiciously using his acceleration, Pataki zipped ahead of them, dodging any newcomers, maintaining a few tantalising metres between himself and his collection of pursuers. He spurted round the corner of the Ministry taking a wake of guards with him, leaving the frontage of the White House deguarded, motionless and summery.

After a longer time than seemed possible, Pataki reemerged from the rear of the building and made his finishing line his starting point where he had left his tracksuit, looking satisfied that he had encircled the White House with his buttocks as his uniformed retinue caught up with him. The guards having apprehended Pataki's unhidden hide were uncertain what to do. Finally a blanket and then a police van swallowed Pataki.

'Oh, well,' Bokros summed up. 'The engine needs a rebore anyway.'

Most of the Locomotive team had decided to visit relatives in the countryside, to take lengthy hikes in the hills, or to reside at someone else's address for a few days. Gyuri waited for the retributional spill-over at home, braced for interrogation and ready with a four-dimensional denial.

Five days after Pataki had blasted the White House with both his buttocks, Gyuri returned home to find Pataki about to take a shower. He was a bit stinky and his hair needed combing but otherwise he looked remarkably intact. 'I hope you've brought your own soap, you free-loading bastard,' Gyuri remonstrated and then unable to combat his curiosity any longer: 'What happened?'

'What do you mean?' Pataki shouted from the shower 'What do you mean, what happened?'

Pataki was soaping himself and Gyuri could see Pataki wasn't going to give him the story just like that. 'I thought the talent scouts from the AVO signed you up.'

'Oh, *that*. Isn't it obvious? I'm insane. Would anyone sane run naked around the Ministry of the Interior? You're looking at an escaped lunatic. Could you fix me something to eat? We nutters eat the same sort of thing as you sane people.'

Pataki came into the kitchen, reading a letter which had been posted just before his escapade. The letter was from the Ministry of Sport informing him that his application for a scholarship abroad had been turned down. A slogan had been rubber-stamped further down the page, below the terse refusal: 'Fight for Peace'.

'Look at this,' said Pataki waving the letter in disgust. 'How can they expect me to live in a country where they put idiotic rubbish like this on every letter? I'm off.'

Pataki for some time had been trying to raise the subject of getting out. This had meant that Pataki talked about it while Gyuri was in earshot. The subject had become fascinating for Pataki, chiefly because Bánhegyi had been moved to work in the international freight department of the railways. Bánhegyi, like all the Locomotive players, wasn't actually required to work, but when he popped in to collect his wages he had access to all the information. It was an extremely hazardous way to get out, but then there were only extremely hazardous ways to get out. If it hadn't been for Jadwiga, if Gyuri had been on his own, he would have given it a go, but he wasn't willing to expose Jadwiga to the risk, although knowing her, she wouldn't refuse. He had something to lose. Pataki should have taken up the offer in '47.

Pataki insisted that they should hunt down Bánhegyi. 'I feel like leaving before the doctors catch me.' Providence was evidently in the mood to grant Pataki his wish because they found Bánhegyi just returning from a dislocation-certifying session with the doctor. 'Yes,' he said, 'there are trains going out but I can't be sure where the trains are going to. They chop and change the forms a lot.' Bánhegyi wanted to wait a few days to study the opportunities, but Pataki wouldn't hear of it. 'Thinking about it isn't going to make it any easier,' he said. So at midnight they went down to the sidings and breaking the seal on a freight-wagon, prized it open. It was full of shoes. 'Shoes are risky,' said Bánhegyi, 'they can go East or West.'

'Is there anything else available tonight?' asked Pataki.

'No.'

'Fine. This will do.' He climbed aboard with a bag containing two loaves, cheese, six apples, a bottle of mineral water and three bottles of Czech beer whose last place of residence had been the Fischer flat. 'Getting drunk is one of the few amusements possible in a dark freight-wagon full of shoes,' said Pataki defending his choice of company.

They agreed on means of communication. 'Even if it's Siberia, do drop us a postcard,' urged Gyuri.

'Sure,' said Pataki. 'And let my parents know in a day or two. Tell them I would have told them but it's easier for everyone this way.' He handed Gyuri an envelope. 'That's a blanket apology for them. And tell them not to look for granddad's wedding ring. I've got that. Does anyone know how many years you can get for this?' He looked at Gyuri. 'You're really not coming, are you?'

'Things can't go on like this much longer.'

They closed the door and Bánhegyi resealed the wagon with the official implement.

23rd October 1956

On his way to the Ministry of Sport (as everyone referred to the National Committee for Physical Education and Sport which liked to pretend it wasn't a ministry, since a ministry would detract from the atmosphere of amateurism they tried to cultivate) Gyuri spotted a ticket-inspector getting on the tram. Gyuri didn't have a ticket. He never had a ticket. He had never had a ticket. Gyuri hadn't paid a filler for public transport since the last years of the war. Furthermore, in all that time he had never even so much as contemplated paying. Not for a moment. This was, firstly, because he didn't feel like handing over any of his money to the state, however trivial the sum, and secondly, because the trams were normally so crowded, only a risible percentage of his body got in. Most of the time, he had to hang on by one hand, with one foot perched on the running-board, in the company of several similarly positioned citizens and he didn't feel that such a posture justified payment.

Seated for once, Gyuri was wondering at what point he should vacate the tram, when at the other end, a blue-overalled worker suddenly barked at the ticket-inspector: 'When the state starts paying me valid money, that's when I'll have a valid ticket, okay?' The ferocity of the outburst was astonishing, much more than one would have believed the question of a tram ticket could have elicited even in the most extreme of circumstances. It hushed the whole tram and centred every-one's attention in anticipation of some good transport theatre. Ordinarily, people who weren't interested in paying or weren't able to jumped off the tram at the approach of the authorities, as Gyuri did, like a tree losing its leaves.

The ticket-inspector had obviously tripped on a long-festering rage. His inquiry had opened the door to a crowd of resentments, and the rebuff's raw savagery, with its billboarded promise of corporeal damage, both imminent and merciless, persuaded him to move on. Gyuri had only witnessed total refusal once before. An elderly man, flanked on both sides by enormous, slavering Alsatians that he was having difficulty restraining, had smiled at the request to produce his ticket and stated: 'I honestly don't feel like paying.' He hadn't.

His dignity imperilled, the ticket-inspector had got off at the Astoria. Looking out, Gyuri could see slim groups of students milling around with placards. They had been quiet for a while, cowed by some of the best brutality available on the planet, but now the Hungarians were back at it again, the national pastime: complaining. Everyone seemed to be at it. Even the Writers' Union, the home of moral malnutrition, was at it, suddenly disclaiming all the things they had written in the last few years. The Union had pulled its head out of Rákosi's arse and now stood blinking in the daylight.

Setting out for the disciplinary hearing, Gyuri had heard from Laci, Pataki's younger brother, that the students from the Technical University were going to hold a demonstration. 'You know, a real demonstration; one that was *our* idea.' There was dispute as to whether permission had been granted for it or not. Some rulers said yes, some said no. The students didn't care apparently.

The demonstration wouldn't make any difference to anything. Gyuri hadn't said so to Laci, since Laci had been so delighted by the prospect, but he had been tempted to quote the words of Dr Hepp: 'Gentlemen, you can turn bearshit upside down. You can take it for a trip to the Balaton.

You can put it in a nice box with a blue ribbon. You can shout at it or compose an ode in its honour. It will remain bearshit.'

So what if they changed the Party leader as they had in Poland? So what if the new leader vilified the old leader? What if they had a Gerő instead of a Rákosi? Or a Nagy instead of a Gerő? They were all turds off the same conveyor belt. It was like making a fuss about changing a light bulb. What if the new leader blamed everything on the old leader? It was political leapfrog, musical chairs in the Central Committee. Why get excited by it?

Gyuri's view of the morning was soured by his attendance being required at a disciplinary hearing, but he was cheered up by the AVO incident.

At the Astoria, an AVO officer got on (uniformed AVO were harder to spot on the streets now – they seemed ill at ease). He was carrying a smart briefcase smartly. He exuded a vigorous belief in his importance, it was as if his importance was flamboyantly doing chin-ups in the tram. A group of labourers was next to him. Dirty, hardy, work-darkened figures who would no doubt place head-kicking at the head of their leisure pursuits. You could see it coming. They took their time, though, eyeing up the officer as the tram rattled along. At the next stop, one of them leaned over and asked him stentoriously to the accompaniment of pálinka fumes: 'Tell me, did you brush your teeth this morning?'

'What?' asked the AVO, puzzled by this forewordless inquiry.

'Did you brush your teeth this morning?' insisted his interrogator.'Yes,' was the only thing the AVO could think of as a reply.

'Excellent. In that case, just this once, you can lick my arse.'

The detonation of laughter practically blew the AVO officer off the tram. Gyuri felt privileged to be in at the making of an anecdote that would enliven many an evening in a kocsma. Carrying his massive discomfiture awkwardly, the AVO noticed his stop had arrived and alighted.

At the Ministry of Sport, Hepp was waiting outside, looking at his watch angrily as if it were colluding with Gyuri's tardiness. They weren't late for the hearing but Hepp always liked to be ten minutes ahead of events. Gyuri really went out of his way to be there on the dot for Hepp, because if you weren't, you'd pay for it. 'But we said eleven o' clock,' Hepp would say, sincerely bewildered as to why such a clear agreement hadn't been respected. And he would keep on saying it until you feared for your sanity. If you pleaded tram-famine, earthquake, your home suddenly combusting, Hepp would merely say: 'Why didn't you start earlier?'.

Being late was incomprehensible to him, dug-up tablets in some ancient tongue. It was more confusion than anger: 'But we said eleven o' clock'. He would repeat this, on and on, tonally turning it up and down, with the determination of a code-breaker trying to crack an unbreakable code. Hepp's solar punctuality never failed him. As far as anyone knew he had only been late for an appointment once in his life and that was when Pataki, forewarned Hepp was due at a coaches' seminar, had slipped into Hepp's office just as Hepp was getting ready to leave. Under the cover of some anodyne conversation, Pataki had withdrawn, palming the key to Hepp's office door. He had then locked the door from the corridor and had joined everyone outside, on the other side of the street, where they had a good view of Hepp's office. Within minutes Hepp was loudly ordering them to let him out, shouting at times with great pathos from his second floor window. Eventually, he prevailed on a passer-by to provide a ladder but by that point he was an irrecuperable fifteen minutes late.

Matasits was, naturally enough, behind Gyuri's appearance in front of the disciplinary tribunal. It was boring, in a way. Every time Gyuri played a game with Matasits refereeing, Gyuri would speedily accumulate his five fouls and be sent off before he could cover the length of the court, whether or not he was actually doing any fouling or even getting into the ball's neighbourhood. Matasits's compulsion to blow his whistle every time he saw Gyuri had long before made it clear to Gyuri that Matasits had him down as a bad element, a committed recidivist.

While Gyuri would have freely conceded that the referees wouldn't be voting him the sportingest player on the nation's basketball courts, the accruing of this fictional blame was irritating. No matter how exemplary Gyuri was on court, no matter how preposterously courteous he was – handing over the ball on a silver plate to the opposition at the slightest suggestion they had an interest in it, shunning contact with the opposing players as if they were radioactive lepers, if Matasits was there, he was off. There was a rumour that Matasits believed Gyuri responsible for a delivery of two hundred pairs of Soviet spectacles to his home and was seeking revenge for this insult by freight.

However, getting to the tribunal was a first for Gyuri. His gift for lurking in the referees' blind spots usually enabled him to nobble the opposition with impunity; he had also developed a prestidigitator's talent for sending the referees' attention the wrong way so he could elbow, grab trousers and tread on feet under the nose of authority. Hepp would even evaluate the quality of his fouling during the post-match analysis, 'adequate', 'stylish' or on the day he had head-butted Princz (a man who regarded basketball matches as an unlimited opportunity for the grabbing of testicles) and got Princz stretchered off, 'world-class'.

However, with Matasits on the sidelines, Gyuri would stick resolutely, if futilely, to nobility. But during a match with the Army, which the Army, despite Pataki's absence, was scarcely winning, Gyuri and an Army player had gone up for a ball. The Army player had got the ball and had Gyuri crash to the ground where he had remained while the Army player winged his way to Locomotive's basket and dumped the ball through the ring for two easy points. Like everyone else, Róka had looked on Gyuri's collapse as an overly histrionic attempt to get the ball back 'It's okay,' Róka had said to the slumped Gyuri, 'you can get up now.'

But Gyuri hadn't got up because he was firmly unconscious. Matasits booked him for wilfully obstructing the course of play, saying in all his years of refereeing he had never seen such blatant fakery and that this was going to the basketball council, particularly as, when Gyuri had regained contact with the world and learned what was going on, he had made a groggy attempt to strangle Matasits.

The tribunal was composed of three inert, overflowingly bored gentlemen behind a sweeping desk: they looked as if they were left in the room when the tribunal wasn't sitting.

Matasits kicked off. 'Esteemed tribunal, we are dealing here with a debaser of what is most sacred to man.' He read badly from notes. Gyuri settled down, judging from the depth of Matasits's sheets that it would be a long haul. Matasits had been leaning on his dictionary. In a number of rehashes, he denounced Gyuri as the fountain of all evil, a homicidal neanderthal, who wandered around the court on his knuckles, only employing his limited power of speech to heap abuse on duly empowered officials. To Matasits's gaugeable and progressive disappointment, the tribunal didn't gasp with horror but took notes emotionlessly albeit diligently. Having counted on something on the lines of a burning at the stake, with a little quartering thrown in for good measure, Matasits left the room, dejected at the coolness of his reception. The bored faces buoyed Gyuri a little, although he had a strong awareness of how even bored people could really disembowel a career.

Then it was Hepp's turn: 'Gentlemen, while I can in no way whatsoever condone Fischer's behaviour, I should like to point out that he has been under enormous, *enormous,* pressures. His mother died recently, and this bereavement combined with his voluntary coaching at the Ferencváros orphanage, in addition to his outstanding work-record at his place of employment...' It was good stuff, though Gyuri wasn't sure there was an orphanage in Ferencváros.

To conclude, he was asked to stand and make any additional mitigation. 'I'd like to apologise, gentlemen, for wasting your valuable time and I can assure you this will be the last time you will see me in such circumstances –' The tribunal could endure no more. They were paid to sit, not to listen. It was lunch time and Gyuri was cut off by the man in the middle. 'Fine of fifty forints' was the verdict. Gyuri, overwhelmed by the modesty of the fine, had a rash impulse to offer to round it up to a hundred if he could punch Matasits in the mouth.

'Aren't you going to the demonstration?' Hepp asked outside. 'Everyone else seems to be.'

'If I thought it could make the slightest difference, I'd be leading it.'

Gyuri debated whether to go to work. It was a short debate. The Feather Processing Enterprise could do without him for an afternoon. It had done pretty well without him in the two months he had been there. Hepp had fixed a job for him there; as a good amateur basketball player, Gyuri needed a job. Once he had qualified as an accountant he resolved he should have a position with more status, more prospects and more pay than knocking out the occasional morse code for the railways.

The post of planner had been wangled for him at the Feather Processing Enterprise. Obviously, one didn't want a job where there was a danger of work but it would have been nice to have had stimulating or glamorous surroundings in which to collect one's wages.

All Gyuri had done in his two months of employment, out of curiosity, was to take the figures supplied by the Ministry stipulating the amounts the factory should be producing according to the Five Year Plan, and divide these totals by the number of units in the factory. Then, having discovered the unit production figures he added it all up again to get the production figure desired by the Plan. What was actually happening in the factory, he didn't know. Gyuri doubted that anyone knew or even wanted to know. Most of the little time that he was in his office, his fellow economist, Zalán, and he, would flick matches (fired from the abrasive strip on the matchbox) at each other's desks, taking bets on which stacks of paper would ignite.

He had only got the Plan details by accident after he encountered Fekete, the director of the Feather Processing Enterprise, as he was belting down a corridor with a couple of fishing-rods. He recognised Fekete because he had been a celebrated all-in wrestler before the war, known as 'The Fat Boa'. The rumour was he had lent money to members of the Central Committee in the days of their illegality, when they shared the same boarding-house.

'Pleased to meet you,' Fekete had said, shaking his hand warmly and giving the rippling-biceped smile of a former showman. 'I'm in a terrible rush, but a copy of the Plan is in my office. Do help yourself.' That was the only time Gyuri saw Fekete mainly because Fekete only came into the office when he needed was a convenient site for his extramarital ventures, and also because there wasn't anything to discuss.

Gyuri went to Fekete's office and with the aid of one of his secretaries who had come in that day to water the plants, searched it thoroughly. No sign of the Plan. Because he was new to the job, feeling inquisitive, and slightly intoxicated by his responsibility, Gyuri decided to phone the Ministry to get some information.

He talked to three people before he realised that simply finding out what he was supposed to be doing would exhaust him and would be going well beyond the call of duty. Gyuri counted, for his own amusement, that he explained twenty-two times that he was phoning from the Feather Processing Enterprise and he wished to obtain correct and up-to-date figures for the Plan. Finally, he was connected to a voice whose hostility and reticence convinced him that he had at last reached the right person in the right department.

'You expect me to tell you all this on the phone?' reiterated the irate voice. 'How do I know you're not an American spy?'

'Look at it this way,' said Gyuri, chewing over this epistemological doubt, 'would an American spy tell you to fuck your mother?'

Ashamed of having tried to do his job, Gyuri had sauntered out of the plant. Passing through the guard's lodge at the entrance, his eye had been drawn to the vigilant defender of proletarian power vivisecting some dog-ends on his table to frankenstein together a new cigarette. Gyuri noticed that the guard was tearing off a leaf of paper from a document entitled, *The Hungarian Feather Processing Enterprise: Revised Five-Year Plan Figures, 1955.*

When in doubt, go home, go to bed, Gyuri thought. He had had a restless night fretting over the prospect of the disciplinary session and elaborating his defence, reckoning the tribunal would be the occasion for a backlog of overdue bad luck to unload on him. He opted to go home and file himself between the sheets.

He found Elek trying to persuade some used ground coffee to do an encore and produce more black soup. 'You've just missed Jadwiga,' he said. 'She's come up to Budapest for the demonstration.' Gyuri swivelled on his heel and went out.

From the other side of the river, he saw the crowd around the Bem statue as he started to cross the Margit Bridge. Bem had been the Polish General who was confused about which revolution he was in, and zealously led the Hungarian Army of Independence in 1848 against the Habsburgs and led it very successfully, until the Russians were called in and the Army of Independence proved how Hungarian it was by getting wiped out. But at least it went down to vastly superior forces, though, apocryphally, when he heard that the ten-times-greater Russian force was attacking, Bem had remarked: 'Good, I was worried they'd get away.'

The students had chosen to gather around Bem, since one of the goals of the demonstration was to express their approval of the political changes in Poland (Jadwiga had gone on about them with great enthusiasm) which were the sort of changes they wanted in Hungary: a friendly, ideology-next-door, happy-go-lucky sort of Communism. They didn't seem alone in this wish.

Not only was the Bem square a lawn of heads but the entire embankment around it was one huge dollop of humanity. Thirty, forty thousand people and more drifting in at the edges. It was a vomiting up of an indigestible system. It had all the makings of uncontrollability.

'Gyuri!' He turned around to see Laci with two friends who were carrying a huge Hungarian flag. It was the first occasion Gyuri could recall that he had experienced the sensation of feeling old, gazing enviously on those younger than himself, those who hadn't expended their optimism and could believe that carrying a flag around could change things.

'Jadwiga's here somewhere,' said Laci, looking back at the crowd. 'She's here with some friends from Szeged.' Gyuri surveyed the throng. It could take him the rest of the day to find her if their destinies weren't synchronised.

'I must congratulate you. I never thought I'd ever see anything like this' commented Gyuri, taken aback by the scale of the protest. 'Have you seen the sixteen points?' asked Laci, unfolding a sheet of paper and passing it to Gyuri. 'We started drawing them up yesterday at the University and we just kept going.'

The first demand that Gyuri read was for a change in the leadership of the Hungarian Working People's Party. That was the sort of thing that, say in 1950, just thinking about it would have got you a ten-year stretch in an unlit cellar with swollen kidneys and icy water up to your knees. Now, what with Stalin smelling the violets by their roots, and Uncle Nikita rubbishing all his predecessors, that sort of thing was negotiable if you were accompanied by a very, very large crowd. The Communist movement, in the best tradition of bankrupt capitalists, was highly adept at changing name and premises and continuing to trade under a new veneer.

The demands grew more demanding. Imre Nagy in, Soviet

troops out. Free elections, free press. Gyuri wondered, Why not throw in a requirement for eternal life and compulsory millionaireships for all Hungarians? There was also a demand for the secret files on everyone to be opened up.

'Good list,' he said. 'Good crowd.'

'The authorities were against it till we started,' said Laci, 'but now we've got plenty of gatecrashers from the Party. I suppose they want it to look as if they were behind it.'

The idea of Jadwiga demonstrating against the Party had dismayed Gyuri greatly when he heard about it. Apart from the more physical risks such as beating or death, the threat of deportation had gnawed at his innards. Poland for him, as a member of the passportless masses, was as inaccessible as the South Pole. But he could see the crowd was too big to have problems. It was a crowd so huge you couldn't shoot at it or try to disperse it. The leaders and speech-makers would doubtless be soon invited in to some subterranean cell for a little chat and damage to their structures. But on the streets, the crowd was too much: like an unwelcome relative coming to call, all you could do was humour it until it decided to go home. Everything would be all right as long as Jadwiga could restrain herself from haranguing the populace or reciting some inflammatory poetry. 'We're going off to the parliament now,' said Laci, 'we're going to stay there until they make Imre Nagy Prime Minister again.' Gyuri watched them walk off along the bridge. Laci was only four, five years younger than him, but his idealism made Gyuri feel like a grandfather. Strange how two brothers could contain so many differences and similarities. Pataki had always harnessed his intelligence to the service of his willy and winding people up as much as possible. Laci was self-effacing, studious; every time Gyuri had been in the Pataki flat Laci had been attached to a book, often extremely dull text-books. Though you didn't notice him, he was always around. It had been no surprise when he won a scholarship to the University, a considerable achievement for someone whose father wasn't in the Central Committee. However, his mischief had merely been more undercover, more insidious, biding its time. Laci hadn't said anything about it but Gyuri was sure he was leading rather than following at the Technical University.

Scanning the crowd, Gyuri tried to catch a fragment of Jadwiga. He was heartened not to see her addressing the demonstrators with a loud-hailer. The people milling around were no longer predominantly students, the demonstration was snowballing: soldiers, old folk, nonentities, water-polo players, housewives, office staff, all those who saw the demonstration and the placards and who realised this wasn't a stage-managed, Communist-led affair, that it wasn't an out of season May Day, abandoned their business and joined in with an air of why-didn't-we-think-of-this-before?

* * *

There were dozens of people trying to pull down the statue of Stalin, imps gathered around his boots. There were many more people giving advice on how it should be done. The assays and the advice had been going on for some time. Sledgehammers, hacksaws, chains attached to lorries, as well as copious abuse had all been directed at the eight-metre-high statue. It remained highly indifferent to the flurry around its legs.

Gyuri was very glad that he was there. If he hadn't been out searching for Jadwiga he probably would have missed this – it was a definite bet that Budapest Radio wouldn't be broadcasting the news that a once-only performance of idol-toppling would be taking place that night.

It was going to be, indisputably, a historic moment, one of those things that grandchildren would be hearing about whether they felt like it or not. Gyuri had never derived such intense satisfaction from anything before like this; pleasure yes, but nothing that had made his soul throw back its head and just laugh. However, it would be nice, Gyuri reflected, if the historic moment could hurry up and get on with it, because it was really too cold to be standing about even for a once in a lifetime sensation and having patrolled the streets all day he was tired. Gyuri also couldn't quite suppress the feeling that this was going a bit too far. He had carefully positioned himself to have a good view, but equally should penalties arrive, to have a good exit. It was like that moment of schoolboy exuberance when the teacher was going to walk in and curtail the pranks.

There was nothing to give substance to his unease though. A few policemen were circulating but they looked as if they were rather enjoying it and Gyuri had heard the one with the moustache suggest that an acetylene torch would do the job nicely. Two more senior, fatter policemen had been present an hour ago. The fattest, presumably most senior one had endeavoured to disperse the crowd but after issuing a few warnings, he got tired of being laughed at and vanished with his megaphone to more pressing matters elsewhere.

Whatever the outcome of the day, it had been the most enjoyable day, on all counts, that Gyuri had spent for ... well, he couldn't remember the last time precisely but the reign of boredom had lifted for a day.

A lorry pulled up and two workers who handled the acetylene equipment with practised lightness pulled themselves up onto the plinth to amputate Uncle Joe at the boot tops. A ripple of applause rose as the flame bit into Stalin's calf, a miniature sun in the night's darkness. The audience for such a monumental event could have been larger; there couldn't have been more than three thousand gathered around the statue, a mere fraction of those out on the streets that night who would have undergone a quiver of pleasure at the toppling of the bronze abomination. Still, Gyuri knew, tomorrow everyone would be claiming they had been there.

Gyuri assumed that most people were still back in the centre of the city, around the parliament where Imre Nagy had waved sheepishly to the hundred thousand people assembled there and begun his address to them: 'Comrades...' This had exactly the opposite effect to what Nagy had wanted. Despite the fact that the crowd wanted him to take over, his opening malapropism brought boos and a rhythmic chant of 'There are no comrades.' Nagy had handled the rest of his speech better, urging coolness and good sense. It wasn't a brilliant performance, but then, as a Communist, Nagy wasn't familiar with the concept of an audience that wanted to hear him speak. People weren't overjoyed, but it had been getting late and most of them, content with a good day's demonstrating, started to go home. Gyuri had seen nearly everyone he had met in his life at the Parliament Square, but not Jadwiga. He was on his way home to check for her there when he happened upon Stalin about to come a cropper.

With some guided combustion, Stalin was tripped up by the will of the people and came crashing down with a clanging slap that dwarfed the ovation of the souvenir-hunters who closed in to feast on the fallen carcass with sledgehammers and pickaxes. Gyuri quite fancied a piece of Stalin as a sort of talisman, a memento of evil not always having its way, but he settled for making one more trip to the Radio to look for Jadwiga if she wasn't at the flat. She wasn't. So he took the tram down to Kálvin Square.

The whole network of streets around the Radio in Sándor Bródy utca was full, packed with people. It was like a replay of the World Cup protest, except this time the number of extras had quadrupled. Gyuri heard that a delegation of students had made its way to the Radio in the late afternoon to politely ask for their points to be read out to the rest of the country. More delegations, more well-wishers of democracy, more politeness had arrived throughout the evening and now by eleven o' clock, the politeness was being discarded and the student idealism was being replaced by proletarian bellicosity. Gyuri hoped Jadwiga wasn't around here (though he guessed his presence would produce her absence) since he was adamant that the Radio was where the Party would draw the line. The Stalin statue, that was allowing people to let off steam, since, after all Stalin was rather dead and *passé,* and it saved them the embarrassment of removing it themselves. But the Radio was real here-and-now power, it could pour the unrest all over the sleepier parts of the capital and the nation...

Gyuri spotted Laci and his gang by the main entrance. He squeezed his way through, earning a great deal of rancour from the people he had to shove and step on to reach them. 'You haven't seen Jadwiga?' he inquired. 'Yes,' replied Laci, 'she was here a minute ago.' Adding proudly: 'They're going to read out the points.'

There was a stir around the entrance way and a suit full of shit started to shout: 'The points are being read out now. Please go home. The points are being read out as I speak. Please go home.' He sounded familiar and he had a booming voice; Gyuri assumed that he must be one of the presenters. The radio man stressed that the points were being read out and that people should go home. Then, from a window in one of the flats opposite the Radio entrance, a woman with the look of a harried housewife materialised. Balancing her wireless with some difficulty on the windowsill so that everyone in the street could faintly sample the broadcast, she shouted: 'You evil liar! There's nothing but music.'

The tear gas followed swiftly after this. It failed all round. The AVO didn't have gas masks, most of the gas billowed back onto them, and since the street was so narrow and full, even those people who wanted to leave couldn't do much about it. There was a lot of coughing and crying but more than anything else, there was a large amount of anger. It was something you could watch growing, like a darkening sky presaging rain. Gyuri dropped back to search for Jadwiga and because he knew it was coming. The Communists might not be good at organising the economy but if there was one thing they knew it was how to organise security.

By the time he had forced his way to the sanctuary of the nearby National Museum, not on a direct bullet line from the Radio entrance and endowed with walls and pillars so thick that gunfire would be no more effective than rain, the shooting started. It was the most sickening sound he had ever heard. His fear was overtaken by nausea at people being shot for standing in the wrong place. The streets, of course, were emptying as fast as possible.

In a doorway opposite, revealed sporadically as people ran past, Gyuri saw a tubby man slumped against the door, his legs straight out in front of him, like a propped up teddy-bear. He had a great red patch on his stomach. A companion was whispering in his ear, perhaps trying to talk him out of bleeding to death. Gyuri could discern two motionless bodies lying in front of the Radio. He was surprised how nauseous the sight made him. He had thought he had seen enough corpses during the war to be immune to queasiness, but obviously you had to keep your hand in when it came to indifference to death. And the anger. He had thought he had wanted to kill people before, but now he knew what the real thing felt like, that he truly wanted to, that it wouldn't be a problem; the desire that had been unperceived in the wings now made its entrance, ready for action.

The shouts and running went on for some time. Then something happened that Gyuri hadn't foreseen. Shooting started, *towards* the Radio. Windows began to shatter and Gyuri spied a young man taking advantage of a street corner to snipe at the building. He was dressed in civilian clothes. Where had he got the rifle from? Looking back towards Kálvin Square, Gyuri could see what looked like a parked Army lorry They must have been handing out weapons, because the sound of sniping commenced from every direction.

It would be funny, mused Gyuri, if a second revolution were to start here at the National Museum. It was here on these steps that Petöfi had read out one of his poems cutting the ribbon, as it were, to inaugurate the 1848 revolution.

A couple of workers appeared, wearing the obligatory berets that explained they came from Csepel, swathed in belts of ammunition and carrying a heavy machine-gun. They were thinking out loud about how to get onto the roof of the museum from where they would have a superb arc of fire onto the Radio. 'Never come to the Radio without your machine gun,' one remarked.

A curly-haired, lanky guy also appeared, and taking up position behind a pillar, began to adjust the sights on his newly-acquired rifle. The payback for forcing everyone to do military training, thought Gyuri. He was positive he knew the man, the face was struggling to be named and placed. Looking at each other, there was a sudden ocular transfer of thought from the aspiring sharpshooter: Yes. It's what we've been praying for. Armed revenge. He smiled widely at Gyuri. Maybe he did know him, maybe it was just the instant camaraderie of that night. 'I feel so lucky,' said the man. 'This is simply wonderful. Wonderful.' He fired off two rounds without much aim.

It was a long and bewildering night. Most of the shooting was just at the Radio, rather than any particular part of it or any specific target. People had fun simply shooting at the bricks. There was also a protracted exchange of fire with the other end of Sándor Bródy utca during a fear of AVO reinforcements coming. It turned out to be another group of self-armed listeners of the Radio wishing to register their complaints.

Tired and cold, Gyuri nevertheless came to the conclusion he could never forgive himself if he didn't do a stint of shooting. He sidled up to one well-dressed combatant and asked him where he had obtained his gun. 'A soldier gave it to me. But if you want one, please take mine. I have to go. It pulls a little to the left.' Here he peered lengthily at his watch in the dark. 'I was hoping to knock off an AVO but the wife will be wondering where I am. A gunfight at the Radio won't be an acceptable excuse.'

At about two in the morning, Gyuri and some others slipped into an adjacent courtyard to see if they could gain entry to a top-floor flat. They found a group of five AVO men huddled in a corner, without weapons and without any inclination to fight.

'Shouldn't you be in the Radio building? Defending the gains of the people?' asked one of Gyuri's group sarcastically.

'Do you think we're going to die for a bunch of fucking Communists?' retorted one of the AVO men indignantly. Unfortunately they were so pathetic, no one even wanted to kick them a bit. As they were pondering what to do with them, a charming pensioner appeared in her dressing gown and asked if anyone would like tea or coffee. 'I've got a few crackers as well,' she said, 'but nothing more. I wasn't counting on company.' She brought them all a drink and got very angry when someone tried to give her some money. 'It's the least I can do.'

After his tea, Gyuri who still hadn't fired a shot, went into the old lady's flat, introduced himself to her husband, opened their windows and fired off three shots in the general direction of the Radio. He closed the window and thanked the couple for their co-operation. He felt much, much better. He had taken part.

Around six o' clock it dawned on the people besieging that there was no one inside trying to stop them getting in. Going in, they found a few AVO rigors, but to their embarrassment it looked as if most of the garrison had slipped out a back door. One or two shamefaced broadcasters were discovered hiding under desks or in broom-cupboards. One enthusiastic youth, who couldn't have been more than fifteen, called them brothers and exhorted them to take up arms for the revolution. You could tell it was a revolution because this appeal didn't sound ridiculous. Revolution. It was the first time Gyuri had heard the word mentioned in regard to the proceedings. And why not? Not surprisingly the presenters readily expressed their readiness to do what was requested. It's amazing how much respect people have for you when you have a gun and they don't, thought Gyuri.

The studios were empty, with the signs of hasty retreat, but from a radio they could hear music being played as if it were a normal Wednesday morning. They were transmitting from somewhere else. 'Now what do we do?' said one of the victors putting his finger on the issue. Gyuri passed his rifle to another enthusiastic but unarmed youth and walked home.

In front of the Keleti Station he saw a convoy of unmistakably Soviet armoured personnel carriers and tanks clattering along. Well, it had been a laugh while it lasted.

He got home to find Elek breakfasting modestly in the kitchen.

'Don't tell me you've missed her,' he said, looking shocked. Without waiting for further illumination, Gyuri ran out and explored the neighbouring streets persistently. It was ridiculous. He was going to stick to his philosophy of staying in bed (Pataki's departure had brought him a new sleep machine to replace the one he had burned in Spartan ardour) until Jadwiga turned up.

'Imre Nagy has been on the radio,' said Elek. 'Did you hear?'

'No, I missed that.'

'He's Prime Minister again. He's asked everyone to calm down.'

'He's going to have to ask very hard indeed,' mumbled Gyuri from his bed.

* * *

On his way to the Technical University, he saw an AVO man taking a flying lesson. He had woken on the afternoon after an unsatisfying six hours' repose, romance and other adrenalin-pumpers marring his sleep, and he had determined to head to the University since all the studenty activities were probably being co-ordinated from there. 'Listen,' he said to Elek, who felt events justified a day off at home, 'I'll be back at eight on the dot, regardless of how interesting the revolution is. Tell Jadwiga she should *wait* if she comes home.'

Outside, there was the sound of remote gunfire, at the right sort of distance to be piquant but not trouser-soiling. At the

Lenin Körút, people had obtained ladders to help pull down the street signs with Lenin Körút on them. A crowd had formed to enjoy this but suddenly there was a scuffle, and a round-faced man in a raincoat was seized by those around him to shrieks of 'AVO! AVO!' Gyuri couldn't tell what had given him away, but there was no doubt that the charge was correct. The round-faced man produced a pistol, and ended his career by firing off two shots, severely wounding a tree. Held by eight pairs of hands, his documents were examined. Then someone said: 'Let's give him a flying lesson.'

So they did. He was conducted to a rooftop and made to walk a non-existent plank. The AVO man wasn't much good at flying. He came straight down and squandered all his energy on screaming.

People didn't cheer this but nor were they bothered. It was about right. Some public-spirited citizens started to drag the body out of the road, and as they were doing this, a diminutive, silent fellow next to Gyuri, who had been watching all this as if waiting for a bus, threw himself on the body without warning, stabbing away with a penknife as if he were hammering on a door, shouting 'You killed my brother, you killed my brother' with the same monotony as his stabbing. The others were perplexed as to what to do, but interrupting his rage would have been impolite.

Gyuri had thought the disturbances would be over by now, that the flirtation with liberty would be a one-night stand. But clearly, people were still doing whatever they felt like. What were the Russians up to?

In the centre of the city, closer to the University, Gyuri saw Russian tanks parked menacingly here and there, trying to look aggressive and unobtrusive at the same time but he didn't witness any fighting.

Immediately, at the university, Gyuri found Laci, with a tricolour band around his arm and sporting a pistol in a holster. Clearly he was in Laci's orbit just as he was out of Jadwiga's. In the main hallway of the University the standard fashion accessory seemed to be a firearm, either a davai guitar, or as a minimum, a revolver. Gyuri was expecting Laci to tell him that Jadwiga had just been looking for him, but he hadn't seen her at all.

Laci was shaken: 'We were attacked this morning. Some AVO men in a car drove past, they opened up, killed one of us. I had a machine gun, I had them in my sights... Gyuri, I simply couldn't pull the trigger.'

So there it was. The shock of being an idealist. Some people can't tell jokes or touch their toes. Laci can't pull a trigger. It was funny, his brother would have been trotting around with extra magazines. As Gyuri commiserated with him, another student joined them. 'Hey, Gyuri, are you enjoying the revolution? Do you want to see our AVO collection?'

The chemistry lecture hall contained twelve predictably miserable AVO employees who had been acquired by student patrols. They were being tortured by a student who was outlining their prospects under the principles of international law and natural justice; how they would be formally, correctly and legally investigated by a properly constituted body and if they had committed any illegal acts they would have to stand trial. Surveying the hunched figures, surrounded by half-eaten plates of spinach casserole (which even starving students found hard work), Gyuri thought how lucky they were to be captured by students, and not walking non-existent planks.

Someone called his name. It was, Gyuri realised, Elemér, the dog-catching mailed-fist of the proletariat. 'Gyuri, Gyuri, why don't you explain to everyone who I am? Tell them I only worked in the stationery and office supplies department. They don't understand I'm no one important.'

Gyuri was so taken aback that he was left fumbling for emotions and responses. Later on, he would wonder whether Elemér's consummate invertebratery wasn't in some senses admirable, such a remarkable absence of moral backbone being as worthy of attention as a circus contortionist. The ability to survive surely being a laudable thing. Elemér's tone would have been apt for greeting a long unseen friend at a party. Gyuri settled for staring at him, aghast that he wasn't standing between a Radio building and a loaded submachine gun. It was a case of either beating him to death or doing nothing. Since he knew the students would be upset at his tarnishing the propriety and decorum of their AVO reservation, giving Elemér a look that he knew would affect his digestion, Gyuri left.

Outside, he could still hear a muted battle raging, like the muffled argument of a domestic dispute a wall away. Trams had become a rare species, hardly glimpsed, but a tram appeared to take Gyuri across the Zsigmond Móricz Square, where he had a good, close-up view of two Soviet tanks shelling what he assumed were freedom-fighter strongholds. Once the tram was over the bridge track in Pest, things were quieter, a few streetsweepers were brushing the pavements clean with their customary sluggish swishes; their union evidently hadn't called them out.

While keeping a look-out for any discharging tanks, Gyuri reflected on the corpse of the student killed that morning, now laid out in state in front of the University by some trees, surrounded by impromptu wreathes and flowers, and table-clothed by a national flag that had been draped over him. It was one of the old fashioned tricolours that must have been stored away somewhere, not one of the new-style flags that everyone was parading around, minus the centre where the Communist coat-of-arms had been cut out.

The makeshift catafalque had been moving but didn't even start to make up for the death. A whole lifetime poured down the drain. The person gone, and a lifesize effigy, a livid, well-observed caricature left. All those beliefs, emotions, memories carefully stored up over twenty-three years junked. Twenty-three years. What? 200,000 hours, a Hungarian Second Army of tooth brushing, cleaning behind the ears, blackhead squeezing, small talk, waiting for public transport, wiped out. An identity, spring-cleaned out. A whole being just left as a resumé in a few memories, until those repositories were disposed of as well. Abridged away. Nothing like death, thought Gyuri climbing out of the morbidity, for making life look good.

He got off the tram at the Körút. Although most of the shops were closed, he remembered that the day-and-night people's buffet (a delicatessen short on the delicacies) had been open earlier, and he decided to investigate what was going in the way of edibles.

Near the buffet, lying in the middle of the road like a giant's abandoned football, was the head from Stalin's statue, dragged there by a jubilant public as a mark of their triumph, displaying the traitor's head on a gargantuan scale. A gentleman was seeking to knock off a chunk with the aid of a pickaxe, and it occurred to Gyuri that he should take a souvenir as well. He queued up patiently behind the man, when the Soviet tank appeared.

It roared into the middle of the Körút and opened fire on Gyuri.

Sheltering behind Stalin's head with the other souvenir-hunter, the first and only thing that occurred to Gyuri as the bullets smashed into the shops and cut down tree branches, was how much he wanted to live. He had never been aware of how enormous, how global this desire was deep down, a desire that was in no way smaller than the universe – how he would do anything, absolutely anything to live, to live for even a few more seconds. If life meant huddling up to Stalin's head for the next forty years or so, that would be quite satisfactory as long as he could stay alive. Rolled up tighter than a foetus, he closed his eyes not questioning whether that could be of any use.

The shooting stopped, and there was no movement apart from some shards of glass keeling over; those who had taken up assorted positions on the ground were evidently quite happy with them and were in no rush to move. Gyuri could still hear the rumbling of the tank engine unpleasantly close. An old man embracing the pavement next to a tree, with his bag of shopping beside him, yards away from Gyuri, was protesting with amazing persistence and volume: 'Two world Wars. *Two* world wars and now this.' Gyuri considered whether it might be a wiser investment in self-preservation to run to a more secure and spacious sanctuary but while he had faith in his speed, the notion of having only air between himself and the barrel of the heavy machine gun on the tank was too disturbing. Unless the tank closed in, he was going to sweat it out behind Stalin. The rumbling of the tank continued at the same remove; Gyuri became curious as to what they were up to but he wasn't going to have a look

'I never thought I'd be grateful to Stalin,' commented Gyuri's companion whom Gyuri was half-crushing. They were there for what may or may not have been a long time but certainly felt like it. Gyuri didn't mind waiting; it was one of those activities you could only do alive. His co-huddler had been in Recsk, the labour camp that had been set up as an extermination centre in the middle of the Hungarian countryside. Gyuri knew nothing about it except that it had existed and been shut down under Nagy; one of István's friends had been an inmate but had given him only the most elliptical of accounts.

Normally, Gyuri avoided the offers of life stories offered in the traditional Hungarian style of expanded self-history, the vocal autobiographies that all Hungarians seemed to be working on continually but he didn't have much choice and besides, Miklós's extracts were quite gripping. Gyuri had always rated himself unlucky but now he realised he was only a weekend player in misfortune.

'The Germans, what a cultured people when they're not invading your country,' Miklós explained. Miklós had done a stint in the anti-Nazi resistance. Caught, the Hungarians were too lazy to execute him and passed him to the Germans who put him in Dachau where he had been dying of cholera when the Americans arrived. He got better. 'It seemed a bit pointless to die when you'd just been liberated.'

He came back to Hungary. 'Talk about being stupid.' Where he worked for the Smallholders' Party. 'Talk about asking for it.' Then he got a free ride in a black car which led to him being imprisoned in Recsk. The concept of Recsk was that you went in but you didn't come out. 'Its scope was modest compared to the Soviet or German models, I suppose,' Miklós conceded, 'but we're a small country, after all: there were only fifteen hundred of us.' For three years Miklós and the others had no news from outside. 'The only news we got was from shitty newspaper we filched from the guards' latrine and let's be honest, the papers aren't much to talk about in the first place. We only found out about Stalin's death when one of us noticed a black border around his picture in the main office.'

Miklós was very talkative despite the discomfort of his position, pinioned by a first division basketball player. 'You know what the worst thing was? It's all crap about how important freedom, friendship all that abstract stuff is. You know what matters? Sleep and food. The hunger was unimaginable. You thought it was bad during the War? I tell you, a few weeks, a couple of months of going hungry – it's nothing, nothing. A doddle. A year... two years...three years without enough to eat,' he was now shouting, 'it's beyond human belief. Ever since I got out, I always carry this.' With some difficulty, he unwrapped a cloth containing a piece of cheese, a hunk of bread and some radishes. 'I have to carry supplies with me all the time. I hardly ever use it. I just have to have it with me.' He offered Gyuri a tired-looking radish.

'No. Thanks. So are you going to be looking up your old guards while you have a chance to express your gratitude?'

'That's an interesting question. We used to discuss that a lot at Recsk. What sort of people could beat someone to death just for the hell of it? There was disagreement about this in the camp, as there's always disagreement when you get two Hungarians together. You know how the 23rd of October is going to be described in the history books? The day the Hungarians agreed.

'Anyway, my view was that the guards at Recsk were basically very ordinary, if not too bright lads. They'd been told we were the scum of the earth, the most evil, degenerate, child-murdering, odious, verminous parasites to be found in creation: in short the sort of people who would run concentration camps. What use was it us trying to explain we were there because we had voted the wrong way?

'The other thing is that, you know, someone who is jailed falsely for a long time, not a year or two, but three or more, tends to go to one extreme or the other. Judging from my experience you either become excessively forgiving or excessively vengeful. I feel we should remember Recsk. People should know what happened. But we should also forget about it and get on with other things. When the tanks go.'

A moving-off rumble came. Having made its point and intimidated the vicinity, the tank moved off. When Gyuri saw people emerging from the buffet he knew he could safely stand again. His clothes were soaked with sweat, the nostril-curling stench of fear. 'Nice meeting you,' he said, shaking Miklós's hand, 'hope you like the revolution.'

He bought some food. It was after seven, and because he had made eight the rendezvous time with Jadwiga and because his luck was sorely depleted, Gyuri was very keen to get home. Moving up to the Keleti Station he was annoyed to see the revolution strengthening. Dead Russian soldiers were lying in gutters and against buildings like inebriated vagrants. While Gyuri had no objection to dead Russian soldiers, it suggested that he was moving closer to the fighting rather than away from it as he desired. His hands were still shaking from his time out on the target range. His stomach would be mulling over the terror for weeks. Ridiculously, in the middle of the shooting he had had the impulse to shout at the tank crew: 'Stop! You don't understand. I'm a coward. This isn't fair. Find some brave people to shoot at.'

A Soviet armoured personnel carrier that had erupted, probably by grenade, was proving a big hit with the locals because, apparently, it had a headless Russian on display inside. People vied to peer into the charred interior. Gyuri was totally unmoved by the sight of the Russian dead. He had heard all the arguments about how the Russians were people, how everyone is the same, what a great composer Tchaikovsky was; nevertheless he couldn't help wishing that the Russians would fuck off and be people and the same, back in the Soviet Union. An incinerated corpse at his feet failed to elicit any compassion. Probably a conscript – he didn't give a toss.

All around the Keleti Station, there were groups of tanks cutting off his intended route home. The Russian tanks weren't doing anything but they didn't seem to want to move. They were just occupying space. No one, Gyuri noticed, was strolling around close to them. The streets were full of people, no one wanted to stay at home, but a peopleless belt extended for hundreds of metres round the tanks. The streetcorner militia that had formed on the Rákoczi út were discussing what to do. There were two soldiers, several new teenagers (two on roller-skates) and a hotchpotch of individuals you'd find waiting for a bus, including two postwomen. 'We need petrol bombs. That's what they're using at the Corvin. Who can get some empty bottles?' asked one of the soldiers.

It was nearly eight. Gyuri cut down a sidestreet to see if he could sidestep the Red Army.

An hour later making his final approach, closing in from the direction of the Zoo, Gyuri was annoyed to discover that the Red Army had completely surrounded his flat. He was getting angry enough to attack one of the tanks.

As he was observing the tank blocking the end of Benczur utca and trying to think of a way of blowing it up, safely, without risk, with his bare hands, from an enormous distance he saw a man walk out of one of the blocks of flats at the end of the street and start to knock on the side of the tank, as if he were knocking on a door. He knocked very assiduously and after a few minutes, the turret opened and a leather-helmeted head popped out. What was the man doing? Asking them for a light? Hoping that the Russians would be less likely to open fire in mid-conversation, Gyuri galloped over. When he ran past, despite his grudging Russian, he realised that the man was haranguing the tank crew. 'What are you doing here?' the man demanded.

'We're here to protect you from hooligans and reactionaries,' the officer protested.

'Where are the hooligans? Where are the reactionaries?' It was an intriguing exchange, but Gyuri had had enough current affairs for one day. Going up the stairs, he met Jadwiga coming down.

'You're late,' she said sternly.

'Time flies when you're having a revolution.'

Inside, Elek greeted them with the news that Imre Nagy had formed a new government. 'I'm pleased for him,' said Gyuri, 'but if you'll excuse us, there are some urgent aspects of Hungarian–Polish relations to consider.'

***

Why shouldn't things be conducted in comfortable conditions? thought Gyuri, glad that he had obtained a fully-qualified bed from Pataki as his farewell present. Worn out by history, worry, fear and his conjugal work, he was reclining into sleep when Jadwiga said apropos of nothing:

'We are winning. It will be Poland next.'

He loved her craziness. Did it really matter what went outside the bedroom where they had established a bad-free zone? 'Who knows, maybe even the Czechs will do something?' Jadwiga continued, recounting her day out in the revolution and how she had come to Budapest. On Saturday, the students at Szeged University had held a meeting, as was suddenly the fashion, to discuss the pervasive iniquity of things. 'It was the first time in my life I've seen anything that could even loosely be called democratic. Strange that I had to wait twenty-two years to see someone saying what they thought in public; there was something almost improper about it. So we voted to withdraw from that Communist-guided student union and to set up our own. I told them we had to do it. I remembered what you said about fighting all the way. That pushed me.'

Gyuri strained his memory but he couldn't recall any such dictum.

The Szeged students had then voted to send a delegation to the university youth of Budapest to urge them to do the same. Jadwiga had arrived in Budapest on Monday night but hadn't wanted to come and break the back of Gyuri's sleep by saying hello at four in the morning. She had then been touring the collapse of the Party's power. While Gyuri had been sheltering behind Stalin, she had been at the Corvin cinema, with one of the best seats in town to watch the fighting. Gyuri related his various encounters with Soviet tanks.

'Were you afraid?' she asked.

'No,' he lied, choosing a tone of cool indifference to the lethal nature of Soviet armour but not one of scorn, since he didn't want to overdo it.

'I wasn't afraid either,' she said. Not for the first time, Gyuri registered that Jadwiga was much braver than he was. A soul as firm as her breasts, beauty and fortitude, Venus and Mars in one. And her bravery was a self-fuelling, independent, detached bravery, the sort that would work alone, in the dark, in the gas chamber. What is she doing with me? Gyuri could envision rustling up some bravado if there was an audience or some support, but the sort of solo bravery that exists even though there is no one to witness or mark it was, he knew, beyond him.

Could doing brave things make you brave, as push-ups made you stronger? Was courage bone or muscle? Something that was meted out at birth or something that was up to you?

They vacated the bedroom to merge the food Gyuri had bought into an omelette. After they had eaten, Jadwiga went out of the kitchen and reappeared with a submachine-gun, the classic davai guitar, which she placed on the table. 'Do you have anything to clean this with?' she asked. Gyuri caught Elek looking at him with vast amusement.

* * *

The only thing that would have been more unlikely than a revolution, thought Gyuri arriving at the British Embassy with a folder full of AVO documents showing that a British diplomat had been spying for the AVO, would have been my arriving at the British Embassy with a folder full of AVO documents showing that a British diplomat had been spying for the AVO.

He rang the bell. After a suitably dignified pause, the door was opened, Gyuri was pleased to see, by Nigel. 'Good morning,' said Gyuri in his floweriest pronunciation. 'How are you, Nigel? Do you know if the Ambassador is free?'

'Actually, he's a Minister Plenipotentiary, but don't let that stop you.' Gyuri had no idea what Nigel was talking about but didn't want his status as a star English speaker to be diminished. He had met Nigel three days earlier, during the heaviest of the fighting. The agreement had been that anything moving down the Nádor utca would get it. They had a heavy machine-gun set up ready to rip, which was hogged by a surly, burly coal miner from Tatabánya, who didn't like anyone coming anywhere near it. 'I was a gunner in the Army, all right? I know how to use this thing. I don't want anyone messing around with it, I don't want anyone fucking it up.'

He didn't take any breaks and he urinated on the spot, because he didn't want to let go of the machine-gun or let it out of his sight. When the car appeared, the miner immediately misfired the gun, which was just as well since it gave everyone time to distinguish the Union Jack tied sloppily to the bonnet of the car. The car trundled up respectfully to their position, and as the miner continued to swear, to curse the quality of Soviet manufacturing standards and to eject cartridges left, right and centre, Nigel had got out and said cheerfully, 'Good afternoon. Is there by any chance anyone here who speaks English *and* who knows the way to the British Legation?' Gyuri had earned this conversation.

Nigel had the elegant garb of a top spy, a rising diplomat: someone, in short, well worth getting to know. But in fact he said he was an aspiring opera singer, studying in Vienna. With a friend, he had driven to Budapest to deliver medical supplies. There was no one else who spoke English, but even if there had been they wouldn't have had a chance. Gyuri took charge, exulting in every well-spent forint of his English lessons. 'And how do you like Budapest, Nigel? Let me escort you to the Embassy. And do tell me what you think of Viennese women.'

A week after the start of the revolution it was all over, barring the history-writing. To Gyuri's amazement, to everyone's amazement, and no doubt most of all, to the Russians' amazement, the part-timers of Budapest had beaten the Red Army. True, a lot of the Russians hadn't been very eager to fight, most of them had been based in Hungary for some time and seemed to understand what they were being asked to do and that they weren't combating international fascism or the Hungarian underworld but the populace of Budapest. Indeed the only Russian Gyuri had seen who was wholly enthusiastic about trigger-pulling had been a Russian deserter he had met at the Corvin who had been fighting his former colleagues.

But the main problem for the Russians, who had been counting on the AVO to pull their weight, had been that, without proper infantry support, their tanks had been bizarrely vulnerable in the streets of Budapest. People simply waited for a tank to pass and then for the price of a good drink, lobbed their petrol bomb on the rear of the tank, where the burning fuel would be sucked in through the ventilation grilles of the T-34s and into the engine, turning the occupants of the tank into charcoal sticks; those fast enough to avoid being burned were shot as they clambered out.

Imre Nagy formed a new new government, one this time with a few people who hadn't been in the Communist Party. Ceasefire. Exultation. Hungarians had fought their way to paradise.

Along with many other curious folk, Gyuri and Jadwiga had taken a look in the White House, which appropriately enough for a revolution looked as if it had been turned upside down, all the drawers and shelves emptied as people indulged their prurience or just enjoyed themselves making a mess. 'You always choose the most romantic places for outings, Gyuri,' she remarked. The first document Gyuri picked up to read was a file detailing the blackmailing of a British diplomat who had been apprehended smuggling gold and then moulded by the AVO. Gyuri grabbed the file and headed for the British Embassy, pleased that he had found a bridge to more civilised parts, leaving Jadwiga to studiously read, slowly and carefully the way she always did, from the vast anthologies of turpitude.

With remarkable speed and ease, perhaps because of a good word from Nigel, perhaps because of the informality of the times, Gyuri was shown in to see the Ambassador, who received the file with courtesy. He puffed on his pipe, manifestly at home in the revolution and pored over the first few pages. 'Ah. Dawson. Yes,' he thought out loud.

'Thank you very much, Mr Fischer. It's very kind of you to bring this round.' It took fifty seconds; Gyuri was out almost as fast as he had got in. He hadn't been expecting anything in particular, though some gold bullion, a British passport, a job offer, something like that would have been quite acceptable. A little excitement and incredulity as a minimum. The Ambassador showed him out as if he had just return a stray button from the Ambassador's overcoat.

In the waiting-room, next to the entrance, Nigel was chatting with a man whom Gyuri had met before, *The Times* correspondent. Gyuri had been excited to meet him because *The Times* was *The Times*, and also because everyone knew that their foreign correspondents worked for British Intelligence, although the correspondent did a good job of disguising it. In fact his behaviour was rather dim. Brilliant cover. Gyuri admired professionalism. There was also a broad, military figure who looked as if he would be happiest inspecting rifles, who sure enough, was introduced to Gyuri as the military attaché.

'What do you make of the new government?' asked *The Times*, presumably looking for some good quote.

'It's fine. I approve of it, while it lasts.'

'What do you mean?'

'The Russians will be back.'

There was gentle British scoffing at this statement. In the few days he had been dealing with live Brits, Gyuri had rapidly become attuned to how the British had reached a level of civilisation where they could clearly tell you how stupid you were, without actually having to say so; that's what cricket and centuries of parliamentary democracy could do for you.

'The Russians have given an undertaking to leave. I saw Mikoyan in the parliament with my own eyes, the man was in tears over losing Hungary,' explained the correspondent. 'They're leaving. They have no choice.'

Gyuri had had the same argument that morning with Elek who was cock-a-hoop over the news. 'I told you this couldn't go on much longer,' Elek had said. Gyuri summoned up a simplified, profanity-free version of his thesis for British consumption.'I know the Russians have lost one fight. They are leaving. But I do not believe they will say: "Oh. You want to be independent. We're so sorry we didn't understand that you didn't want us here." They will return.'

There was more quivering of stiff upper lips in amusement at the wary Hungarian who had no grasp of the international situation. 'No,' pronounced the military attaché, 'they're finished here.'

'Indeed,' said *The Times*, 'I'm willing to bet you five pounds that they don't come back. You can give me a few Hungarian lessons when I win.'

'I hope you do win,' said Gyuri.

Jadwiga had told Gyuri to meet her at the Corvin and going there he stopped on the Körút to buy a newspaper. A Soviet corpse was still lying there, an unusual sight now, since the dead had been mostly packed away out of sight. Something metallic glinted on his wrist. It looked familiar: an Omega watch, like the one the Red Army had relieved him of back in '44, exactly the same model. He undid the strap, and looked on the back of the watch. There were the initials Gy. F. 'Thanks very much for looking after it,' he said, pocketing the watch.

Walking across to the newsagent, a shout stopped him. It was Róka. 'Hey class alien! This is what you want,' he said, handing Gyuri one of the stack of papers he was nursing. 'Kill anyone interesting?' he enquired. 'Not really,' Gyuri replied, 'but I was being choosy.' Róka had spent most of the livefire time chasing a lorryload of AVO who were keen on surprise atrocities; they would flip open the flaps on the lorry's rear and blast away at anyone in view, male or female, young or old, unarmed or unarmed. Róka's crew had missed them several times by seconds. The story ended with the AVO being last seen motoring in the direction of the Angyalföld. 'They couldn't have lasted more than ten minutes,' Róka obituarised. The paper that Róka had handed over was entitled *The Truth*. 'I'm working on the editorial committee,' he explained proudly. 'Oh, before I forget, Hepp wants everyone out at the club at Hepp-time, Monday morning. He says we've wasted enough time.' With a parting injunction to look up Gyurkovics, who had managed to get himself put in charge of the distribution of a vast amount of processed cheese from Switzerland, Róka carried on down the street dishing out his journal to anyone willing to take it.

Gyuri had never thought he would ever in his life earnestly want to read a Hungarian newspaper. Newspapers were now teeming with the sort of increases that could normally only be found in the production figures of Communist enterprises.

The old papers had changed, they had received editorial transplants and new ones were springing up like mushrooms. They weren't much good but you did have the novel sensation of wanting to read what they had to say. You couldn't tell before you read the paper what would be in it; now you got all those things that hadn't been there for nearly ten years, opinions that weren't the Party's. Casting his eye over *The Truth*, Gyuri read some soggy new poetry, some exhausted old poetry and some articles about the 23rd which hardly counted as news. It was still a pleasure to read.

After the fighting, the tidying up. Everywhere, shattered glass, masonry and martial litter was being victoriously swept up by the city-proud populace. Soviet wreckage was being pushed out of roads so that traffic could circulate properly. Everyone was on their best behaviour as if the Revolution was an honoured guest they wanted to impress with their hospitality and civility. A bubble of decency had risen out of the earth's core and burst in Budapest. Peasants were driving in from the countryside with their carts to distribute food to whoever they came across, dishing out sacks of potatoes, apples, marrows, some late melons. In a broken jewellers' window Gyuri saw a note explaining that the contents had been taken to the flat above for safe-keeping. There were cardboard boxes on pavements marked 'for the fallen', overflowing with banknotes contributed for the dependents of the dead.

The worst fighting or the best fighting depending on how you felt about it had all been around the Corvin Cinema. The Corvin Cinema was not a very salubrious or comfortable cinema, as a cinema it wasn't much to brag about, but as if with astonishing forethought, it couldn't have been better designed for street fighting. The circular cinema was surrounded by a ring of flats with lots of convenient alleyways in and out.

But the Corvin had not been the only streetfighting club. All over Budapest they had jack-in-the-boxed. Even around the

Corvin, there had been stiff competition: the Práter utca school, just behind the Corvin, and, just across the road, on the other side of the Üllői út, the Kilián Barracks, the home of a 'C' battalion, a collection of soldiers considered by the authorities to have no commitment to the cause of Communism, who had been down for even more than the usual excessive ditch-digging and road-laying and who generally had a menial, unpaid, unfed time and who had been particularly interested to hear about the Revolution.

As if that wasn't enough, running parallel to the Üllői út which had been the major route into Budapest for the Soviet troops, was the Túzoltó út, a ludicrously narrow street which had sired its own warriors, known locally reasonably enough, as the Túzoltó boys, who had pulled off one of the neatest coups of the fighting, known locally as the Túzoltó massacre. Seeing that his comrades were having nasty, mainly fatal, accidents on the Üllői út as they came to look for hooligans and reactionaries, a Soviet tank commander had made the decision to go down Túzolto út. Five tanks had gone in, but none had come out.

'We got the first tank and we got the last tank,' one of the participants (a leading water-polo player) had related to Gyuri. 'So the other three were stuck there. They weren't going anywhere. We had a break for lunch and then we finished them off.' So gorged was Túzoltó út with bits of Soviet tanks that the boys had to move their operations to another street.

When Gyuri arrived at the Corvin, as always there were lots of groups congregated outside the cinema; the necessity to be out on the street hadn't diminished. People wanted to see history with their own eyes. The anti-tank gun was still out by the entrance with a sign 'retained by popular demand' propped up on the barrel; people were still carrying their weapons, despite the call for people to start handing them in. Jankó, the commander of the Corvin's single anti-tank battery, was hobbling about on his wooden leg and didn't look as if he would be paying heed. He had a rifle in his hand, a greatly-prized AK-47, the latest Soviet assault rifle, slung over his back, a holstered pistol and a bayonet peeking out of the top of the boot on his good foot. Indisputably a man who was afraid of missing an opportunity of killing some Russians, Jankó had certainly done a faultless job on the anti-tank gun, six tanks burst open like popcorn, one shot apiece. Not surprisingly in a man with such homicidal proficiency and a knack for the gadgets of death, he had a mean set to his face. Gyuri could imagine him working as a rat-catcher, getting a kick out of killing small mammals, until larger, more Soviet ones came along.

Jadwiga, true to form, was nowhere to be seen where she should have been seen. Gyuri glanced in at a few of the meetings that were taking place, but he couldn't see her. Now the fighting was over, people were doing one of two things, either holding meetings or painting the old national insignia on everything. The meetings, initially bracing and euphoric, were lurching towards tedium. The absence of free association had been wearing, but it was like not reading a book for five years and then trying to read five at the same time to make up. Creedal orgies, nationwide.

All sorts of organisations were coming into existence; the old political parties carrying on from mid-sentence where they stopped in 1947 and all sorts of societies for political prisoners, for students, for office workers, for economists, for revolutionary water-polo players. The old joke about two Hungarians on a desert island resulting in three political parties had been enacted in earnest. There was probably already an association of one-legged freedom-fighters for Jankó to join.

Gyuri sauntered around the Corvin yard. The faces of the fighters were young, most of them not out of their teens (he again felt somewhat obsolete); they were working-class generally and well, most of them not too bright. But then would anyone intelligent spend their leisure time taunting Soviet tanks? No, the educated, intelligent people chiefly stayed at home producing pamphlets and let the poor and stupid do the dying for them, coming out to wave the flags at appropriate moments.

The Corvin was in the sort of district that appreciated a good fight, whether it was with rival football supporters or the Red Army. Gyuri kept expecting to see Tamás; the Corvin was his sort of event, and there could be no doubt that if Tamás were alive, Russians would be dying. But there were so many other thriving locations apart from the Corvin to choose from. Still, familiar faces were at the Corvin; he had seen Noughts, arguing with two girls kitted out with submachine-guns. Gyuri had said hello but suspected that Noughts hadn't placed him, Noughts having played a larger role as Gyuri's cellmate, than Gyuri with his walk-on part on Noughts's stage.

Gyuri kept expecting to see Pataki as well. Backs, profiles, haircuts, overcoats, remote forms would imitate Pataki or give off Patakiness. He imagined Pataki might be on his way back to Hungary, he wouldn't want to miss this. One man coming out of the parliament resembled Pataki so closely, moved so much like him, that Gyuri was getting the joy and the greetings ready and only the absence of any recognition in the irises of the impostor gave him away at the last moment...

In the end, far down the Üllői út by some scenic rubble, Gyuri found Jadwiga having her picture taken by a couple of Western photographers. They seemed to have a fondness for attractive women with weapons. Gyuri didn't like this at all. Jadwiga was merely handing out one of her polite smiles, her toothy calling card, but they weren't to know that.

Gyuri came up to glower at the photographers at close quarters but they had already finished and were on the move to their next snap. Viktor the Soviet deserter and another Pole, whom Gyuri thought was called Witold, were leaning on the husk of a tank, where they had been watching the photo session.

Jadwiga was wearing her quilted Soviet jacket, the pelt of a dead Soviet soldier, Gyuri thought bleakly. He had taken weapons from the dead internationalists, but weapons were somehow faithless, they didn't belong to anyone, they were just carried. Jadwiga's blue jacket, approximately a third of her small wardrobe, had got ripped to shreds on the 26th as they were crawling along under Soviet fire at the Corvin. The noise of the tanks, more than anything else, had been terrifying. It was no more dangerous, rationally, than being shot at by infantry but it sounded more dangerous. When Jankó fired the anti-tank gun in reply, Gyuri had believed he was going to die of fear. As he lay on the ground, using muscles he had been unaware of to propel himself into the pavement, impressed more forcefully than if an elephant had been standing on him, he pondered how it would only take one of the hundreds of bullets zooming through the Corvin to unanchor him from the continuum, and wondered why everybody didn't just run away, Jadwiga was only upset by her jacket failing her in combat conditions, and tattering during her sniping. During one of her shopping expeditions in the lulls to collect ammunition and weapons from inoperative Soviets, she had returned with the tough jacket.

'So how is the great optimist?' she said to Gyuri. Jadwiga had sided of course with Elek in the morning, insisting that the Red Army had had enough and that Gyuri didn't want to face up to the fact that he was now free to do whatever he wanted since he could no longer reach for the handy excuse of an inane, dictatorial regime preventing him from being a great success.

'Budapest today, Warsaw next week. Right, Witold?' Witold nodded in agreement. Then she added in Russian: 'Moscow, let's be realistic, one month.' Viktor grinned in approval.

'That's why they have to stop it here,' said Gyuri. 'This can't go on much longer'

'You're so miserable,' Jadwiga remonstrated. 'I hope our children will have none of that. When I will tell them how stupid their father was, they'll laugh.'

Having secured a promise from her that she would return

home soon, Gyuri started back for Damjanich utca. Passing by a bookshop that had puked out its contents into the street, it occurred to him the household was short of paper, and because he wanted to carry out a scientific experiment, Gyuri gathered up a few volumes that hadn't been burned or only just nibbled by the flames.

At home, relaxed on the loo, he tried out the books. Révai, the Party ideologue, was disappointing. It was an imposing volume, *We Knew How to Use Freedom* (684pp), but the paper was too shiny to merit the diploma of bottom-wiping. Méray, the journalist who had fearlessly invented and then exposed American atrocities in Korea in his illustrated *Testimony* (213 pp) looked promising. Gyuri had no idea what had really happened in Korea but he was quite willing to stake his life that the only things in the book that weren't downright lies were the author's name and the commas. Nevertheless, Méray afforded a greater degree of absorbency. Coming to Rákosi's *Selected Speeches and Articles* (559pp), there was still a perceptible failure to carry out the work in hand. The most effective nether napkin was Rákosi's *The Turning Point* (359pp), an earlier offering, from 1946, on coarse paper which almost worked.

Gyuri was trying to enjoy his sojourn at the hindquarters' headquarters with extracts from these books but although the idea had been highly pleasing, the reality wasn't as satisfactory. The Communists couldn't even hack it as toilet paper. You could imagine Rákosi, forecasting that people might well one day seize his books with a hankering to convert them into arse-fodder, ordering that his works should be printed on the most unaccommodating of paper. Still, it would make an amusing paragraph when he wrote to Pataki.

Where were Révai, Rákosi and the others? Gyuri wondered. Where were all those bastards, the beloved favourite sons of the people? The Russians probably had them tucked away in the basement of their Embassy, in storage for future necessity, labelled 'spare dictators'.

The last book Gyuri turned to was in English, *Eastern Europe in the Socialist World* by Hewlett Johnson who was supposed to be the Dean of Canterbury. The book was a paean to the Socialist order. Either the book was a forgery, or else the Dean must have been caught wanking off small boys in Warsaw and blackmailed into writing this, thought Gyuri, because no one could be stupid enough to write things like this of their own volition.

* * *

It was the largest park in Hamburg, full of ducks, but he still couldn't manage to catch one. Ducks were brainier and faster than they looked and Pataki was disadvantaged by having to keep looking over his shoulder to make sure he wasn't arrested. He was sure there would be some by-law protecting German ducks from hungry refugees. He tried improvising traps with string and dry bread, he tried netting them with his overcoat, he tried a straight grab and wring. As it got dark, Pataki resigned himself to dining on boiled eggs again. He had explored all the options for cooking eggs and somehow boiled seemed the least dispiriting. Eggs were far better than nothing but after months of unrelenting eggs, non-egg edibles had deployed an unprecedented fascination.

But, as he strolled past an off-licence, Pataki snapped and resolved to blow a little money. Two beers to celebrate the Revolution. There was one pinguid German in front of him at the counter who stupidly seemed to be buying more beer than he could possibly carry. As the man struggled to find a way of managing his impossible load, Pataki was about to ask for two bottles of beer, when a hand landed on his shoulder. He turned to see a long-haired figure behind him say in German: 'I'm a Hungarian, let me buy you a drink.' Insane? Drunk? Uncontrollably gregarious? Just Hungarian?

'I'm Hungarian too, and I'll let you buy me a drink,' Pataki responded in the mother tongue. His host was called Kincses and he was evidently a man used to going to great lengths for company. His room was virtually above the boozery, so they repaired there to drink. Kincses was very pleased he didn't need to employ his appallingly accented German and that he could really get loquacious. Kincses had been in West Germany for over three years. He had done some work as an artist's model, but a vogue for abstract expressionism had dried up most of his employment and he was now working as factotum in one of the liveliest brothels. 'It was all very German. There was an interview. They asked whether I had any previous experience of working in a knocking-shop. They were perfectly serious; they were terrified of taking on unqualified help. What do you do?'

'I'm the head of the postage-stamp acquisition department in a bank,' replied Pataki. 'I'm the one they send down to the post-office.' They drank to the revolution.

'I tried to go back yesterday. Got as far as the Austrian border,' said Kincses. 'But the Austrians wouldn't let me in. They were convinced there were enough Hungarians in Hungary. Mind you, I don't know why I wanted to go back so badly when I think of the trouble I had getting out. I had to waltz through the minefields. What about you?'

'My personalised railwagon. You must have wanted to get out quite badly to go out that way.'

'I didn't have much choice really. That always makes things easier. You see, I'd walked out of a place called Recsk, a labour camp.' Kincses outlined the inspiration behind Recsk. 'Lots of people helped with my escape. It took us months to scrape together a guard's uniform. It was very cheeky, very dramatic. A big brass neck, a dark winter evening, bored, dim guards and I was out. I just walked out. There was no hope of staying at liberty in Hungary so I knew I had to leave.

'We all thought it important that the world should know about Recsk. I memorised everyone's name, their date of birth, occupation and the city they lived in. I was working on the addresses when the uniform was completed.'

'So what did the world say?' asked Pataki.

'Nothing much. Walk out of a labour camp, that's heroic; walk out of a labour camp *and* walk through an Iron Curtain and you'll find you've walked round the moral globe and it's not heroic, but extremely suspicious. Everyone was very polite, but I had the impression they thought I was on a payroll somewhere in Moscow.' (Pataki remembered his debriefers: 'Ach, Herr Pataki, we understand you are saying you were sent out by the AVO but we have been told by people who were sent out by the AVO that people who are sent out by the AVO are told to say that they have been sent out by the AVO.' The meeting had been a stalemate; he was staying in the country but without a generous salary from the security services.)

'Are you going to go back?' Kincses inquired.

'When I leave, I leave.'

* * *

'You don't think I should tell him?' Jadwiga asked.

'No. Best not to interfere in that sort of emotional traffic,' Elek answered.

'But there can't be any doubt; the documents were very clear.'

Elek looked unhappy. 'The documents might have been very clear. But you didn't really know Pataki. He was as fast off the court as on. His sun-bathing stunt outside their front door would have been a hard one to talk his way out of but he's slippery. The AVO might have *thought* he was working for them, but he probably agreed just to get out.' He lit a long-saved cigarette. 'And I bet he got an advance out of them.'

* * *

It was the artillery that woke them up. Faraway, but forceful. Gyuri looked out of the window. Darkness, stillness. No sign of dawn or the Russians but both were coming. Switching on the radio, they heard Imre Nagy announce the obvious attack by the Russians and state that Hungarian forces were fighting. This was followed by an appeal for help from abroad. He got dressed, since misfortune had to be faced in trousers, the juices in his stomach can-canning.

'We must go to the Corvin,' said Jadwiga. Gyuri really didn't want to go to the Corvin. He wasn't at all pleased at being right. Being right, he discovered, doesn't necessarily do any more good than being wrong. He had thought he had been angry before but he realised his previous rages had only been false starts compared to his present anger. Thanks to the Red Army, he was going to explode, but he didn't want to fight. He was trembling from a mixture of ninety per cent fury and ten per cent fright. He wanted to suggest going to the border, but he knew Jadwiga wouldn't listen. He suggested it anyway, knowing he would regret it more if he didn't. 'Let's go to Austria,' he said.

'You don't mean that,' she retorted.

They ran out into the streets, Jadwiga carrying her favourite gun. There were few people, and those that were out, whether armed or unarmed, didn't seem to know what to do. He tried to keep the thoughts submerged because he didn't want them to come into the world because they wouldn't help but he couldn't keep them down; they floated up to the surface. *We're going to lose. We're going to be killed.* They bobbed around in his mind. The other people looked to Gyuri as if they were holding down the same prompts. Stealthily, they reached the Körút, which Gyuri suddenly recognised as the street where he was going to die. 'I feel safe with you,' said Jadwiga cocking her weapon, which was intriguing because Gyuri certainly didn't feel safe with himself.

Kurucz was also making his way along the Körút, slithering along the doorways, a couple of grenades in his belt, carrying his gun ready to use it; Kurucz was one of the professional soldiers who had ended up at the Corvin. The sight of Kurucz cheered Gyuri up; Kurucz was a close personal friend of surviving.

Clever. Lucky. Kurucz didn't make mistakes and would take a lot of killing. Being close to him might cast some protection on them. Gyuri noticed his pullover was on back to front.

'You heard about Maléter?' Kurucz asked. Gyuri shook his head. Colonel Maléter had been appointed Minister of Defence a few days earlier on the strength of his activities at the Kilián Barracks. 'Went to have supper last night with the Soviet High Command, didn't come back.' More good news, thought Gyuri, deafened by the voice that was shouting *you're going to die* in his ear.

'Well, military leadership was never this country's strong point,' observed Kurucz. It was stupid, but Gyuri couldn't help thinking things would have been different if Pataki had stayed. Pataki wouldn't have let this happen. Pataki wouldn't have been conned by a load of fat Soviet generals. He wouldn't have let them shit all over the country. Gyuri couldn't see how but somehow Pataki would have foxed them, or at least not lost the match before the start.

'If only Pataki were here...' he said, trying to think what to do.

'If you were better read you wouldn't say such things,' snapped Jadwiga. Gyuri didn't understand what she meant but she was always having bouts of Slav mysticism.

The Corvin seemed to be getting the brunt of the attack, the price of celebrity, a murderous tribute to its teenage army. Aircraft, artillery and new, larger tanks were all in action. They inched down the Körút but it looked suicidal trying to get any closer. They were behind a pile of sandbags, remnants of the earlier round of fighting, when one of the tanks, hundreds of yards away, opened fire.

Half the building behind them disappeared. It took Gyuri a while to convince himself he was still alive and that all the components of his body were in the right places and still working. Jadwiga was next to him, covered in dust and debris. When he saw her wound two thoughts raced through him, the axiom that stomach wounds were always fatal, and the other that his sanity couldn't cope with this. Holding her as if that would help, he tried to keep the horror from his face, the knowledge that he was about to see the last thing anyone wanted to see, the death of the one he loved.

She knew anyway. 'You won't forget me,' she said.

* * *

Nigel was whiling away the time before the start of World War Three by polishing all the shoes he could lay his hands on in the Legation.

The phone was ringing. Nigel had answered it once. 'Hello, British Legation,' he had said.

'We are trapped. We are going to die,' a voice had said. It was a rich, deep, calm voice that spoke fluent English with only enough of a Hungarian accent to give a pleasing colour; you could imagine the voice belonging to a professor of English literature. Nigel didn't know what to say. Clearly commiserations were in order, but there was nothing at hand in his immediate etiquette to cover a situation like this. The voice carried on though, fortunately, without giving Nigel a chance to participate. 'Our building is completely surrounded by Russians. We will fight to the last bullet, but we will die. We don't matter, but you must help our country. Hungary must be free –' The line had gone dead.

Everyone was chipping in, running things in the Legation but Nigel wasn't going to answer the phone any more. The building was a refuge for a strange mixture of Britons, well-wishing students, adventurers, journalists, holidaymakers and two businessmen whose unflinching devotion to marketing their brand of razor-blade in the face of history was remarkable. No one talked about it but there was an unspoken assumption that war was going to break out and they would be well behind enemy lines; whatever was going to happen it wouldn't be pleasant. Everyone had been presented with a copy of their own death.

Nigel had opted to clean shoes since it gave him something

to do and as he joked, 'We want to look good when the Russians capture us. My old housemaster would never forgive me if I met my end with dulled footwear.' The BBC journalist was roaming up and down the building, clutching a bottle of vodka, and repeatedly accosting any female on sight with 'Anybody for a fuck?' Nigel could see the Minister would be making representations to the BBC when this was over, if he were in a position to do so. The Minister took a dim view of journalists; the correspondent of the *Daily Worker* had almost been barred by him. 'Shouldn't you be outside with your Communist friends?'

The political attaché and the military attaché strolled up to where Nigel had set up his shoe-cleaning business.

'Kádár has finally resurfaced. He's been broadcasting from somewhere saying he's established a workers–peasants' government which has invited the Russians to tidy up. I'd love to count the number of workers and peasants in his government,' remarked the political.

'Who's Kádár?' asked Nigel.

'Was Minister of the Interior under Rákosi. Home-grown Communist as opposed to the Muscovites. Was also a Minister in Nagy's latest government but he seemed to get tired of it and disappeared a few days ago.'

'Anyone know where he's been?' asked the military attaché.

'Somewhere safely Soviet, I'd venture. He's probably spent the week trying to think up a new configuration of socialist/worker/party to name his new outfit. But he's stuck with the Hungarian Socialist Workers' Party, which Nagy thought up. I suppose all the variants have been used up.'

'Mmmm. I suppose it's time to earn the King's shilling,' said the military attaché, stepping out into the Revolution.

* * *

You don't get any braver, you just get tired, bored with fear, thought Gyuri as he scrambled over the wall to land in the

Kerepesi Cemetery. He and Kurucz ran through, dodging gravestones and undergrowth. Where were the others? Gyuri wondered. Looking back, he could see the Mongols coming over the wall.

The return of the Red Army relied largely on troops from Central Asia or some slant-eyed part of the Union. Unlike troops who had been stationed in Hungary and had some idea what was going on, Gyuri had heard the Mongols thought they were fighting at the Suez Canal. They certainly didn't mind killing people.

Kurucz signalled that they should make a stand. Gyuri still had enough energy to savour the irony of having a shoot-out in a cemetery; very convenient for the people who had to clean up afterwards. The Mongols moved cautiously, as if expecting American paratroopers to open up on them at any moment. All day Gyuri had been hearing stories about American paratroopers arriving all over Hungary, particularly in places where they weren't needed. Well, if they didn't hurry up, it would soon be over.

A lot of Party people are buried here, Gyuri noted, hoping he could find a cadre tombstone to shelter behind so that it would get shot up.

Kurucz gave their pursuers a magazine's worth, really working their cardiovascular systems, maybe nicking one of the yellow bastards. He and Kurucz fell back a few yards further to a gigantic mausoleum, a sort of mini-history of architecture, composed of a dozen different styles, perhaps to cover any changes in fashion up to Judgment Day. It looked awful but must have cost a fortune. 'In memory of the Gerebend family' read the inscription. The Gerebend family are going to take some punishment, thought Gyuri.

He and Kurucz were both short of ammunition. Kurucz still had one grenade but that was it. They could start throwing rocks after that. The Mongols argued loudly about their strategy, a long way off. After a few minutes, one of them appeared, crawling on his belly, weapon cradled in his arms in the textbook manner but out in the open. Did he think he was invisible? It was insulting.

Gyuri felt a flash of anger on his emotional palate. He'd missed his targets all morning but with his last two rounds he hit the serpentine Mongol. The Mongol turned out to be a screamer, expressing eloquently in a universal language how painful it was to be shot.

There was more hurried, Asiatic consultation and then from a wide front came small arms fire, chipping away at the Gerebend family's final abode. Gyuri could tell Kurucz wanted to hang around and try and gouge their eyes out but he indicated they should leave. It was easy. They left the cemetery while the shooting continued with a bit of perfunctory grenade-lobbing. The Mongols would be there for hours before they realised they had used the back door.

'I'm going down the Üllői út,' said Kurucz.

'You won't come back,' said Gyuri, noting by the sound of his voice he was hysterical. He wouldn't have believed he had enough vigour for that. The Üllői út was a preview of the end of the world, a little localised armageddon. It was safer firing a revolver in your mouth.

'I lived like a worm for a long time,' said Kurucz, although Gyuri couldn't envisage Kurucz doing so. 'I'm glad I can die like a man. Where are you going?'

'Out. West. Austria,' replied Gyuri.

'You won't come back either.'

Gyuri threw away his empty gun. If he needed another gun, he could pick one up off any street-corner, and carrying one didn't do you any favours. 'The Red Army won't forget about its outing in Budapest,' said Kurucz. 'It's been ... well, people will write about us.'

Clinging to walls all the way home, Gyuri crashed into the British military attaché, recessed in a doorway, observing the proceedings. The way Gyuri greeted him in English made the attaché realise they were acquainted, though he obviously couldn't place Gyuri. 'Awesome, these new tanks,' he said gesturing at a herd on the other side of Hősök Square, 'those new guns too, formidable rate of fire.' Gyuri nodded because he was unable to add anything to the conversation. He merely smiled politely in the way one does when one's country has been invaded by interesting new tanks. The attaché was carrying an umbrella, Gyuri observed, as all Englishmen should.

At home, the flat was empty. Elek had, along with everyone else in the block, taken refuge in the cellar, just as they had done during the siege in '44. In a final act of defiance and rebellion, Gyuri climbed into his bed and slept indefatigably for the next twenty hours in truly passive resistance.

* * *

He was woken by István moving around in the lounge. István was taking down a landscape picture off the wall, an oil painting so ghastly that it had been snubbed by legions of plundering Soviet soldiers and even when they had been starving Elek had been unable to find anyone willing to take it off their hands for a few forints. 'A tank put a machine-gun round through our still life,' said István. 'Ilona insisted that I find something to replace it. Been fighting, have you? I can tell you, you look frightening enough.'

Gyuri rummaged in the kitchen for food, out of reflex rather than hunger. 'Where's Jadwiga?' asked István. The look that Gyuri gave him made everything plain.

Gyuri started putting on layers of clothing. When he got to his overcoat, he reached into a pocket and put Jadwiga's effects, some identity cards and rings, on the table. He kept the passport. 'I need a favour. When things get settled, could you send these to Poland?' Grabbing his scarf, he said to István. 'I'm off. Have a good life and so on.'

Hamstrung by sadness, it was a long walk. *Dear God*, thought Gyuri, *does it really have to be like this?* It was colder than usual for November, and it seemed much blacker at six than it should have been, as if the Russians had imported extra darkness with themselves and dawn had given up. There weren't many trains running, but the Keleti Station had a train, greatly over-subscribed, getting ready to leave. It wasn't a train taking people anywhere in Hungary, although nominally it had a Hungarian destination. Although no one said so, everyone knew it was the slow train to Vienna.

The centre of the city had quietened but as the train chugged out of Budapest, passing Csepel Island, explosions could be heard. Csepel, always referred to officially as 'red', since it was inhabited exclusively by industrial workers, was the last part of Budapest to hold out. They had a munitions factory. They had anti-aircraft batteries so powerful they could be used to turn most tanks into Swiss cheeses. Their own leaders had told them to give up. They had been instructed to go to hell. Huge columns of smoke had hung immobile over the island all day as if pinned there. People who lived in Csepel had a reputation for tenacity, toughness and an implausible degree of violence second only to Angyalföld.

There were two people on the train that Gyuri knew. The first, Kórodi, who lived at the other end of Damjanich utca. Gyuri hadn't seen him for years despite his proximity, and it was ironic to bump into him in a dash to see if the border was still open. Clutching his violin-case like a life-belt, Kórodi was very pleased to see Gyuri. 'Haven't seen you for a long time,' said Gyuri sitting next to him in the buffetless buffet car.

'No one's seen me for a long time,' said Kórodi laughing. 'I've spent all my time practising. Fourteen hours a day sometimes. No evenings without a violin. No romance. No long baths. No trashy novels. No good novels. I may not be the greatest violinist alive, but I've been the hardest working. I cut everything out, because I knew, I *knew* one day I'd get out and then it would all be worth it. Those lazy bastards in the West won't know what hit them.'

'The streets may not be paved with gold,' said a part of Gyuri's mind responsible for repartee.

'You know what? I don't care if they're paved with turds.'

Gyuri's other acquaintance was Kurucz. Looking for a seat, Gyuri hadn't recognised him immediately because most of his face was swathed with bandages. He was leaning on a crutch. What Gyuri could see of his face looked awful, worse than some of the corpses that had been lying around for a couple of days. They didn't acknowledge each other at first, the old caution having silently returned but an hour out of Budapest, Gyuri noticed Kurucz having a cigarette in the corridor. They had enough space for a hushed conversation.

'What happened?' asked Gyuri.

'I got killed,' said Kurucz, speaking with the mellowness of someone who hasn't eaten or slept for days. 'Near the Rákoczi út. We were surrounded. Ammunition gone. Have you ever tried to kick a tank in the balls? There was a chance if we surrendered we might live. Not that we were expecting much. There were twelve of us, mostly lads. They lined us up on the spot, shot us and tossed a couple of grenades in for good measure. I was hit in the neck and I don't have much left ear left. Not to mention a generous helping of shrapnel. It must have looked bad, thank goodness. Next thing I knew I was in a flat being patched up, thinking what lousy wallpaper heaven has; the people who helped me said I was the only one alive.'

They stared at the blackness outside the window. Solid gloom, a sinister aspic. No features from outside made it through.

'Did we kill too many? Not enough?' asked Kurucz speaking apropos of the AVO and the Party. 'They always seem to find replacements. Quislings, shits, like hope, spring eternal.' Kurucz had done a spell of military service at the border; he offered to take Gyuri through a very green part of it.

* * *

Elek, bored in the flat and not eager to find out if he had a job to go to at the hospital, greeted István warmly when he appeared.

'Have you seen Gyuri? I'm getting worried. I managed to buy his favourite cakes. Can you imagine in the middle of all this, the patisserie's back at work?'

István sighed at Gyuri's untidiness. 'He's gone,' he said. That November there was no need to say more.

'Just as he was getting interesting,' remarked Elek.

* * *

People got off the train at different points once it reached Western Hungary, depending on how they saw their escape. There were families with two, three or even four children and innumerable suitcases, solitary voyagers, couples just carrying each other's hands, and even a farmer who had voiced intentions of trying to smuggle his prize pig out. There was an atmosphere of a grim holiday excursion.

Kurucz seemed to know what he was doing, although well on the way to being dead. This, at least, saved Gyuri some thinking. He couldn't be bothered to be afraid; the events had quelled his terror, if at great cost. They walked slowly towards the border, warily appraising any other figures, most of whom shunned them with as much alacrity and distance as they did. The plan was to get within a kilometre or so of the border, wait till dark, then move.

There was a thin carpet of snow. Why did it have to be so cold? Gyuri had thought he would remain unmoved by his circumstances but the cold was coming through loud and clear. He wasn't at all hungry. Nothing like death to dispel appetite; he couldn't even imagine wanting to eat. He would have happily traded some cold for hunger. However, he couldn't really complain. Kurucz, who had so much more material to work with, hadn't grumbled once.

'They've taken up the mines, haven't they?' asked Gyuri almost as an afterthought, recalling that as an act of friendliness towards Austria, an announcement had been made that most of the fortifications and minefields would be removed.

'Yes, the minefields should have been taken up,' said Kurucz, continuing, 'but can you tell me one thing that's ever been done properly in this country?'

Towards dusk, according to Kurucz, they were in sight of Austria. There were just trees and snow on all sides. Austria looked remarkably like Hungary. Waiting in the woods, it was so chilling that Gyuri lost touch with several extremities. Circling around to prevent himself completely freezing up, Gyuri stumbled across three bodies, lightly covered with snow: two women, one boy. His emotions, he discovered, were as numb as his fingers.

The moon was fullish, which wasn't very encouraging. But, probably because of the cold, they could see the huge light of fires where shadowy sentinels of unknown nationality were gathered, beacons which drew them away. Gyuri and Kurucz moved very unhurriedly, very carefully, but still tripped up and stumbled a lot on a surprisingly uneven border. They were especially circumspect when they reached an open strip which was presumably the former minefield. Although his feet had become very uncommunicative, somehow Gyuri suddenly felt there was something unfield-like under his right foot. He seized up completely.

Eventually, in a tiptoeing whisper, Kurucz, anxiety and anger split fifty-fifty, asked 'What's wrong?'

'Nothing. I think I just trod on a mine.' Gyuri had deduced by the thin light that he was standing on what resembled an unearthed mine. Finally, he walked on, surmising that if the mine was going to explode it would have already done so. Soviet rubbish.

They found a barn. It was no warmer than outside, but it at least gave them the possibility of believing it was. Gyuri spent a few hours in attempted sleep, quivering with cold and misery. As soon as there was a suspicion of dawn, he went out to piss. He could hardly find his dick, it had been so reduced by the cold.

'Right. Let's find somewhere warm,' said Kurucz as soon as

there was enough light to navigate by. Looking back, Gyuri could see that they were out, because of a faraway row of guard-towers behind them. He was out. Suddenly, unexpectedly, he started to cry. He walked half backwards, as best he could, so that Kurucz wouldn't see.

Tears, in teams, abseiled down his face.